The One

Annaliese Plowright

All characters in this publication are fictitious and any resemblance to any persons, living or dead, is purely coincidental

ISBN: 1-4751-3294-8
ISBN-13: 9781475132946

Dedication

For my son, Angus

Prologue

"Drink, Morgen, and forget Arwan's betrayal!" My sister, Annora, offered her wooden ladle. The strange, transparent, purple potion threatened to spill over, such was the force of her wrath, and, as if in sympathy, her cauldron boiled and frothed angrily nearby. "Walk with mortals and never think again of Arwan; it's the only way you'll ever again know peace, Sister." Her earth brown eyes were adamant; Annora felt rage. I felt only pain.

"Are you sure, Annora? Are you sure you saw them together?" I shook my head in a fruitless attempt to dislodge the vision Annora's words had planted in my mind, that of my beloved Arwan in the throes of a secret affair. My heart was desperately hoping she'd been mistaken; he'd sworn that his life was mine every day since we met. How could this be the truth?

The ancient jewelled floor was cold beneath my knees, where I'd been since the moment Annora had told me what she'd witnessed. My hands rubbed at my chest in circular motions. I realised that the searing pain that had been there since I'd been told Arwan couldn't love me was my heart beginning to crack, fragmenting into pieces.

Annora gathered her long red gown and kneeled down before me, her beautiful oval face level with mine.

"I can barely believe it myself, Morgen, but can you live through an eternity seeing another in his arms?" Her words were the last rip to my heart. The final pieces of tissue still holding my vitality together tore in two. I was broken. My eyes swelled with moisture, blurring my vision, until tears streaked freely down my face.

Annora was right. I had no other choice. I would not stay in Achren to see him with another. No, I would not stay to see that. Annora offered me the only future I could live with, the only way I could face an eternal existence without the all-consuming misery and pain I felt at that moment.

"Thank you, Sister." I reached for the steaming ladle. "You have never failed me."

As I drank the bitter potion, a triumphant smile spread over Annora's face, and for a brief moment I was confused by her reaction to my total devastation.

My final thought, however, was an image, the image of Arwan's face...

chapter

ONE

It hadn't stopped raining since the moment my ancient green hatchback had crossed over the Scottish border almost an hour ago. It seemed the heavens were officially christening me into my new life in Scotland. I had left Colchester, Essex, at first light, and, if the instructions I'd been given were accurate, I had to be getting close to Claremont, my final destination.

I sighed, peering through the rain, whilst setting the windscreen wipers to comically fast, and I wondered how on earth I had managed to get myself into such a mess.

As of seven o'clock that morning, I was officially under a Witness Protection Program—the individual I was hiding from, my own husband of seven years, Adam Fleming.

Adam, believing I would back him up, had told the police he had been at home with me the night a business rival had been murdered. Everybody, including me, always did what Adam wanted. That's just how it was. Adam frightened people. Outwardly he was a respectable businessman, articulate and intelligent, but that was the surface layer.

Something much less palatable lay beneath. Adam believed in his own complete autonomy, and he was a control freak in every aspect, from his employees to me. So I don't know where I summoned the courage to betray him, but I will never forget the look of absolute disbelief on his usually contained face when I told a jury of twelve that I had no idea where my husband was the night of 14 November, 2010.

The man he was convicted of murdering, execution style, was no better or worse than himself, a money laundering, drug dealing gangster operating under a charade of legitimate business. It didn't matter to me. I wasn't going to lie for Adam, not in this. How could I and still sleep at night?

Adam was sentenced to fifteen years in a maximum security prison. I was advised, for my own safety, to lose myself in society and start again, a new life. Adam was a powerful, connected man, and even confined to a high security prison, posed a serious threat to anyone who betrayed him. His parting words to me, as he was led from the dock, "I'm in the shadows Brook; don't ever forget that," had me agreeing to witness protection.

Packing my entire life up and leaving Essex for good was maybe not quite the wrench it could have been. I had no friends, Adam wouldn't allow me to socialise independently, and my relationship with my parents had always been difficult. They divorced when I was two, and I spent the following fourteen years of my youth being nudged back and forth between them and their new spouses. As my mother liked to frequently point out, I had been an odd child, prone to daydreaming and wandering off. Like once when I was four, although I have no recollection of it, apparently my mother had woken one morning to discover my bed empty and the back door to the garden wide open. I was found several hours later, deep in the woods that surrounded my mother's isolated house, unharmed and curled up amongst the roots of a tree. That was the first of several similar incidents, all of which I have no memory of. Odd, I'll admit, but I had always felt lost as a little girl, a stranger amongst familiar faces.

I often wondered if it was my empty childhood and distant relationship with my parents that drove me so quickly into marrying somebody like Adam Fleming. As soon as I was old enough, I had all but cut ties with them. I hadn't seen my Mother or Father since my wedding day. It was a sad reality that I didn't have much to leave behind and had nobody there to miss me when I had gone.

From what I could make of the official website, Claremont was a quiet country village on the west coast of Scotland, about an hour and a half drive from Glasgow.

My little car was completely loaded up with my most precious possessions, art books and various sculptures and sculpting tools. The rest of my stuff had been boxed and picked up the day before by removal men, and with any luck would be waiting for me when I arrived.

I glanced down at the dashboard, where a crumpled piece of paper rested, and read my messy scribble for the hundredth time: 9 Mistletoe Street, Claremont. I felt exhausted from the early start, and the relentless rain was an added strain to my tired eyes. I had to be close now. In fact, according to the street map that I had only a moment earlier felt confident enough to shove back in the glove compartment, I should simply follow the winding country road I was travelling, and it would eventually lead me right into Claremont.

"You have got to be kidding me!" It was suddenly apparent that my poor little car had decided that it, too, had had enough for one day. An ominous, tinny, whirring sound shrieked out from under the bonnet as a red light began to flash angrily at me from the dash. My heart sank as I realised I would have to pull over.

After sticking my hazards on, I rubbed at my gritty eyes and tried to think what to do next. Why now, when I had to be just a few miles away? After a moment, I reached down to the floor of the passenger seat, yanked my handbag up into my lap, and foraged for my mobile phone. Great—no signal. Things were going from worse to worse. How had I managed to breakdown on the only road in the country where there was no mobile phone signal? I didn't think there was anywhere left on the planet that wasn't within coverage. Apparently I was wrong.

I glared out of every streaming window at the same dense green smudge as the rain drummed noisily on the roof of the car. Not a house in sight, and the rain, oh my god, the rain was relentless. I thought this was supposed to be the height of summer? There was no sun, just grey, sodden bleakness. I had left the sun in Essex that morning. It couldn't be a good sign. Whose idea was Scotland? I couldn't remember; maybe it was mine. I had initially suggested Spain, but had been bluntly told by the police that I would be outside their jurisdiction and that it was safer for me to remain within the United Kingdom.

I sighed in defeat. I would have to walk the last few miles into Claremont, jacketless.

I flung my handbag up over my arm and was about to push the door open when I spotted a break in the line of trees on my right-hand side. I wondered if it was a driveway. It was worth a look, at least. I pulled a breakdown card out of my purse and shoved my handbag under the passenger seat. Not that there was much chance of purse snatchers wandering around out here, I mused, but I was used to urban living, and old habits die hard.

A moment later, I slammed the car door under a battering of rain and turned to step into the road with the intent of crossing it, when the almighty holler of a truck horn stopped my heart and knocked the air from my lungs. I froze rigid against the car as a monstrous articulated truck thundered angrily past, spraying me with muddy water, only missing me by what seemed a cat's whisker.

"Sorry," I croaked in apology to the speedily departing rear end, fright paralysing my voice box. What next? If I believed in omens, I would be seriously worried by now.

The rain, of course, I had been expecting, but the chilly cold air I had not. I wrapped my arms uselessly around my middle as I jogged towards the opening in the trees. It did indeed appear to be a track of sorts, but there was no house visible from the road. I hesitated at the foot of the drive, debating whether to proceed or to follow the road into the village.

"What the heck?" I muttered eventually. What did I have to lose? There were only so many degrees of wet, and either way, I was going for a maximum soaking. I might as well try my luck with the driveway first.

The driveway was in fact no more than a narrow, rusty gravel track, but with a thick wedge of green running down its centre like a punk rocker's mohawk. A dense line of mature trees hugged the driveway, and I wondered who would want to live out here in the middle of nowhere. I knew it was only my present mood and predicament that made the location seem so unappealing. It was probably very peaceful when it wasn't raining torrentially, and how blissful it would be to be surrounded by so many beautiful trees.

In fact, I loved to sculpt unusual tree trunks. Something about their curves and twists held me in rapture and willed me to recreate their beauty with my own hands. Over the years of my marriage, I had mostly copied from photographs in books, never having the freedom to take myself off into the countryside and seek out my own living subjects. In Claremont, however, it appeared I was to be surrounded.

A strong wind blew my hair over my shoulders as I jogged my way up the seemingly never-ending driveway. It felt like a storm was brewing. Under normal circumstances I would have been thrilled at the prospect. Despite hating dreary weather, I had always loved storms. Even as a child I relished the electricity and anticipation that filled the atmosphere on the approach of moody weather. Thunder and lightning reminded me how fragile earth's inhabitants were when compared to the all-encompassing strength and might of Mother Nature. A storm gave perspective. It was a leveller; maybe we are not quite as big as we think we are. I found that thought comforting. It brought me back to the clay of the planet, to the earth, making me feel part of a much bigger makeup.

In acknowledgement of my accolade, the first roll of thunder cracked loudly around me, and the air took on a static quality as it anticipated lightning.

As predicted, I was completely soaked by the time I veered the last corner and a striking white mansion came into sight. I stopped at the top of the drive for a moment, panting from my jog, hands on my knees, startled to have come across such a grand property hidden away in the woods. I noticed a flash white Audi Q7 sitting directly out front of the somehow arcane looking house. A sign that someone was home.

The house was imposing and intimidating from the outside, and doubt niggled as to whether this had been such a great idea. The building had to be at least two hundred years old, but even through the rain, I could see it was in excellent upkeep. The entrance was grand in the extreme. Wide curved steps led up to a large porch supported by four tall, graceful columns dressed in thick green ivy, which had spread from the main body of the building. Large windows looked out over the driveway. I counted at least three stories. "Grand" was an understatement.

The mansion was set within simple, immaculate gardens, which seemed to draw the eye naturally towards the woods that, other than the driveway, completely surrounded the house. Despite the garden being understated, several life-sized sculptures stood in strategic places on a neatly cropped lawn to the front of the house. I couldn't clearly make out much of their detail through the rain, but they generally appeared to be Renaissance nudes. I would desperately have loved a closer examination, but the rain and the fear of upsetting whoever owned this spectacular property had me making the final dash up the steps to the front door.

I tapped a highly polished bronze knocker three times, stood back, and waited as butterflies gathered in the pit of my stomach. I was nervous, very nervous, but for what reasons I wasn't entirely sure. The house was clearly imposing, but that didn't mean there weren't nice, helpful people inside. A flash of lightning momentarily illuminated the porch in white light, and I swirled on my feet to scan the horizon above the line of the woods. Until the lightning, I hadn't realised how much darker the world had become as the storm prepared to pick up its pace.

I didn't hear the door open, and I jumped and yelped simultaneously as I turned back to find a man standing in the doorframe watching me—a breathtakingly handsome man. Or perhaps, more accurately, a breathtakingly handsome *angry* looking man. A strange feeling of familiarity swept over me, a kind of déjà vu, as if I'd at some time before experienced the unnerving gaze of this man. That couldn't be possible, I told myself. I wouldn't forget meeting this man; nobody would. It occurred to me that maybe he was an actor

I'd seen in some film, or a model from one of the glossy magazines I picked up from time to time. Who'd have thought Claremont would be home to the rich and famous?

Famous or not, he was clearly furious. His ice-cold eyes bored into my face with such intent that I wondered if they cut through me to the garden beyond. My knees felt weak. Why hadn't I just jogged into Claremont? This guy clearly didn't appreciate interruptions, but did he really have to look so angry? It was almost frightening.

"Um, hi," I said, finding my voice and hoping to somehow ease the tension radiating from the man before me. His anger seemed almost tangible, like the wind that lashed around us on the porch. I waited a heartbeat, but he gave no answer, his belligerent expression unwavering. I wondered if he had heard me over the increasing noise of the elements. My hair was whipping my face, and I used my hands to hold it back as I looked up at him. I started again, raising my voice slightly against the storm, heart hammering in my chest at the hostile emotion emanating from this absurdly handsome man.

"I'm really sorry to have disturbed you, but I've just broken down on the road back there," I said, flinging my thumb over my shoulder in the general direction whilst trying to ignore the peculiar stirring sensations that continued to move in the pit of my stomach. "I can't get a signal and wondered if I could possibly use your phone?" I pulled my breakdown card out of my back pocket and held it up for him to see, but he wouldn't take his cold eyes from my face to look at it. I waited again for a response...nothing.

"I just need to call a mechanic," I added lamely. Why was this man being so damn rude? I was disorientated, tired, and wet, and the temporary surge of heat the jog up the driveway had provided was rapidly evaporating, with a chill chomping at the bit to pick up the slack. All I wanted to do was take a hot shower and crawl into a warm bed. If only I'd just jogged into Claremont, I'd probably be sitting in a cosy cafe by now, sipping a skinny latte while waiting for a mechanic. Instead, I was stuck on some arrogant actor's doorstep, practically pleading with him to let me use his phone as he shot me with ice daggers from his eyes!

I was about to open my mouth to tell him to forget it, when he stepped back into the house and held the door wide for me to enter. For one rapid heartbeat, I considered turning and running back the opposite way. This man seriously had my nerves on edge. But in the next beat, a cold gust of wind sent a shudder through my rain soaked body, making my decision for me. I didn't want to admit that part of me was a little intrigued.

"Ah, thanks," I muttered, avoiding his gaze as I stepped apprehensively over the threshold, my heart going ten to a dozen.

A moment later, I found myself in a square reception hall that was truly something to behold. I let my eyes gaze around, soaking up the ambience as he closed the door behind me. I gasped in amazement. The hall was dripping in opulent Renaissance art; I had never seen a collection like it outside a gallery. Magnificent paintings adorned the walls, and most appeared maternal in nature, depicting mother and child. Was that a Raphael? I felt my jaw drop. It had to be a reproduction, but the quality was exquisite. All the furniture was antique and looked in mint condition. A glorious crystal chandelier hung from the centre of the ceiling, its shape reminding me of a telescope pointed to the stars. A spectacular staircase with an ornately carved oak banister swept up to the second floor and beyond; my eyes followed its smooth curve, admiring the fine craftsmanship.

I felt the burn of eyes, and turned to find the proprietor of the house intently watching my rovings. He appeared to have some of his anger in check, his handsome face more contained, expressionless. Only a hint of his former rage betrayed him about the line of his mouth—that, as well as his hands, thrust deep into his trouser pockets. There was nothing casual about the gesture; it was as if he were restraining the urge to close the distance between us and throttle me.

My eyes locked in with his, and I swam in the spellbinding blue of his relentless gaze. I felt intoxicated, hypnotized—the only sound a steady drip, like the ticking of a grandfather clock, as the water from my soaked clothes hit the floor. A small but growing puddle spread out from my feet.

It was his eyes that trapped me. Piercing bright blue, with an unusual tint of purple like tanzanite stars, breathtaking. Coal-black hair, long enough to touch the collar of his shirt, added to their vividness. The slightest hollow to his cheeks emphasised the perfect planes of his finely sculpted face and straight nose. My fingertips tingled at my sides as I fought an urge to run them down the line of his jaw. I wanted to reach out and feel the glorious skin that conjured images of dusky sunlight on still water in my confused mind. He was strong looking, athletic, and well over six feet tall. My five foot four inches felt tiny by comparison; he literally towered over me.

I was distracted from my hypnotic appraisal when he suddenly disappeared through a nearby door, leaving me alone, only to reappear an instant later holding a white towel, which he offered me. I stared at it vacantly for a moment, eyes blinking heavily, as my head swam in what felt like the opposite direction to my body. I took a deep breath, attempting to pull myself together, and looked up to meet his gaze. He thrust the towel closer as a loud roll of thunder from outside suddenly snapped me out of my confusion.

"Thank you," I said quietly, reaching to take the towel. My hand accidentally brushed his, and I gasped in surprise. He grimaced in return. His hand had been so incredibly warm against my cold skin that it had almost burned. There were no windows to the outside from the reception hall, but I had the oddest notion that at the exact moment we touched, lightning split the black sky outside. His anger broke through his features again. He looked even angrier than before, if that were possible. My heart kicked up a gear in response. It had to be blurring in my chest.

I tried to towel some of the water from my hair and clothes, looking anywhere but into the face of this unnerving man. What was his problem? I had to get out of here before his anger ignited me in flames. It was strange, and I had to be imagining it, but every glare and brusque move he made seemed to coincide with the sounds of the escalating storm outside.

I continued to feebly dab at my hair, when I spotted an old-fashioned dial phone on a sideboard across the hall.

"I'll just make that call and get out of your hair." I was mortified to hear my voice pitch out in a nervous squeak, telling the tale of the state of my nerves. I handed him back the towel, careful not to touch him again, and almost ran across the hall to the phone, breakdown card still clutched in hand. I didn't think I could face his anger a moment longer, and turned my back to him as I dialled the number from the card. Of course my shaking index finger wouldn't do what I wanted it to, and I had to hang up twice and start again. It was like being trapped in a nightmare where the only way out was a phone call my stupid sluggish fingers wouldn't let me make! I dreaded to think about the look that would be on the man's face behind me, as I fumbled away with the old-fashioned dial.

I finally had the right sequence of numbers and waited for somebody, anybody, to pick up at the other end. I drummed the fingers of my free hand on the sideboard, to fill the heavy, oppressive silence within the hall around me. If it weren't for the burn of his eyes on my back and the static heat his mood seemed to create in the room, I would have thought I was alone. He didn't make a sound.

"Good afternoon, breakdown service. How may I help you?"

I exhaled in relief.

Several minutes later I hung up the phone. "I'm in luck," I said, taking a deep breath and reluctantly turning back to face the man behind me. Just as I thought, he hadn't moved a muscle, but his beautiful face was now completely void of emotion. At least he didn't look angry anymore. I could deal with anything else.

"There's a mechanic in the area, ten minutes away, max," I said, biting my lip self-consciously and tucking my hands in the back pockets of my soaked jeans. Recent events with Adam aside, I'd never felt like such an inconvenience in all my life.

"What is your name?" His sudden decision to communicate verbally, and the fact that I liked the sound of his voice, took me by surprise. His accent was subtle and hard to place, but I didn't think he sounded Scottish. I needed a moment to gather myself to answer him. I cleared my throat.

"Umm, Brook."

"Brook!" he scoffed. I watched him, taken aback and confused by his attitude. He ran a hand through his black hair, appearing frustrated. What difference did it make to him what my name was? I felt a flush of anger heat my cheeks.

"Is there something wrong with my name?"

"It doesn't suit you." His eyes were hard and cold again.

I'd had about enough for one day and could feel a snap imminent. My emotions were already frayed by the trauma of the last six months, and the knife-edge they'd been balancing on since I walked into this bloody house hadn't helped. Who did he think he was? He could be angry that I'd interrupted whatever it was he'd been doing when I showed up, it was after all his house, but I wasn't about to let him insult me.

"Is that so? So what name would suit me then? Sarah? Jane?" My voice was conversational, but dripped with sarcasm. "You must enlighten me, and I'll swing by the name registrar and have it changed immediately. You're clearly some sort of *name* expert." I pressed a temporary pause on my rant to pull in a much needed breath, when something like mirth flashed in his eyes and the merest ghost of a smile played about his mouth. I sighed. Why was I prolonging this agony? I'd used his phone, and help was on the way. I could make good my escape.

"Well, thanks for your opinion on my name and the use of your phone," I said haughtily, "but I'd better get back to my car." I felt like I was the one being rude now, and hated it, but honestly, what did he expect?

I had started for the door when I froze dead in my wet tracks at the sight of two massive wolflike creatures that had suddenly appeared through one of the many doors off the hall. I shrank away from them instinctively; their sheer size alone was intimidating and strange. My eyes widened in fright as they padded over to sit by their master's feet. They sat down on their haunches and raised their heads to watch me.

Relief flooded through me as I picked up no tension in their demeanour. Instead, their tails wagged simultaneously, making a light sweeping noise as they swathed back and forth across the wooden floor. They were spectacular, like no dogs I'd ever seen before. Their heads easily came to my chest, and they were covered in long, shaggy hair that was so white it looked sterile. Their ears, in stark contrast to the fur, were bright pink, almost red, making me think, rather morbidly, of spilt blood on fresh snow. Both tails wagged furiously as they looked from me to their master in complete unison, mouths open, lips pulled back over fangs in excited doggy grins. I wondered, feeling slightly foolish, if they were asking his permission to greet me.

"They're beautiful," I said, forgetting my initial fear and my earlier agitation with their owner. I stepped forward, reaching out both hands to be sniffed. The dogs looked back at their master, who nodded stiffly and, unbelievably, both dogs lifted their heads to meet my hand. I braced myself to be bowled over with clumsy paws and swishing tails, but they were remarkably gentle, as if they were aware of their size. Their fur felt as lush as it looked, soft, thick, and warm. After a few moments of mutual appreciation, the dogs pulled back to sit at their master's feet.

I looked back up to the handsome face of the black-haired man and saw something like curiosity in his expression. I found myself staring into the depths of his purplish blue eyes, again seeking the answer to the question my brain had been yelling at me since I entered the house. From where did I recognise him? The sound of deep laughter broke through my trance. He was laughing at me. What an idiot I was. I had blatantly been appraising him, practically ogling him. I hadn't been able to stop myself, and now he mocked me. I had to get out of there. Maybe he was a famous actor? So what! He had no right to treat me like this.

I made for the door, but was hindered as he suddenly stepped in my way. My breath caught in my throat at his unexpected close proximity. I looked up at him questioningly, and saw something I couldn't fathom in the depths of his eyes. After a long moment, he stepped aside and opened the door for me.

"I think we shall be seeing each other again." His tone was matter-of-fact. Not if I can help it, I thought.

“Um, yep...okay...thanks again,” I mumbled, confused. I hadn’t told him I was moving to Claremont. For all he knew, I might only be passing through to another destination, or might just be a tourist.

I stepped out onto the porch, and after a fleeting glance over my shoulder told me he was still there, still watching, fled down the steps. To my surprise, the dogs shot out beside me into the storm, keeping pace on either side as I jogged from their master’s land through the still-pouring rain. I didn’t notice the cold air this time.

I expected to feel relief when I was back at the car, and to a large extent I did, but there was something inside me that longed to be in the company of that rude, arrogant, stunning man again. I felt I must be mad. But as I waited for the mechanic, it occurred to me that the whole time I had been in his house, I hadn’t once thought of Adam and the fear of his catching up with me. I had felt, despite the hostility, strangely safe.

chapter

TWO

Half an hour and a new fan belt later, I arrived in Claremont's centre. The static and tension of the storm had ebbed while the mechanic worked on my car, but a steady downpour of rain remained, escorting me into the village.

There was barely a soul on the street; it was a ghost town. I guessed the weather kept everybody indoors, but I was relieved to see all the usual amenities: bank, post office, bakery, pub, even a small library. Despite the bad weather, the village was picturesque, quaint even. Surely it didn't rain here every day? Scotland did not have a good reputation on the weather front, but I was determined to stay optimistic. I felt a smidgen of hope at the sight of half barrels brimming with summer flowers, albeit rain battered, and lining the pavement, benches for idling the afternoon away. Of course, all were vacant of idlers today.

A torrent of rainwater gushed down the gutter of the wide cobbled High Street. No doubt it was headed for the River Byron, which I had glimpsed from the car as it snaked close to the road before disappearing into the dense woods just ahead of the village boundary.

Once I was on the High Street, Mistletoe Street was easy to find. My hand shook with momentum as the key I had been given several days earlier, in anticipation of this moment, turned in the lock, opening the door.

I don't know what I'd been expecting, but I was pleasantly surprised with my new home, a compact, white, 1930s bungalow with one double bedroom, a bathroom, a small lounge, and a smaller kitchen/diner. Small was good, safe.

The inside had been carpeted throughout in sensible beige, with every wall painted to match the outside. Everything was white and bland, a blank canvas, perfect. It would be fun to decorate my own place, something I'd never been allowed to do in the past. Maybe when I got settled, I could take a drive into Logan Mills, the nearest large town, and get some wallpaper.

The biggest surprise, however, was a small, mature garden backing out onto the thick woods that dominated so much of the landscape in Claremont. The garden was a little wild and neglected, but I didn't mind; it was natural, almost part of the woods behind.

After the day I'd had, I was relieved to see that my stuff had arrived and that the removal men had even put the right boxes in the relevant rooms. After a hot shower, I spent a few hours unpacking and ate a pot noodle I'd found in one of the boxes. I hung several of my paintings on hooks provided by the previous occupier, and found homes for some of my sculptures. It was a long way from homey, but it was certainly an improvement.

Having been desperate to crawl into a bed earlier in the day, I was now growing increasingly reluctant to get undressed, get into bed, and turn the light out on my strange surroundings. Exhaustion won over fear in the end. I closed my eyes and expected to see Adam's face, but it was another face that glared in my mind's eye as I drifted off to sleep.

I woke up relatively fresh the next morning, surprisingly having slept the whole night through. My clock radio flashed seven fifteen, in neon red, from the bedside table. The thick bedroom curtains let no light in from outside, but I had left a small lamp on while I slept, unable to face total darkness. But besides my needing a lamp to sleep, the night felt like a milestone. If I could get through the first night, surely the ones that followed would be easier? This was a new start for me in more ways than one, and if I didn't let my fear of Adam somehow finding me become overwhelming, I could actually make a go of things here.

I was apprehensive about the new life that faced me, but a big part of me was excited. In many ways it was a *new* life, a fresh start, a chance to get things right. Whatever awful circumstances brought me to this life, it was *my* life. Not Adam's, mine. It was like being reborn at twenty-six.

I sat up and ran my fingers through my tangled hair. I was perplexed to find myself thinking again of the moody, rude man of yesterday. His attitude had affected me more than I liked to admit. I still felt the burn of his eyes on my face. But I had other things to think about this morning.

Today I started one of two part-time jobs. I had contacted a local employment agency several weeks earlier, but due to a lack of local full-time opportunities, had to accept two part-time positions, one as a private housekeeper at somewhere called Avallon House, and the other as a recreation officer at The Shades Residential Retirement Home. The latter I was excited about. I thought perhaps I could incorporate art classes within the recreational program.

After I had graduated from high school, I went on to study art history at college. I was doing well and making some friends, and then I had met Adam in my second year. Somehow I let him convince me that finishing my course wasn't important. I could still remember the way his blonde brows had furrowed over his eyes in disapproval when I had told him I wanted to be a sculptor. "Art is for people with too much time on their hands," he had said. I dropped out, but carried on studying and practising art at home, unable to break away from it completely, much to Adam's annoyance.

I pulled the duvet back and padded over to a box that still contained most of my clothes. What to wear? Jeans never failed, but maybe that was too casual for a first day at work. I opted for a black knee length pencil skirt, only slightly creased, and a red short-sleeved turtleneck. I slipped on my favourite pair of patent black pumps, then examined my reflection in a mirror tacked to the back of the bedroom door. I sighed.

I had been told plenty in my life that I was a good-looking woman, even beautiful, but today my chestnut brown hair seemed to be curling into every direction possible, and my dark eyes were framed by darker circles, which my fair complexion seemed only to emphasise. It had been a tough six months.

I rummaged through my still-packed toiletries bag and found my brush. I could never understand why girls with straight hair always wanted curls. They had no idea of the work involved. I spent ten minutes trying to brush myself into some sort of order before deciding it was what it was.

I pulled back the heavy brown curtains to see what kind of morning awaited me. A harsh light flooded in through the window from a sky suffused with garish orange and red. The neutral, bland tones of my new bedroom seemed to greedily soak up the livid colours of the sky outside, creating a sinister orange atmosphere that instantly dashed my hopes of suppressing any anxiety.

I was devastated to realise how thin and easily shattered my earlier veneer of optimism was. I didn't like admitting it, but I was freaked out by most things lately: sudden noises, crowds, shadows. I had been living in a perpetual state of heightened anxiety since Adam had been arrested.

I took a moment to collect myself. It was, after all, just light from the sky, nothing foreboding. What was the old saying, "Red sky in morning, shepherds..."

Suddenly my mobile trilled out from the bedside table, sending my heart into palpitations. I glared down at the phone. It was a private number. I hated not knowing who was on the other end. My head pounded in protest at the sudden surge of panic reverberating through me.

"Okay, okay," I tried to convince myself. "Breathe. You know it can't be him. Answer the phone." I took a deep breath and reached for the mobile, placing it to my ear.

"Hello?" I said, my voice pitching on the "o".

"Brook?"

"Yes," I answered, relieved. It was a man's voice, but definitely not Adam's.

"Hi, Brook. This is DI Thompson; I'm with the Witness Protection Office in Essex." Of course, I'd forgotten they said they would call first thing this morning.

"Hi, I..."

"Well, it sounds like you got there okay." It wasn't a question. "Remember," he continued in a rush of halfhearted words, "stick to the truth as much as possible. You moved to Claremont after your marriage broke down for a new start, blah, blah, blah."

"I was wondering if..." I tried again, but he steamrolled over me.

"Oh, and don't forget, you're Brook Davenport now, forget Fleming."

"Yes, but..."

"Your new passport and driver's license are being sent recorded delivery in the next couple of days. A lot of expense has gone into relocating you in Claremont, Miss *Davenport,*" he said, emphasising the "Davenport" for my benefit, "so try not to mess it up. It gets expensive having to keep moving people around."

"I'll do my best," I sighed, defeated.

"Well I'm sure you're busy, first day in a new place and all. Any questions, pick up the phone." Click. The line went dead.

It appeared I'd served my purpose as far as the police were concerned. I really was alone.

I walked back over to the window with my arms wrapped around my centre. The handsome face of the man from the previous day suddenly came back to mind. I let myself think about him for a moment, a distraction from the wave of loneliness and unease I felt. I just wished I knew why he'd been so mad. You couldn't hate somebody on first meeting them, could you? People talked of love at first sight, so I supposed, why not hate? I wondered whether I would bump into him again at some point; after all, the nearest shops to him were here in Claremont. Presumably even famous people did their own shopping from time to time. Would I acknowledge him? Probably. "Hi" seemed to come out of my mouth involuntarily whenever I saw anybody vaguely familiar. If Adam walked past me in the street, I'd probably say "Hi," before collapsing in a terrified heap on the pavement.

Suddenly my eyes focused on a soft orange movement at the back of the garden, distracting me from my thoughts. A stag! A magnificent stag! My arms goose pimpled as I realised with awe that the creature was pure snow white and only cast orange in the light radiated by the sky. It raised its great head to my window, staring at me with intelligent, knowing black eyes. I knew it could only be my imagination, but I thought I saw recognition in their depths. Steam bellowed out around its nose, as hot breath met with cool morning air and rose to the sky through antlers at least three feet high. I couldn't look away for an immeasurable moment, as our eyes locked together. The creature was perfectly still, like a marble statue; then, as quickly as it appeared, it disappeared back into the woods.

I drew in a deep breath, enchanted by the majesty and beauty of such a creature. It felt strangely spiritual in some way, like we were connected. I had never before seen anything so beautiful—other than the moody proprietor of the white house in the woods, I thought involuntarily. Seeing the rare white stag had been like sneaking a peek into another more magical realm. I felt truly honoured at having glimpsed it.

The stag had lifted my mood immensely, and it was with a lighter heart that I left for my first morning at The Shades Residential Home.

I headed along the High Street, with a small map the employment agency had provided clutched in one hand, and a basket filled with a few art supplies in the other. The livid colours in the early morning sky had begun to subside by the time I actually left the house, and chalky blue had won the fight for supremacy overhead. Despite a slight nip in the air, I began to have hope for the weather today. Bumblebees so plump that they reminded me of winged mice droned hypnotically, drawn to hanging baskets outside the post office, lifted my hopes further still. Maybe summer came to Scotland after all.

Shopkeepers could be seen in their windows, preparing to open for the day ahead, as the street around began to fill with early morning shoppers and others making their way to work.

There was a lovely buzz to the village that I hadn't expected. It had a nice feeling about it, a pulse through the day-to-day noises of people going about their business. Claremont had heart, but it was more than that. There was something about the place that I couldn't quite put my finger on. Maybe it was just glimpsing the mystical stag in my garden that morning making me sentimental, but the place felt almost enigmatic. Like there was more just above the line of conscious awareness going on here.

Being the new girl in town, I received my share of surreptitious glances, but more often, friendly smiles. That was good; I was keen to blend in as quickly as possible.

A newspaper stand outside what was obviously the local newsagent caught my eye, and the headline: "Local Youth Dies Using Contaminated Heroin." A stark reminder that even small villages like this had their share of problems. Drugs frightened the hell out of me. So many kids seemed to fall into using them and ruin their lives.

I had wanted children at one time. At that moment, I almost felt relief, not to have any such worry about children of my own. Hunching in my coat as a shudder rippled through me, I continued along the High Street.

The Shades turned out to be an attractive 1920s Art Deco style building that had been converted to operate as an old folks' home. Despite being almost a hundred years old, the building was probably one of the more recent builds in Claremont.

As I walked up the short driveway, admiring the classic geometrical lines, I found a path that took me directly to the front door. I pushed the buzzer as first-day nerves kicked in.

"Hello?" A voice crackled through the intercom.

"Hi there, it's Brook Flem...Davenport. I'm starting work here today." I couldn't believe I had slipped up already. I would definitely have to be more careful.

I was buzzed in and met instantly by a short (despite three-inch stilettos), attractive, plump, middle-aged lady with a tight red perm. She thrust her hand at me to shake.

"So glad to meet you, Brook; I'm Ruth, the home manager." Her face was genuinely welcoming, but there was something distracted in her countenance.

"Hi, Ruth, nice to meet you too," I smiled nervously.

After a brief exchange of pleasantries, Ruth led me down a long green corridor, passing several open doors on the way. I noticed a TV room and another room where elderly people were quietly reading as we passed by.

The home appeared spotlessly clean, but there was an overall whiff of neglect about the place. The carpets were fading and dated, wallpaper had started to curl from corners, and all the furnishings were beginning to show signs of stress. It wasn't quite shabby, but like most council-run institutions, it was definitely in need of a cash injection.

I moved to the far left of the corridor to let past a tall woman, dressed in a clinical white uniform. She pushed in front of her a trolley housing what looked like various types of bottled medication that clinked together in chorus as she walked along.

"Morag?" said Ruth, resting her hand lightly on my arm in introduction. "This is Brook, the new part-time recreation lady." Morag looked in her late thirties and was incredibly thin. She had a short, sharp blonde bob framing her almost severe features, but she smiled warmly at me in greeting, and it completely transformed her face. I noticed what pretty green eyes she had.

"Oh right, the newbie," she said. "Welcome."

"Thanks," I smiled back as she passed, and Ruth and I carried on down the corridor.

"Here we are." Ruth came to a stop and opened a door to her right, revealing a small office. I followed her in and watched as she lifted a stack of paperwork off a swivel chair and indicated for me to sit. Then she added the papers in her arms to another stack on her desk, before sitting in a chair behind it. It was the untidiest office I had ever seen. The desk looked like it would collapse at any moment, like an overloaded donkey. The clutter didn't stop at the desk, but overflowed to cover most of the floor as well. I wondered how she could work in such an environment. I guessed that explained Ruth's air of distraction. I wouldn't be able to concentrate on anything 100 percent if I knew this lot waited for me in my office.

I sat through a half hour induction chat with Ruth, where she outlined staff policy and handed me several brochures and papers to look through when I got home. I was just pleased to relieve her of some paper. To my own relief, she only asked a few questions about my time at Art College and life in Essex, but nothing particularly specific about my personal circumstances, not even why I had moved to Claremont. After all, how much did people really want to know about you?

I didn't like lying. It really went against the grain to now find myself in a situation where it was highly likely I was going to have to lie on a regular basis. I hoped everybody was going to be as easy as Ruth.

I followed her back down the corridor towards the front of the building and into a spacious room that had the benefit of large windows flooding the room with natural light.

"Morning everyone." Ruth addressed a table where eight of the home's residents sat, apparently awaiting my arrival. "This is Brook Davenport, the young lady I told you about, who will be organising various recreational things for you to do." I sucked in a deep breath and smiled at the faces before me. Four of the faces that looked back smiled in welcome. That was promising. Two were somewhat indifferent. One was hostile, and the last was unconscious, snoring.

Ruth began introductions. Starting from left to right were Joe, Bob, Doreen, Emily, Arthur, Peggy, and Edith, and the lady sleeping was Marion. Ruth didn't bother to wake her.

"Well then, I'll leave you to it," and after a quick reassuring pat on the arm, Ruth left. I was petrified.

"What's in the basket?" It was the hostile looking lady, Edith, who spoke. I was too nervous to catch the mockery in her tone. I looked down at my basket, like I'd never seen it before.

"Um, I've brought some clay," I said finally. "I thought we could do some pottery or sculpting." Edith burst out laughing, and I felt myself physically slump.

"What are we doing tomorrow, gymnastics?" Any fragments of confidence I had managed to muster disappeared at the sound of her laughter. Whatever possessed me to think that a group of old-age pensioners would want to sit around playing with clay?

"I thought you might enjoy it," I tried. I felt so humiliated. Edith grabbed the hand of Peggy, the lady next to her, making her jump, and held it up for me to see.

"With hands like these?" I winced at the scorn in her tone. "Silly English lassie."

How could I have been so stupid and thoughtless? Sculpting had been a ridiculous idea. Peggy's hand was so badly deformed with severe arthritis that I doubted she could hold clay, let alone sculpt. I didn't know what to say. Blood charged to my cheeks as I realised how foolish I'd been.

Then Peggy snatched her hand from Edith's grip and said with an encouraging smile, her eyes twinkling at me, "I'm looking forward to doing some sculpting, Brook. I used to enjoy pottery as a bairn. Ignore Edith; she's trying to unnerve you. Don't let her." This little speech was greeted with several ayes from around the table.

Edith sat back, somewhat defeated, and crossed her arms dramatically in front of her chest, apparently sulking.

"Aye, and dinnae rule out the gymnastics either," said the man called Joe, in his broad Scot's accent. "Just have a paramedic on standby, ye ken."

I exhaled with relief, and something inside of me relaxed just a little.

"We can start with cartwheels, and see how we go," I said, attempting a shaky smile.

The two-hour session flew by, and to my immense relief and satisfaction, I thought everybody enjoyed themselves, even Edith. She had reluctantly joined in after seeing everybody else getting involved and, despite several age-related hindrances, by the end, the group turned out some pretty impressive pinch pots.

Joe and Peggy chatted away throughout the morning, helping me to relax a little, and gave plenty of suggestions for day trips in the local vicinity. A place called Ross Cove seemed quite popular with everyone, and I promised to see what I could arrange.

Marion, who had been sleeping when I arrived, woke up about halfway through the session, confused and not quite sure where she was. But after a moment, she seemed content to join in.

It was, of course, the frosty Edith who bombarded me with the most probing of questions. Where was I from? Why did I leave? Why did I come here? So on and so on. I took DI Thompson's advice of earlier in the day, and stuck to the truth as far as possible. Generally, everybody listened politely and seemed to accept my answers as they would anybody else's. After all, what possible reason would I have to lie to them? Only from Edith did I feel any scepticism. Her shrewd eyes surveyed me with intense interest as I answered her questions, and her curt responses told me she saw what I wasn't saying. I ignored her acute intuition. What else could I do?

I was packing up at the end of the session when a voice interrupted my thoughts.

"Hi." I turned to see Morag, the staff member Ruth had introduced earlier, just standing inside the doorway. She was carrying a pile of pressed white sheets in her arms. "How did your first morning go?" I was relieved to see that her sharp face was smiling.

"A little shaky to begin with, but I think it turned out okay," I replied, suddenly vulnerable again as I remembered Edith's taunts at the beginning of the session.

"Let me guess. Edith, right?" she asked, dumping the sheets down on a chair beside her and putting her hands on her hips. Her smile had disappeared, her face suddenly severe.

"How did you know?" I asked suspiciously.

"She did the same to me on my first day. Edith likes to see if she can push your buttons, but it looks like you survived," she said. A smile of approval returned to her mouth. I noticed again how her face transformed and came to life when she smiled. "Her bark's worse than her bite," she added. "Once she sees that she can't get a rise out of you, she quietens down. Trust me." Morag, too, had obviously been put through her paces by Edith. It was a relief to know I hadn't been singled out for attention.

"I wasn't expecting such a tough audience," I admitted.

"Never underestimate the old timers," she laughed. "Joe and Peggy are lovely. In fact, they all are, really. At least you only have one first day to worry about. It will be easier here on in," she said reassuringly.

"Actually, I've got another first day tomorrow," I said, suddenly distracted. I hadn't given much thought to the second job I was due to start tomorrow. It also occurred to me that I didn't have a clue where Avallon House was. The agency had only provided directions for the care home.

"Another first day?" Morag asked, confused.

"I'm starting a housekeeping position at Avallon House tomorrow," I explained. "I don't suppose you know where it is?"

Morag's eyebrows shot up when I mentioned Avallon House, giving me hope that she would be able to provide directions. "You're going to be working at Avallon House?"

"Um...yes, I think so." I looked down into my basket, to see if my letter from the agency was handy to confirm.

"Sure, it's just a few miles out the village." She began sounding almost excited. "You have to really keep your eyes open for the driveway; it's unmarked, just a gravel track amongst the trees that leads up to the house."

I groaned, and my shoulders slumped. Surely not? It couldn't be the same place. That would just be cruel. It did, however, explain his certainty that we would see each other again. The agency would of course have told him the name of his new housekeeper.

"Are you okay?" Morag asked, concerned by my reaction.

"I think I met my new employer yesterday," I said, tortured. I couldn't go back there and face that rude man again. I wouldn't.

"You met Arwan Jones?" My heart skipped a beat as I finally had a name for the angry face.

"My car broke down on my way into Claremont yesterday. I stopped by a house to use a phone," I explained. "It sounds like it was Avallon House."

"So what's the problem?" Morag asked. Her tone wasn't at all snippy, just curious. I frowned, shaking my head.

"He's the rudest man I ever met. He barely uttered three words to me, and when he did, it was an insult." I could feel my cheeks flaming as I remembered his scoff at my name, but was more overwhelmed by the stirring, pulling sensation in my centre. It was the same feeling I'd had when in his presence the day before.

"That doesn't sound like him," Morag said, clearly taken aback by my account. "I've seen him once or twice in the village, and haven't actually met him, but those who have say he's charming and charismatic."

I was startled by what I was hearing, and even more confused by his behaviour towards me. Why had he treated me with such blatant coldness and hostility?

"There was little charm afforded to me," I muttered.

Morag shrugged her slender shoulders. "Well, you'll be the envy of the village," she said, bending to retrieve her sheets. I guessed she was referring to how good-looking he was, but who on earth would want to work for such an arrogant, rude man?

"He's famous, isn't he, an actor or something?" I asked, hoping to finally pinpoint why he seemed so familiar to me.

"No," she laughed, "although he could be, right?"

"Sure," I said. "He's very handsome." I hoped I sounded as blasé as I intended. I wasn't prepared to admit just how beautiful I thought Arwan Jones was.

"He's an art and antiques dealer." That was a shock, although it did explain the amazing art collection. But it didn't explain where I recognised him from. Presumably his work would take him all over the country. Maybe I had seen him in an art gallery in Essex at some time, on the rare occasions I'd escaped the shackles of Adam. Morag snapped me from my thoughts.

"I better go make the beds up," she sighed. "Don't worry about tomorrow. You must have caught him on a bad day or something." I had a feeling I was really going to like Morag. The longer I was in her presence, the more I seemed to. I hoped I'd maybe made my first friend.

"Thanks, Morag. I'm sure you're right," I said, not feeling the conviction of my tone.

There was no way in the world I was stepping foot in that place again. A girl had her pride. The job could go hang! Something else would come along eventually.

chapter

THREE

The following morning, I got up as soon as it was light and went for a run. I had to put the previous night behind me.

The day before, I had noticed a path running through the trees, not far from my garden boundary. It looked well-established, so I set off, hoping to find some inner calm before tackling the day ahead. It wasn't long before the combined sound of my steady breathing and my pounding trainers began to do the trick.

I was delighted to discover that the path, after half a mile or so, met directly with the river. The footpath then continued to run alongside its banks. The sound of the silver water tumbling over rocks filled my senses and seemed to flush out my mind, clearing it of the shadow of the previous evening.

Unlike my first night in Claremont, I had barely slept a wink the night before. Every groan and creak of the settling, unfamiliar house had me imagining Adam creeping into my bedroom, hell-bent on revenge, and as a result, I had spent most of the night in a state of terror. The only way I had been able to eventually calm down enough to sleep had been to let my mind wander to Arwan Jones.

I knew that only a crazy person would want to put themselves on the receiving end of anger from that man for a second time. Clearly I *was* crazy, because despite my complete resolve the day before that I was under no circumstances returning to that house—"A girl has her pride", and so on—I had decided at some point after midnight that I was going to do exactly that, and show up to work the following morning. Curiosity had got the better of me. Morag had said he was charming and charismatic. I needed to see how he would react to me on a second meeting. I had to admit that my already fragile ego had been dented.

Although Adam had not allowed me to have friends of my own, that didn't mean I wasn't capable of making and keeping them. I had a few friends at school and college, and nobody that I knew of had ever disliked me on the spot. There had to be an explanation. Maybe he had been working on something vitally important the morning I knocked on his door? Or received some terrible news just moments before I arrived? Anything could have happened, prior to my turning up, that might *just* justify his behaviour towards me.

After my run, I took a hot shower and had the usual wardrobe crisis. I set off at eight o'clock, worrying unnecessarily that I wouldn't be able to find the obscure driveway. But it was like I was drawn to it. My foot was braking and I'd put the indicator on before I'd even consciously made the decision. It wasn't pouring with rain, which probably helped. In fact, it was a bright, clear morning. The sun brought the landscape to life around me, throwing the multitudes of rich greens from the woods into clarity.

I drove purposely slowly up the winding drive, giving myself some needed time to get a grip. The peculiar pulling sensation in my centre, which I had experienced when in his company only forty-eight hours earlier, had returned, and my heart thumped heavily in my chest. I was nervous as hell. I had to pull myself together before I saw him. I was being ridiculous.

The huge dogs were waiting for me when I pulled up, and they bounded over with unreserved excitement when I stepped apprehensively from the car. I was struck again by their unusual bright white coats, not to mention the sheer size of them. They trotted ecstatically alongside me as I headed for the porch, my own personal entourage.

My legs shook as I walked up the steps. I lifted my hand to raise the bronze knocker, but was startled to find the front door ajar. I stuck my head through the open door and called, "Hello?" in as loud a voice as I dared. I waited. No response came. No angry man charging down the oak staircase to reduce me to a pile of smouldering ashes with his anger. I tried calling again, this time managing to lift my voice an octave.

"Mr Jones? It's Brook Davenport. I'm your new housekeeper." My voice sounded loud and obtrusive as it echoed around the huge reception hall. Again, there was no response. A breath later, I decided to enter.

I stepped into the opulent hallway and turned around in a full circle. It was as breathtaking as I remembered, but this time I was alone. There was no sign of Mr Jones.

I bit my lower lip, glancing nervously around me. I felt like I was intruding again. I stood for a long moment, the dogs circling me, nudging me with their cold noses, as I wondered what on earth I should do.

Then I spotted a note with what looked like my name on it, on the sideboard by the phone I had used only a couple of days earlier. I walked to the sideboard, picked up the note, and read...

'Brook, my apologies I could not be there to greet you this morning. You will find everything you need in the kitchen at the end of the hall and through the door on your right. I only require the ground floor serviced. Yours, Arwan'

I exhaled. I wouldn't have to face him, today at least. I folded his (what I felt to be) very formal note and tucked it into my handbag before walking slowly towards and then past the staircase, feeling like a trespasser.

I opened the door on the south wall to a large, modern kitchen. French double doors let in the bright morning sun, and I wandered over to them, pulled by the light, and looked out onto a beautiful garden.

Unlike the front garden, the back garden was full of flowers of all descriptions. Three miniature manicured hedges in circular shapes dominated the space, with their centres full of summer blossoms. In the heart of the centre circle stood a life-sized naked goddess-like creature made of bronze. It looked old and weatherworn, but that certainly didn't detract from her beauty; instead, it gave the statue an earthiness, almost as if she emerged from the soil beneath to stand tall in the garden, a gift from nature herself. I shook my head in disbelief. This place was incredible.

As stated in Arwan's note, I found everything I would need laid out for me on the island in the kitchen. As I wiped down the already spotless surfaces in the kitchen, I decided that the best emotion to feel was relief, relief that Mr Jones didn't feel it necessary to greet me on my first morning as his housekeeper. It wasn't rude or personal; he was just a very busy man. We had already met, after all. Yes, I was definitely relieved I wouldn't have to face his cold expression that morning. I refused to acknowledge the part of me that felt deflated. I ignored the hint of disappointment that marred my relief at his apparent absence. I admitted curiosity only. I had been curious to see how he would react to me and how I would react to him.

It occurred to me, suddenly, that he could be in the huge house somewhere, as the front door had been left open. Surely he wouldn't have gone out and left the door ajar? Was his car there when I arrived this morning? I couldn't remember seeing it, but I couldn't be sure, I had been so nervous. Of course, if he were in the house, wasn't it particularly rude of him not to have greeted me personally?

I moved about the kitchen, debating the prospect that he was intentionally avoiding me. The most likely explanation was that he was simply too busy to greet me, and had decided to leave the door open so he could get on with his work. That was definitely the most logical reason, and yet I couldn't shake the feeling he was purposely avoiding me. If he felt that strongly, why didn't he just phone the agency and cancel my contract? It was easy enough to do.

I worked into the early afternoon, pausing only for a quick sandwich, which I ate on the bottom step of the staircase. Despite only being required to service the ground floor, I still worked in an area that consisted of the kitchen, drawing room, a large dining room, a library, an art studio full of canvases, and several smaller rooms, all of which were filled with paintings or antiques or both. The two huge dogs never left my side, but the day ended just as it began, through the front door, with no sign of Arwan Jones.

Friday was the same, with no sign of him, and again on the following Tuesday.

It continued like that for some time, and as the weeks passed and the end of summer approached, I settled into my job at the retirement home and loved the time I spent there. By the end of my second week, every able resident at The Shades attended my recreational activities, around twenty-three in total. Ruth was delighted, and so was I. Things at the home were going great. I was absorbed into the team almost instantly, and had even formed some friendships, particularly with Morag, who I'd spent several evenings having dinner with, along with her teenage son, Daniel.

I managed to transform my bland little bungalow into a home that I felt truly proud of. Having free rein over its decoration had been truly liberating, and every time I walked through the front door, it gave me immense pleasure.

Of course, Adam was never far from my thoughts, but that was to be expected. Adam wasn't the only one serving a life sentence, but every other aspect of my new life was definitely heading in the right direction.

It was only the continued absence of Arwan Jones that tarnished the otherwise smooth transition. Why was he avoiding me? I had come to the conclusion that he had to be doing just that, or surely our paths would have crossed in his own home by now.

His house only fuelled my interest in the man himself. Arwan was a complete enigma to me. Even though I'd only met him briefly, something about him didn't fit, didn't feel quite *normal.* Arwan just didn't seem to appear the usual young, handsome, wealthy bachelor. Shouldn't he be living in some city apartment in London or something, schmoozing the night away in expensive restaurants, with beautiful women on his arm? Instead, he chose to live in complete solitude, aside from two dogs, in a huge mansion practically in the middle of nowhere in the Scottish countryside!

I was completely aware that I was stereotyping; maybe I was subconsciously comparing him to Adam, and that wasn't fair. Good-looking and wealthy didn't necessarily add up to sleazy and no morals. Adam was a rotten apple in a big barrel, and I knew better than to judge, but my personal experiences to date made it hard.

Morag had informed me, when I had subtly enquired about the Jones's, that Avallon House had been in their family since as far back as anyone could remember. Apparently th ey had homes all over the country and were very rarely in residence in Claremont. In fact, as far as Morag was aware, the house had been unoccupied for years, until Arwan had showed up six months ago.

"Does anyone know why he suddenly moved in?" I had casually asked.

"Nobody really knows him well enough to ask," Morag informed me. "He's rarely in the village, and when he is, it's usually to see Frank Jefferis at the bank, and Frank would never discuss his wealthiest client's personal circumstances." She smiled to herself, as if remembering something, then continued. "Duncan Buckie took it upon himself to drive out to Avallon House and personally welcome Mr Jones back to Claremont, on behalf of the community."

"Duncan Buckie?" I asked, not knowing who she was talking about.

"Oh aye, he's a financial advisor who works out of a small office above the bakery."

"Oh."

"He didn't make it up the steps, apparently," she laughed.

"Why ever not?" I had asked.

"The guard dogs!" she replied, as if it should have been obvious.

I had laughed out loud. They were huge, but hardly what I'd call guard dogs; they were softies, in fact. I felt silly thinking it, but they seemed so intuitive to me, completely attuned to my daily emotions. The dogs had turned into my shadows over the weeks, rarely leaving my side as I worked my way around the ground floor of Avallon House. They were quiet, but constant and dependable at my side.

They were undoubtedly remarkably unusual, like no other dogs I'd ever seen, but definitely not what I would have called guard dogs. I was surprised they hadn't licked him death.

"Well, Buckie reckons they near killed him," she had continued. "He said they were like wolves, snarling and snapping at him until he got back in his car and drove off." She laughed again. "He actually thought they were going to eat him! I'd love to have seen the look on his face."

I was surprised at the time that Morag found the story so funny; she seemed friendly with everybody in the village, and it didn't seem like her to laugh at another's terror.

But nothing Morag could tell me enlightened the mystery that surrounded Arwan Jones. If anything, it intensified my curiosities about him, and there was, of course, still the niggling feeling, a hunch that I'd known him before, or at the very least that we had met. But no matter how hard I racked my brains, I just couldn't place him.

Five long weeks had passed since I began housekeeping at Avallon House, and I wondered if I would ever lay eyes on my boss again.

I woke after a restless sleep. I had no memory of it, but I was sure I had been dreaming about Adam. My bedclothes had been bunched up in a wrinkled little heap when I woke, as if I'd been fighting with them.

I showered, dressed, and blow-dried my unruly hair. My hair had always frustrated me. It wasn't curly enough to spring into cute ringlets, but it was wavy enough to produce a bird's nest any magpie would be proud of. Of course, it didn't help if there was moisture in the air, like there seemed to be most mornings as autumn approached. I sighed and tied it up out of the way in a loose ponytail, and after applying some light makeup, grabbed my coat and headed out the door.

If I wasn't nervous as I drove out to Avallon House, then it wasn't a normal day.

Despite the fact that I hadn't laid eyes on him again since the day we met, I always felt a strange mixture of dread and excitement on waking on a Tuesday or Friday morning. My mind fired the same questions at me as soon as I opened my eyes from my slumber. Will he be there today? If he is, will he talk to me? Will he be angry? Should I talk to him? So as I turned my little car into his driveway, the anticipation of the possibility of seeing him again grew and grew, as did the fluttering wings of a million butterflies in my stomach.

I had noticed over the last few weeks, as the weather had begun to turn, that Avallon House seemed to cling on to the remnants of summer sunshine. It had been overcast and grey when I had left my house, yet here the sun was out, and it looked like it was shaping up to be a lovely day. Like my employer, the stormy weather of the afternoon that my car had broken down had yet to rematerialize. In fact, I'd noticed what a little suntrap this part of Claremont was. I had heard of unusual weather phenomena before, apparently having something to do with the lie of the land.

Warmed by the sun, I shrugged out of my duffle coat and folded it over my arm as I headed up to the front door. I noticed immediately that the white Audi Q7 that had been parked out the front of the house on the day I broke down was, as usual, nowhere to be seen. My hopes, however, weren't entirely dashed, as I had discovered a double garage round the side of the house one afternoon, when I had decided to cut some flowers from the garden to decorate the dining room table.

Arwan no longer left the door ajar, but it was always unlocked for me to enter. As usual, the dogs had met me at the car and padded alongside me up the curved steps and into the hall. I didn't pause, but headed straight through to the kitchen, to pick up the cleaning things that I stored under the sink.

The house was quiet. There was no sign that Arwan was at home. I sighed as I opened the cupboard under the sink and bent to retrieve my cleaning basket.

"Come on, boys," I said to my two constant companions as I straightened up, "let's get started in the library." They looked up at me with adoring toothy grins, and I couldn't help but smile back at them, as I scratched one behind the ear and then the other.

My footsteps felt weighted as I walked through to the library. I should have expected his absence, and I suppose that on most levels I had, but I couldn't deny the part of me that felt disappointed at its continuance. I knew I shouldn't feel that way. I *must* not feel that way, and yet there it was. I was deflated. Something inside of me collapsed, as it did every Tuesday and Friday morning. I found myself trying not to think about him, trying not to conjure the memory of his glorious face in my mind, but it was a battle I always seemed to lose. Was I becoming fixated upon him? Surely if he just materialised one day, and we had a nice chitchat over a coffee, I could put all this nonsense behind me. I had taken his treatment of me all those weeks ago far too personally. He really couldn't hate me so much that he refused to be in his own home just because I was here. I refused to believe that was the case.

"Oh, get on with it, Brook," I muttered under my breath. I wasn't being paid to ponder over the mysteries of Arwan and his unorthodox behaviour.

I looked around me. The library never failed to impress. It was a massive double-storey room, and three of its four walls were floor to ceiling shelves stocked with the oldest and rarest books you could imagine. Arwan had so many first editions, it would make any book dealer green with envy, and all appeared in immaculate condition, including signed first editions of Tolkien's *The Hobbit* and *Lord of the Rings*. Most astonishing of all was an excellent duplicate of the *Book of Kells*, housed in its very own glass display cabinet. To my untrained eye, it could indeed have been the original. I would have loved nothing more than an opportunity to flick through its almost garishly coloured pages.

The west wall held three large windows, which were permanently closed over with burgundy velvet drapes. No natural light filtered through at all, a measure presumably intended to protect the books. In the centre of the room sat four brown leather chesterfield sofas pushed together in a square, encasing a large coffee table. It was classic, stylish elegance, just as in every other room I had seen in the house.

I don't know why I didn't remove my flats this time, before climbing the ladder that provided access to the tallest shelves. I always remembered to take my shoes off, preferring the feel of the step under my bare foot. I could get a better grip that way. It felt safer.

It was as I ran a yellow cloth duster along the closest shelf to the ceiling that I made my second error in judgment. I took one foot off the ladder and stretched out to try to reach a fraction further with my duster, rather than simply pulling the ladder along. As I moved to put my foot back on the step, my gripless flat shoe slid straight off like butter from a hot knife. Having expected to have both feet back on the step, I had readjusted my weight, and as my foot slipped, I lost my balance on the ladder altogether.

I was aware that I was falling, but the full horror of the likely outcome of that fall didn't really have time to register. Or maybe it was just that my brain wasn't prepared to consider consciously what my subconscious had already accepted, that at best I'd end up in a wheelchair, never able to walk again, or that at worst I'd shatter my skull into a thousand white splinters.

I landed, not as I'd been expecting, with a deathly crack like an axe splitting wood, but with more of a frump, a sound like that of somebody catching a sack of spuds from a considerable height—which, as it turned out, was near enough what had happened. I must have closed my eyes at some point, so I didn't register what had intercepted my drop.

My eyes flew open, and I found myself looking up into the face of Arwan Jones.

My heart, pumping with adrenalin from the fall, seemed to suddenly stop in my chest, and an odd, astonished sound escaped from my lips. I could feel my eyes wide with shock as I stared up at him. He was just as beautiful as I remembered; hair black as night, and those distantly familiar, piercing eyes which, from only inches away, seemed more purple than blue.

I scanned his handsome face, anticipating the rage that would be there. What a klutz he would think I was! I could feel my cheeks begin to burn up with humiliation.

"Brook, are you hurt? Brook?" Something shifted in my core at the sound of his voice. It was a relief that he didn't sound mad; in fact he sounded worried, anxious, even. His black brows furrowed together in concern, his expression grim as he looked deep into my face, waiting for me to answer. I noticed what a glorious smell he had, like rose petals, but somehow not remotely feminine.

"Brook? Will you answer me! Are you hurt?" I realised I was gaping at him, a sure-fire way to make him livid. I was convinced it was my gaping at him that had contributed to his anger on the day we met. I swallowed hard before I could answer.

"No, I don't think so." My voice sounded shrill. I hoped he would put that down to shock at the near death experience rather than shock at being in his arms. He let out a breath, as if he'd been holding it, and I felt some of the tension leave his arms as he held me.

I was suddenly acutely aware of the feel of those arms around me, the feel of his tight chest muscles along the line of my body as he cradled me. He was much bigger and brawnier than I remembered. I felt small, childlike in his arms. I was distantly aware that I seemed more concerned about the fact that I was in Arwan Jones's arms than I was about the small matter of nearly dying.

Instead of setting me down on my feet, he walked over to one of the chesterfields and gently deposited me on it.

"You should be more careful," he said as he released me.

"I know, I know, I always remember to remove my shoes. I don't know what I was thinking, well, clearly I wasn't thinking, because I didn't, and I slipped, and well, if you..." I realised I was rambling like an imbecile. I snapped my mouth shut to stem the flow.

I could feel my face burning again. If I were outside, I was absolutely certain I could be spotted from space, thanks to its glow. What must he think of me? I dreaded to think. Why did it matter so much what he thought of me? That was a question for later.

I watched him warily as he went to sit on the sofa facing me. I wondered if his mood would switch to anger now that he knew I was unharmed and that he was not likely to face any accident lawsuit. But I saw only concern in his face as he studied me. I dropped my gaze to my lap for a moment, not wanting to meet his eyes and become fixated. I knitted my fingers together and circled my thumbs nervously.

Then something odd occurred to me, which I would have realised sooner if anyone other than Arwan had caught me.

"How did you catch me?" I hadn't heard him come in. The floor was hardwood, and the sound of footfalls unavoidable. "I didn't hear you come in before I fell. Don't get me wrong," I added quickly, "I'm glad you did. Thank you, I think you just saved my life, but you weren't in the room before I fell." I folded my legs beneath me on the sofa as I waited for him to answer. He seemed to be debating what to say.

"You must have been preoccupied. I came in the moment before you fell...in search of a book," he said evenly.

I was too utterly confused to pay much attention to the coldness that was creeping into his tone. I definitely had not heard him come into the room. Although I hated to admit it, I listened for him all the time, wanting to see him. I would have heard him if what he was saying was true. I supposed he could have been in the hallway before I fell, but how could he have made it across the room in time to catch me? Was that possible? The room was huge. Could he really have made it from the doorframe, across the room to where I was falling, in a matter of seconds?

I looked to the door, then over to the ladder, then back to Arwan. The look on his face dared me to challenge him. I could tell that he could see I was trying to do the math in my head and coming up with *not bloody likely!* So how did he do it? I didn't see any way it was humanly possible. It was unlikely if, as he said, he'd come into the room before I fell; I *would* have heard, and I would have definitely sensed him. I noticed as I sat on the sofa across from him how the air had changed since he'd been in the room. I could feel it as I watched him watching me.

I was about to challenge his explanation when he suddenly rose from his sofa opposite me and moved towards mine. My breath caught in my lungs, and my insides stirred in that familiar way, as he strode through the space between us with clear resolve. Then suddenly he stopped, as if hitting an invisible wall just feet from me. I looked up into his face to see a myriad of emotions flash across his features, as his hands flexed at his sides. He appeared to be battling with himself, restraining himself, but from what? Anger finally settled on his handsome face, as somehow I knew it eventually would, then he turned stiffly and stalked from the room. The sound of his shoes on the hard wood floor as he left seemed to echo about the room long after he departed, just as the static of his mood continued to hang in the air.

I remained on the sofa for an immeasurable moment, staring after him at the empty doorway, trying to make sense of what had just transpired. I had spent weeks waiting to see him again in the hope of putting to bed the initial hostilities between us and, perhaps, even discovering from where it was that I knew him, but instead, seeing him only seemed to have made things worse, much worse.

chapter

FOUR

Sunday nights were always the hardest. Unlike Saturday, when I nearly always did something with Morag, I was alone all day and night with my relentless thoughts and fears.

I hadn't heard anything else from the Witness Protection Department in Essex since that first morning in Claremont. I supposed that was a good thing. It meant everything was going as it should be, and that Adam was still safely tucked up in his prison cell, doing his time. Every now and then, in quiet moments, I found myself imagining him there, lying on his bunk, in his cell, arms crossed behind his head, pale grey eyes staring up at the ceiling, plotting. Sometimes I thought I could actually feel his hatred for me, travelling in waves over the miles between us, connecting us despite the separation.

I was aware of the fact that Adam would know I was frightened, that no matter where I was, I would be living in fear, and I knew that would comfort him, maybe even give him pleasure. It was hard not to wonder who was the one really being punished.

This particular Sunday, however, my head was otherwise occupied, with Arwan. I had spent the whole weekend trying to come up with some sort of explanation for his superhero-like rescue. It didn't matter what he said, he was not in that room when I fell. As my hands idly played with a chunk of clay, I replayed the incident over and over again in my head, possibly lingering a little longer than necessary on the part when he had me cradled to his chest. I shook my head in disbelief as I looked down to discover that my hands had formed the chiselled planes of a familiar handsome face. I sighed, then quickly squished the clay with both hands.

The following morning, I was relieved to be out of the house and back at The Shades. Joe had asked me if we could watch *Blue Hawaii* during our recreation time. As I was planning a fairly laid-back morning anyway, I readily agreed. I had struggled to stop giggling throughout the duration of the movie. Joe sang along to every song, standing up periodically to swing his narrow hips like a man half his age.

I was still giggling as I walked up the hallway to the staff room at quitting time, hoping on the off chance that I might catch Morag for a coffee on her break. I poked my head round the corner and saw Ruth and Clive, one of The Shade's carers, eating their sandwiches, but saw no sign of Morag.

Ruth waved, clocking me in the doorway.

"Why don't you come join us?"

"Thanks, I will." I pushed through the door and went over to the kitchen area to stick the kettle on.

As I sipped my tea, the chat centred round the forthcoming Halloween celebrations. It appeared that Halloween was quite the event in Claremont. The village's folk prided themselves on throwing the best street party in Scotland. Clive, who was what one might call a stereotypical looking highlander, stocky, ginger, and very hairy, began recounting several tales from previous years, tales that were well on their way to becoming legend.

The highlight of the year before had apparently been when a friend of Clive's, Laurence John, had been tasked with lighting the bonfire. As legend went, when his first and second attempts proved futile, he got a little overzealous with the kerosene. Needless to say, his third attempt was somewhat more successful. The force of the heat from the flames that had suddenly surged from the storey-high pile of sticks and debris had licked poor Laurence John's eyebrows completely off. From what I understood, prior to his brush with fire, he had sported a somewhat rustic set of caterpillars, and the new look was rather startling, to say the least, much to the hilarity of all his friends, naturally. If I wanted, Clive could email me photos.

"You'll have a hoot, lass, just wait and see!" he promised. I didn't have the heart to tell him that there was no way on earth I'd be attending. I couldn't tell Clive that big crowds, scary masks, and loud noises were not a good combination for me. I would definitely be sitting that one out. I made a mental note to get a good excuse ready.

After my chat with Ruth and Clive, I went home to pick up my car. I had planned to head over to Logan Mills and stock up on some art supplies. There was nowhere in Claremont that sold basic sculpting materials, so when I ran low, it was time to take a trip out of the village. It was at moments like this that I really felt the benefit of my new life, even if it had to be under witness protection. I had the freedom to go where I wanted when I wanted, and I didn't need anyone's permission.

A small smile played about my lips as I headed out along the winding road and it started to drizzle again. It had been raining on and off all morning and wasn't showing any sign of letting up. The sky was an intriguing marbled grey, streaked through with white where the daylight tried unsuccessfully to break through. The trees that lined the road had begun to cast off their yellow and orange leaves, and I sighed at the prospect of my first Scottish winter, only a matter of weeks away. I had a sudden mental image of Avallon House, its gardens and the surrounding woods covered in a layer of freshly fallen white snow. Maybe winter wouldn't be so bad after all.

I had decided that I had to accept Arwan's word that he had been in the room when I fell from the ladder in the library. I didn't really have any choice. I couldn't prove that he wasn't, and what other explanation was there?

Maybe I had been preoccupied as he said, preoccupied with him. I was determined to get a handle on that. I thought about him way too much, much more than was healthy. I sighed; easier said than done. Why did he have such an effect on me? Okay, it was obvious to any female, and probably a lot of males too, that he was simply glorious to look at. But I didn't think it was just the way he looked that had me so...umm...*confused?* Yes, "confused" was a good word to describe my feelings for Arwan; I liked it so much more than "obsessed".

Other than a couple of trucks, I hadn't passed a single vehicle. The road out of Claremont was usually quiet at this time of day, so I noticed immediately when the black four-by-four appeared in my rear-view mirror. It seemed to surge up behind me like a rogue wave and sat right on my tail, leaving barely a metre between us.

I drove on along the country road, not adjusting my speed, as my eyes flicked back and forth from the windscreen to the black jeep in the mirror. Crap, this guy was really close. I felt puny in my hatchback, the jeep seeming to loom threateningly over me like some sort of dark menace.

I could feel panic beginning to seep in. Adam had driven a dark four-by-four, and even though I knew it was crazy to think it was him, I couldn't help but imagine his face behind the wheel, peering down at me through the rain, his mouth twisted up in a grin. The windscreen was tinted, so I couldn't even see who was behind the wheel, to put my mind at ease. Not that it would have made much difference; the jeep was so close now that all I could see in my mirror was the steel leer of the grill.

I glanced down at my speedometer. I was hitting eighty-five miles. I hadn't intended to go faster, but my foot had pressed down on the accelerator without my conscious knowledge. It didn't matter; the blacked-out jeep ate my speed up instantly. I never gained an inch on him.

What was this guy's problem? My eyes kept flicking, almost frantically now, to the rearview mirror, as all strength abandoned my legs. It was a mammoth effort just to keep my foot pressed to the accelerator.

I could feel a full-blown panic attack brewing, as my anxious breathing began to fog up the windows.

Had he found me? Had Adam somehow tracked me down and sent somebody to run me off the road? My mind went into complete panic mode. I couldn't think straight, and the awareness of my mental meltdown made me even more frantic. I didn't have a clue what to do. Should I pull over? Speed up? Slow down? Brake hard? What should I do?

I was distantly aware of the fact that I hated feeling so out of control, like my mind was outside my body watching a robot look-alike go through the motions of driving the car. *"The lights are on, but nobody's home"* echoed around somewhere in my brain.

Then it happened; I sucked in a huge breath and released it, as the road ahead straightened out and the black jeep immediately accelerated and overtook in a swoosh of tarmac. It left my little car behind in a splattering of brown water, which rendered my windscreen temporarily useless until the wipers pushed the muck away.

I pulled over on the verge and watched as the black jeep disappeared over an incline in the distance. It had seemed like we had driven along bumper to bumper for hours, but it could only have been minutes, if not seconds.

So much for enjoying the freedoms of my new life! I could almost hear Adam's gravelly laugh ringing in my ears. My complete terror at some loser in a tinted car would have given him a real kick.

After a few minutes, my heart, although still pounding, had begun to slow, and my breathing eventually evened out. I unwound the window, and the cool air that flowed in helped calm me further still.

Okay, so that was a bit of an overreaction, but one I felt was justified, I thought defensively. The man behind the wheel of that jeep had undoubtedly been driving in an aggressive and threatening manner. I just wished I hadn't become so incapable of rational thinking during my panic. I thought randomly of the heroic pilot who had landed a plane in the Hudson River in New York, avoiding a major catastrophe. No chance of a career in aviation for me.

What if something did happen for real? There had to be a likelihood that Adam would try, or why was I in witness protection? I sighed. I had to have faith that the police would keep me secure, but one thing was clear from the incident with the black four-by-four: I would be useless in aiding my own likelihood of survival.

As I sat gazing out the windscreen, musing over my lack of ability to react under pressure, a succession of cars passed by, spraying my car in waves of filthy water.

"Oh great, now there's traffic!" I muttered. "Where were you five minutes ago?" For a moment I felt as tired and washed-out as my little car must have looked, sitting there all alone on the side of the road.

The journey back was uneventful, although it had brightened up slightly. Not to the extent that the sun had come out, but it had stopped raining, and the clouds were more white than grey.

When I pulled up outside the bungalow, I saw something pinned to my front door. It looked like a note. I lifted my box of supplies from the boot and headed up the stone steps to the door.

The note said, *'Making lasagne for dinner. See you around seven if you fancy. Mo'*

My stomach growled in anticipation. I hadn't eaten anything since a bowl of flakes that morning. Morag made a mean lasagne.

I smiled to myself as I pulled her note from the door and let myself inside.

The following morning, I made my way directly to Arwan's studio. I had thought, after our last quite frankly bewildering encounter, that I probably wouldn't see him again for several weeks, if not months. And yet, there he was.

He sat at an easel, in his studio, perfectly still apart from his right hand, which held a paint brush to a canvas. He didn't acknowledge my presence, but had to be aware of it, because I'd practically shrieked in surprise when I noticed him in the room. After an awkward moment, waiting for him to talk to me, I realised that he wasn't going to. It seemed that Arwan found it impossible to communicate with me without losing his temper, and had therefore decided it was best not to bother. I decided to do the same. I could ignore him just as easily. Why would I want to talk to him anyway? The man was beyond irritating!

I decided to carry on as normal, as if he wasn't there. I certainly wasn't going to instigate a conversation after his behaviour towards me. Of course, carrying on as normal is easier said than done when it feels like your whole body trembles from the inside out.

"Stop looking at him, Brook!" I told myself over and over again. It seemed my eyes didn't tire of seeing his face. It was a battle to keep them on my work, as I moved about the room. I thought several times that I could feel his eyes on me, but when I chanced a glance at his face, they were always carefully on his work.

It went on like that for the next few weeks. I worked and he worked, in complete silence. I became accustomed to his presence, but I couldn't get used to it. My heart stuttered and my insides stirred every time I saw him. I had to learn to concentrate and focus, in order to regulate my breathing, to basically make sure I *was* still breathing whenever we shared a room together. Despite that, the silence didn't bother me. In fact, I welcomed it. No questions, no answers, fine with me. I could relax at the mansion in that respect, and I was surprised to notice that I actually enjoyed my days there. It was like an Aladdin's Cave, containing so many ornate and beautiful things. I didn't like to think about the value of the items I dusted. I guessed that most were priceless.

My favourite rooms were his library and studio, which was where I assumed he felt the happiest, as he seemed to spend most of his time in one or the other. When I worked in these rooms, he carried on as if I wasn't there.

I began to realise that despite the lack of interaction between us, I was aware of him on many levels. I was intrigued, and it bothered me immensely to admit it.

I would find myself watching him discreetly from the corner of my eye. His grace was breathtaking. He never wasted a motion on hesitation or indecision; every gesture or step had a purpose. Complete confidence.

I loved to watch him paint, the way his dark head bent to his work, with strong hands and fingers moving so adeptly. My senses had become highly attuned to picking up the slightest sounds he made as he worked, brushstrokes on canvas or the ting of a brush being gently cleaned in water from a jar. He rarely made any sounds himself as he worked, not a cough to clear his throat or a stifled yawn from his perfectly formed mouth.

His finished pieces adorned the walls of the studio. They were mostly oils, with the occasional water colour, but all were of a classical style and of exceptional accomplishment. I had to be careful there, surrounded by his work. I got lost, lost in the worlds created by his hands. They literally made me emotional.

My favourite depicted a creamy-skinned mother and child bathing nude in a pool within a lush forest clearing. The mother smiled serenely down at the boy cherub in her arms, while his chubby fingers playfully tugged a lock of the black hair tumbling down around her shoulders. A green canopy filtered light from an unseen sky, creating orbs of gold that sparkled on the water like jubilant fairies. The mother and child were not alone; they shared the clearing with all manner of creatures, foxes, badgers, rabbits, robins, even snakes foraging amongst the plants and fallen leaves, all in harmony, all enjoying the tranquillity of the forest. None were concerned with the others' presence; they were completely at peace with themselves.

I would mentally bathe with them in the cool water, light and carefree. It was a hard place to leave.

In fact, I was bathing in the forest pool one autumn afternoon, when he spoke to me for the first time since saving me from a premature death.

I swirled on my feet to face him, dropping to the floor the feather duster I'd been holding, as I was ripped from the peace of the picture by his deep tones. He had been in the library engrossed in his books when I walked by the door twenty minutes earlier, and as usual he hadn't acknowledged my presence. What had he said? I'd missed it, having been so caught up in his damn picture.

My heart was pounding in my chest from the fright he'd delivered me. My inner voice spoke up, "*Is that the only reason your heart's pounding?"* Shut up!

Why was he standing there watching me with his piercing purple eyes, anyway? What did he want? I refused to acknowledge my insides shifting, stirring, and pulling in his direction, and again, the recognition of faint but certain familiarity.

"Why did you come to Claremont, Brook?" His face was hard, his tone controlled, apart from when he spoke my name. Then it sounded strained, as if it hurt him to say it. What was wrong with this guy? Could he really dislike me that much?

Alarm bells rang in my head as I digested his line of questioning, but I was getting used to this particular one, remembering always to stick as close to the truth as possible.

"My marriage broke down," I said. "I needed a fresh start, and here seemed as good a place as any." I hoped that would satisfy him, but I knew somehow that it wouldn't. His eyes bored into me as if holding me up. It *felt* like they held me up.

"Did you leave him?"

"Yes."

"Why?" Okay, he had decided to engage me in conversation, albeit belated, but why on earth did he want to know about my marriage? He was staring at me intently, clearly expecting an answer to his question, even though he had uttered not a word to me in weeks.

I'm sure he could hear my heart thudding away obtrusively in my chest, and my stomach felt like I'd left it on a roller coaster somewhere. Why did he now feel it appropriate to ask about my marriage? I opened my mouth to tell him to mind his own business, but found myself saying, "He wasn't the man I thought he was." This was true; he certainly wasn't, but why was I telling Arwan that? I was supposed to be keeping my mouth firmly shut about my past, not blabbing on about it! I was beginning to feel annoyed and apprehensive for being so open with him.

"Who was he?" he asked casually, looking from me to a vase on a table at his side. A lock of black hair fell across his face as his head angled down. I sighed at the sight; he was glorious. He lifted his hand to the rim of the vase, and began circling it with his index finger, as if my answer were of little consequence to him. I sensed that despite his sudden show of indifference, this question was just as pertinent to him as the first.

"He was cruel," I answered sadly, watching as his finger moved around the vase, my voice barely a whisper. I wanted to tell him that my husband was a cold-blooded murderer. I wanted to tell him the words my husband had said to me as he was led from the dock, *"I'm in the shadows Brook, remember that..."*, but I knew I could not. I pressed my mouth into a firm line, willing it to stay shut.

Arwan's eyes remained trained on the vase, but it was impossible to miss the anger suddenly surging from him. It was overwhelming. The air about us seemed denser, warmer, and slightly static. It was like the day we had met, but worse somehow. I was frightened by his reaction and felt an urge to back away from him. I was about to do just that, when all feelings of fear departed, replaced by astonishment.

I squeezed my eyes shut for an instant and reopened them, hoping to see again what I thought I had just glimpsed. I could have sworn Arwan's eyes had flashed a completely different colour to their usual gentian blue.

All fear forgotten, I moved closer to him, trying to get him to look at me, but he avoided my gaze. It didn't matter. His usually tanzanite eyes had flashed a brilliant emerald green. I was desperate for him to look at me so I could see them more clearly. Instead, he turned and walked brusquely from the room without saying another word. I was left staring after him in shock, soaked in an atmosphere dripping with his anger.

What had just happened? The man was driving me crazy! Why did I make him so angry? I would have to have it out with him. This bizarre behaviour couldn't continue. We were both adults; surely we could discuss this, whatever *this* was, and put an end to it.

I glanced down at my watch. Two o'clock; I could leave.

On my way through the hall to the front door, I paused at the sideboard and picked up my wage. Every Tuesday it was there in an envelope, waiting for me. I never had to ask. Anything, it seemed to avoid communication, until just a moment ago.

As usual, the dogs trotted alongside, escorting me to the car. I had grown accustomed to their following me around, and barely noticed it anymore.

My hand reached out for the car door, my mind still occupied with the bizarre encounter with Arwan, when a sudden gust of wind like a miniature tornado picked up across the lawn, sending hundreds of autumnal leaves twirling noisily into the air. The chaotic, swirling leaves rustled and fluttered in my direction at rapid speed. For some reason I couldn't fathom, I was frightened. Every hair on the back of my neck was on end.

"Get a grip, Brook, it's a gust of wind!" I muttered, to shame myself out of a panic attack, as my eyes zeroed in on the approaching wind. "What harm can a little wind do?" I watched the twirling leaves continue to crack and whip their way in my direction. The logical part of my brain said I was being ridiculous; the wind would pass over harmlessly. Why wouldn't it? Another part of me was unconvinced.

Maybe living in a constant state of anxiety was turning me insane, because there was something about the leaves moving towards me that I didn't like, but I couldn't quite put my finger on why. Then it hit me. The leaves weren't moving quite so chaotically as I initially thought; there was sequence to their movements. I could see patterns repeating themselves over and over again as the growing formation continued to head my way. It gave the twirling leaves a sense of life, some sort of purpose, an unseen force come to seek me out and steal me away.

I was frozen to the spot, unable to move, despite my inner voice shrieking at me to jump in the car and slam the door shut. The dogs seemed attuned to my sudden anxiety, as they came to sit by my legs in a protective gesture. I heard them whining softly to each other as they stared in the direction of the spiralling leaves, which surged nearer and nearer to where I stood, heart hammering in my chest. I was fighting a feeling that I was about to be lifted off the ground with the other debris and disappear forever into the surrounding woods. I held my breath as the gust approached, glued to the ground, eyes wide. My hair flew up as the wind passed over, and I raised my arms to my face as a shield.

Ludicrously, I felt relieved to be still standing in the same frozen, terrified position as the tornado disappeared into the woods behind. I remained motionless, not breathing, as I digested what had occurred as the wind passed over me. I hadn't been lifted off the ground as I'd feared, but I had to seriously consider the possibility that I was losing it, because I could have sworn somebody whispered a single word in the air as the flurried leaves battered about me: *Achren.* Other than the dogs, I was completely alone. I had to be losing it.

"Achren." I repeated the word out loud. Something about the way it rolled off my tongue felt natural, familiar even. Where had I heard that before? I felt a peculiar tugging sensation at the back of my mind, as if the whispered word were a pair of hands trying to coax some long-forgotten memory from my subconscious into awareness. There was, of course, the possibility that my stressed mind, in fright, had conjured up the word from nowhere as the wind blew over, but I didn't think that was true. I was sure that the voice had somehow come from within the energy that blew the leaves. This could indeed back up the very real likelihood that I was having a nervous breakdown. After all, as far as I knew, most people didn't hear words whispered in the wind, outside of poetry.

Was there something about Claremont? The place did have an atmosphere, there was no doubt about it. The unusual seemed usual here. Claremont felt like a place where white stags and whispering winds wandered hand-in-hand, and as the days passed, I felt more and more akin to it, part of it. But I really didn't know if I could trust my own judgments. I suddenly felt very lonely, to the point that I had an almost overwhelming urge to run back into the house in front of me and throw myself into the arms of a man who clearly couldn't stand me. No, I certainly didn't need a professional to tell me I was insane.

chapter

FIVE

"Brook, are you okay? You look like you're a million miles away."

I had asked Morag to meet me at Claremont's only bar, the Balmoral, after leaving Arwan's, grateful that it was her day off. I was still shaken up after my peculiar conversation with him, not to mention the strange wind phenomena that occurred as I was leaving.

"Sorry, Morag, I was," I admitted.

Morag and I had grown close quickly. It was almost as if she made it her personal goal in life to draw me into her family and make me feel welcome. She was the first person I thought of when I decided I needed company. It had been a long time since I'd had a real friend of my own.

Other than me and Morag and a young man behind the bar, the cosy old lounge of the Balmoral was empty. A fire crackled and hissed comfortingly in the hearth as flames licked wood, providing welcoming warmth after the cool autumn air outside. I could just make out the gentle hum of voices coming from behind a door that led through to the public bar, along with the occasional chink as snooker balls glanced abruptly off one another.

"Thanks for coming for a drink. I really felt like some company," I said, giving Morag my full attention.

"You know me, any excuse for a drink," she said, smiling. "So are you going to tell me what's got you in such a flap?"

I put my head in my hands and sighed. There was no point in concealing from Morag what had happened; she would see right through any attempt I could make at being dismissive. I peeked at her through my fingers, and was surprised to see her smiling knowingly at me.

"Why are you smiling?"

"You're in love with him already!" she replied, laughing. "He seems to have that effect on people; half the women in the village are dreaming about him, and the other half haven't seen him yet." It felt childish, but I pulled a face at her.

"Well what then?" she demanded, still smiling. I couldn't help feeling a little irritated by her seeming lack of concern for my turmoil.

"Why does he hate me so much?" I asked. "He ignores me completely for weeks, and then when he does finally decide to talk to me, it's through gritted teeth! He can't stand me, and I don't know what I've done to upset him." My shoulders hunched in bafflement as I turned my palms to the ceiling. "I'm serious. I don't know what his problem is."

"If it's that awful, quit."

"Oh great, that's helpful!" I snapped, and was immediately repentant. Morag was right. Why didn't I just quit? I didn't need this grief, not after everything I'd been through, and yet quitting just wasn't an option I could think about.

"Sorry, Mo," I said guiltily.

"Well, it does sound a bit odd," she said, mirth still twinkling in her eyes. "Everybody seems to think he's..."

"I know, I know, so charming and charismatic!"

Morag laughed, then after a moment became thoughtful, taking a sip of her wine. Her eyes lowered in thought, their vivid greenness reminding me of what I thought had happened, but couldn't possibly have seen, in Arwan's eyes that morning. People's eyes didn't flash different colours, for goodness sake. Did they?

"Have you looked in the mirror lately, Brook?" Morag said suddenly. I looked at her, confused. "I'm going to tell you because you seem completely oblivious to just how beautiful you are." She looked me up and down with wide eyes, her hand gesturing from my head to my toes. "Velvet brown eyes, skin like porcelain, high cheekbones, and a figure any woman would kill for. I wouldn't at all be surprised if he wasn't stunned into speechlessness the minute he opened the front door to you."

"Don't be ridiculous," I muttered, embarrassed. I had never taken compliments about my appearance particularly well. It wasn't that I wasn't grateful for them; I just didn't know what to do with them.

"Seriously, Arwan Jones isn't the only one who caused a stir in Claremont when they arrived. It's not just your face either. You've a glow about you. People seem...," she paused, searching for the right word, "*drawn* to you. Every resident at the home shows up to your sessions religiously, and you know how they can be, right? There's something about you. It makes people feel, I don't know...," she paused again, her eyebrows furrowed in thought, "part of something... relevant!" she added with triumph, as the word she was looking for came to her.

"Are you finished?" I asked.

"I guess so," she replied, smiling again at my attempt at curtness.

I decided a change of subject was maybe in order. I had wanted to ask her something anyway. A log on the fire cracked and popped loudly, commandeering our gazes as a little flurry of orange sparks flew up the chimney. I took a deep breath.

"Has anything *weird* ever happened to you?" I asked, turning back to her. I wasn't sure how much I was going to tell her, but I really needed some assurance I wasn't insane. She raised a brow at me. "By weird, I guess I mean sort of *supernatural* weird," I clarified. I don't know how I expected her to answer, but I was full of relief and gratitude that she didn't laugh. Instead, her face took on an intense expression mirroring my own, and I loved her for her empathy.

"The world's a strange place. I think weird stuff happens all the time." She paused again in thought. "I actually think weird, even *supernatural* weird, is completely natural."

I smiled inwardly; I had known she'd make me feel better. I tucked my hair behind my ears, glanced over to check that the barman was suitably occupied, then leant over the table to be slightly nearer her, whispering, "I heard a voice today, as I was leaving Arwan's, just before I got in the car. But I was completely alone." I watched for her face to take on a look that clearly questioned my sanity, the same look I had always seen on my mother's face throughout my childhood, but she surprised me again.

"What did the voice say?" she asked, no nonsense.

"Achren," I answered with no hesitation.

"Achren," she repeated, surprised. "That's a Celtic word for 'Other-world'." We had leant unconsciously further in towards one another, our voices low as we talked.

"'Other-world'," I repeated. "What does that mean?"

I was a little taken aback that Morag had even heard of Achren. I had expected her to be as bewildered about what it meant as I was.

"My late Aunt Rudy, and for that matter, quite a few other people in Claremont at one time, believed in the existence of gateways that lead directly to another world." She hesitated, and this time it was her turn to gauge my reaction. "Achren," she continued, "is what some people call that Other-world. My aunt was convinced there was a gateway here in Claremont."

"You're kidding."

"No, I'm serious. My aunt and her like-minded friends searched this whole area, the woods, the meadows, everywhere. I think they even thought it was something to do with the river."

A shattering crash from the bar split the air like an arrow, making us both jump in our seats. We turned to see an apologetic looking barman bending on one knee, retrieving several broken pint glasses scattered about the hardwood floor. Morag and I looked at one another and burst out laughing at our overreaction, lessening the tension somewhat.

Morag composed herself and shifted the subject.

"I get the feeling that stuff has happened to you in your past that you don't want to talk about, and I'm guessing a lot's to do with your ex-husband." I was surprised and touched by her intuition.

Morag never pressed me for information about myself, but I had moments, like now, when I wanted to tell her everything. I didn't like having secrets from her. Morag had made my transition into witness protection so much easier, and she didn't even know it. I longed to tell her just how much that meant to me. People like Morag were the salt of the earth. She was a single mother raising a teenage boy alone, and she still made the time and effort to bring me into her little fold. I felt the telltale sting of salt in my eyes, and knew that if I didn't take a deep breath, I was going to start blubbering right there in the pub.

Mo placed a warm hand lightly on my arm. "What happened to you before you came here is your business, and I would never probe you. But whatever you went through, it's led you here," she tapped her index finger on the table between us, "to Claremont, and I think there's a reason for that." She took a sip of her wine, leaning back in her chair, then smiled brilliantly. "Don't ask me what it is; it's just what I believe."

I likewise took a sip of wine, digesting her words. "I hope you're right, but whatever happens, I'm glad I came here and met you. A better friend I couldn't ask for."

Neither of us saw the arrival of another in the bar, and considering the newcomer's size, that was quite an achievement. The sound of voices had me turning to see the back of a tall, hugely overweight man, standing at the bar. He had a full head of dark hair swept back with too much gel, and he wore a pale grey, ill-fitting suit. The image had me in mind of a grotesque cartoon character.

"Great," Mo muttered under her breath. I looked from the man at the bar back to her. "Buckie," she whispered, rolling her eyes. So that was Duncan Buckie, the man who Arwan's dogs had menaced.

I watched as Mr Buckie shoved his change into his trouser pocket and turned from the bar, drink in hand.

His eyes alighted on us, and I shivered. There was something immediately dislikeable about the guy. He was a creep, and it stood out a mile, even under the false smile he had fixed on his piggy features.

His face was white and tight, the skin stretched and strained like an overstuffed beanbag ready to split.

"Ladies!" he bellowed in a surprisingly high voice as he strode over to our table, manoeuvring his bulk like it were no more than a child's paper boat on a stream.

"Hi, Mr Buckie," Morag said, the sound of her voice unashamedly monotone. All humour had disappeared from her features, her face severe. I guessed that my intuition about the man was merited. Morag did not seem at all comfortable with his sudden presence.

"You must be Brook?" he asked, pulling a chair from the next table over to ours and sitting down without invitation. He either hadn't picked up on Morag's blatant "leave us alone" face, or chose to ignore it.

"Yes...," I began.

"I'm Duncan Buckie," he said in his strange soprano voice. He thrust a pudgy hand out for me to shake. I knew it would be cold and clammy even before I reluctantly shook it.

"Hi."

"You've probably heard of me," he continued, ignoring Morag. "I'm the only financial advisor in the village. I work out of an office above the baker. They bake the bread, I invest it!" His chins wobbled fascinatingly as he laughed loudly at his joke. Then he paused, his eyes seeming to zero in on my face as a hungry, greedy look flashed over his features. I wasn't sure what he wanted me to say.

"Well...,"

"You're looking after Arwan Jones up at Avallon House, aren't you?" My heart skipped a beat at the change in conversation. I glanced at Morag, who was shaking her head in disbelief, then back to Mr Buckie. In the brief moment my attention had been elsewhere, he had, in true magician style, managed to produce a business card out of thin air. The penny dropped.

"Perhaps when you're next up at Avallon House, you might just give this to Mr Jones?" he said, offering the card to me. "I could be very useful indeed to a man like him." I looked down at the business card clutched in his hand.

"It's really not my place to do that," I said, keeping my hands firmly wrapped around my glass. I didn't want to admit that I was barely on speaking terms with Arwan Jones, let alone making introductions.

The look of the huge man's eyes switched from greed to anger in an instant. He lent slightly closer over the table, in a gesture designed to intimidate. I instinctively pressed back into my chair to increase the distance between us. Was this really happening? Was this guy trying to bully me into giving Arwan a business card?

"Surely it wouldn't hurt for you to mention me to him, would it? A small favour, that's all I'm asking for."

I wasn't frightened of Duncan Buckie, but every instinct in my body seemed to be repelled by him. Indignation ignited inside me as I stared back with disbelief into his uncomfortably close face. I had spent the best part of seven years in a marriage being bullied, and I wasn't about to let anybody ever treat me like that again.

"Actually, it would, Mr Buckie. I'm his housekeeper, and I can't help thinking that passing on business cards would be completely inappropriate." I could see Morag nodding in approval, in my peripheral vision, and mouthing something at me that looked like "Bravo!"

He said nothing for a moment, but stared at me with his furious little eyes. I wondered if he was going to push the subject, but in an instant his jovial facade fell back into place.

"Of course, of course, completely understand!" he said convivially. He abruptly turned his attention to Morag.

"I hope you haven't forgotten the committee meeting for the Halloween party next week, Morag?"

"No, Mr Buckie," she said, in the same deadpan tone.

"I hope you'll be joining in the festivities, Brook?" he said, bringing his eyes back to me. He sounded genuine enough, but his eyes were flint. I was relieved he didn't wait for an answer. Instead, he lifted his bulk, in a surprisingly fluid movement, from the chair, hand clutching his drink.

"I'm afraid you'll have to excuse me, ladies. I'm meeting a client in the public bar next door." He split an overly toothy smile between the two of us and moved swiftly through the adjoining door into the public bar.

Immediately the atmosphere in the room cleared. It was like breaking the surface of the sea after being tumbled by a wave. I hadn't even realised that I'd been holding my breath since he had seated himself at our table. It was a relief he was gone. Morag sat back in her chair, clearly relieved as well.

"What was that all about?" I asked.

"Buckie's been desperate to get Arwan Jones as a client since he moved here. I reckon he's mulled away many an evening, thinking what he could do if he got his hands on his millions. I guess he saw you as his opportunity."

"I didn't think he was going to take no for an answer." I remembered the steely look in Buckie's eye, and shuddered again.

"He's definitely the village creep," Morag said. "Along with an idiot, every village has one." She sipped her wine and glanced in the direction in which Buckie had disappeared. "He seems to have everyone in Claremont duped," she added. "He's a powerful man in this village."

I didn't see how Buckie could dupe anybody; he was beyond creepy. Something about him reminded me of when I was nine years old, and my mum and Frank, my stepfather, had bought an old rundown house in Pitsea, Bowers Gifford. My bedroom had been upstairs at the end of a long, windowless corridor, with the bathroom at the other end. In the middle of the night, when I needed the lavatory, I had to tiptoe along that long, dark corridor to get there, and as I passed the darkened staircase, something always, without fail, made me turn and look over my shoulder. Buckie reminded me of the creep and crawl of that shadowed stairway. I shuddered again and wondered how somebody like that became remotely successful. I wouldn't trust Duncan Buckie with a pound, let alone a fortune.

Morag broke into my thoughts. "You are going to come to the Halloween party, aren't you? I can sort you out with a costume if you like?"

"Um...er...I don't...," I stammered. I'd forgotten all about the excuse I had planned to prepare. "When is it again?"

"Halloween's the same date every year, Brook. October thirty-first remember?"

"Oh yeah, um," I was stammering again. I cracked the knuckles of my right hand absently, as I tried to think of a get-out plan.

"You're not trying to think of an excuse, are you?"

"What? No, of course I'm not," I said unconvincingly. I'd overdone the no, and it came out like "noooooowah", giving the game away.

"I'll count you in, then," she said, beaming.

Great, I groaned inwardly. Maybe I could feign an illness a little closer to the time. I still had a week or so to come up with something. I'd heard a couple of people moaning in the newsagent about flu and fevers and various other colder weather-related ailments. I was sure I could catch one of those. I felt a little relief at the prospect.

As we finished our drinks, the bar had begun to fill up with the evening clientele. The Balmoral had the monopoly on local and tourist revellers seeking an evening out in Claremont, being one of the few places with a liquor licence. We shimmied through the growing throng, smiling and waving to familiar faces.

Outside, it was already dark, despite the fact it couldn't have been much later than six o'clock. For some reason, the street lighting hadn't switched on. That probably wouldn't bother most people, but I wasn't most people, not anymore, anyway. I had come to dread the night and the shadows it brought with it. Morag suddenly stopped.

"Hang on," she said. "My shoelace has come undone." She headed for the nearest bench that sat, almost obscured, beneath a lovely weeping willow that I admired every time I passed it. I sat down next to her, as she began tying her lace.

The pub door abruptly swung open, startling me and breaking the stillness of the evening outside with the escaped sounds of chatter and laughter from within. The dark doorway was briefly illuminated in a warm glow of gold, just before Duncan Buckie stepped out into the frame and recorked it. He then stepped onto the pavement, letting the door swing shut behind him as he pulled a mobile phone out of his waistcoat pocket. He fumbled with it for a moment with his chunky fingers, before putting it to his ear, seemingly not noticing the spectators on the bench off to his right.

"What the hell is it, Douglas? I haven't got time for this; I'm right in the middle of a meeting!" He paused for a moment, presumably allowing the person at the other end the opportunity to explain. Then he resumed his shrill rant down the phone, as he began to walk up the street away from us. "I told you only to contact me on this number in an emergency; otherwise you wait till you bloody well hear from me!"

"What on earth was that all about?" Morag muttered, her eyes following Buckie as he carried on in the opposite direction. He had stopped by a parked car and, with his free hand, was searching for something in his pocket. A moment later, he slid behind the wheel of the car and, once again, I was taken aback by his agility. For such a large man, he manoeuvred almost gracefully into the driver's seat. A few moments later, his shiny metallic blue Jaguar pulled out and drove down the main street, a little faster than the regulatory thirty miles an hour.

"He's driving a brand new car, and has been bragging around the village about a new cruiser he's docked somewhere at Ross Cove. Where on earth does he get all the money from; there's a recession on, right?"

"Beats me," I said, curiously. I was just glad he'd gone. But even in his absence, something of him seemed to remain, tainting the air with its unpleasantness, almost as if he left a trail of toxic slime behind him that lingered until it dried up and disappeared.

Morag's mouth curved up in a cheeky half smile as she continued to gaze in the direction in which Buckie's Jag had disappeared.

"Snog, marry, or avoid?" she asked.

"Without doubt, avoid!" I laughed, though I couldn't help thinking again of that shadowed stairway.

Morag and I parted ways and headed home. I had no appetite, but knew I should eat something, so made do with cheese on toast. I washed, dried, and put away my single plate, and was leaning against the kitchen counter, contemplating what to do for the rest of the night.

Eventually I decided to work on a sculpture of Edith's face, which I had started several weeks earlier.

As I moulded the clay, my mind ran wild. What was Achren? Another world like Mo said, and if so, what did that mean to me? My mind turned to Arwan. Should I have it out with him and confront him about his quite frankly bizarre behaviour towards me? Or should I just let it go and carry on as normal, and hope he would do the same? I simply didn't understand why my marriage, or indeed the breakdown of it, should be of any concern to him. Most worryingly of all, when he questioned me, I seemed unable to stop myself telling him the truth. I had to get myself under control, or the cat could leap from the bag and my identity be blown. Why did everything have to be so damn complicated?

I thought about how I would feel if that were to happen and I had to move away from Claremont. I felt tears on my cheeks and quickly wiped them away. I didn't want to admit just how much it would hurt me if I had to leave this place. I would miss Morag and my friends at the home terribly. I had, for the first time in my life, found somewhere that I felt I almost belonged.

Then there was Arwan, a man who had me so confused and bewildered that I didn't know how on earth I felt about him. I didn't even really know him, and yet on some level, we were connected; I could feel it. Although we had rarely communicated, and not once had it been particularly cordial, there was *something* between us, and there was something about *him*. The very air around him seemed charged, alive, with the energy his moods generated. And those eyes of his, I was certain they had changed for an instant, flashed another colour every bit as vibrant as his usual purplish blue.

The early evening hours flew by as my mind conjured up more questions that I didn't know I'd ever get an answer to. I finally put my scalpel down, exhausted by my mental musings, and decided to have my first early night since arriving in Claremont. Adam usually started creeping into the forefront of my mind around sundown, with the prospect of bed not far away, but tonight I felt so tired, I could barely keep my eyes open.

I wrapped Edith back up in her damp cloth for the night, switched off the lights, and dragged my body down the hall to the bedroom. Moments later, in the dim light of the lamp, I was pulling the duvet up over my shoulders. I drifted off almost instantly.

I knew I was dreaming, because of both the slight blur to the edge of my vision and the fact that I was walking up the driveway to Avallon House barefooted, in a long ivory gown. Strangest of all, however, was that my hand rested on the back of a white stag. We meandered up the drive like two old friends, out for an evening stroll.

As we made our way companionably up the driveway, I marvelled at how real all my dream senses seemed. I could feel the stag's fur, thick and coarse, under my hand, as well as the cold gravel beneath my feet, hindering my pace. My footsteps were noiseless next to the sound from the stag's hooves, which crunched almost continuously into the gravel and overshadowed any other sounds of the woods at night. The evening air was cool, with just the gentlest of breezes to dance the fallen autumn leaves around us. The moon shone high and bright in the black sky, throwing plenty of light to our path.

Presumably, because I was dreaming, there was nothing remotely odd about the fact that I was in the company of a beautiful white stag heading up Arwan's driveway. Instead, it felt completely natural and not in the least strange or uncomfortable. In fact, I felt thrilled that I was going to see Arwan; anticipation coursed through my veins. I knew, even in a dream, that it was crazy to feel that way, but there it was.

As we veered the last bend in the drive and Avallon House stood grandly before us, the stag came to an abrupt stop at my side. I stopped too, confused by the stag's suddenly tense behaviour. Something in his whole demeanour had changed. He was no longer relaxed and at ease, but restless and agitated, his muscles visibly rippling and flexing with tension. I looked up at the house, following the line of his gaze.

It took me a moment to realise what I was looking at. It was a woman, standing amongst the white pillars of the porch. At least, I initially thought she was standing. On closer scrutiny, I realised that she was actually hovering several feet above the ground. I couldn't see her face. It was obscured by a veil of jewels that sparkled and glinted in a rainbow of colours as the moonlight found them. She wore a long, flowing gown, like the one I wore, only red. Rich red hair, the same colour as her dress, flowed and rippled around her hidden face like cascading silk, seeming to have a life all of its own. I flinched unexpectedly as the acidic sound of the strange woman's voice cut through the night to where we stood.

"I will not let her enter, Lugh, she will not see what he keeps." The woman suddenly surged backward through the air, her hair flying forward with the force of the movement. She came to a stop directly at the front door of Avallon House, almost entirely blocking it from view in a mass of red satin and swirling hair.

"You must know your attempts to stop it will be fruitless? A potion has been prepared; she will reclaim her status." I turned in wonder to look at the beast at my side. I should have been flabbergasted that it spoke, but I wasn't. Instead, its majestic tone, deep and soothing, made my heart stutter.

"Ah yes, but will she be willing to return? I don't think so." the veiled woman replied, her sharp voice trailing into mockery. The wind had picked up, and her crimson gown rippled up behind her in a flame of fabric, straining the front so it clung to her body, outlining her distinctly feminine shape. I gasped at the sheer presence of the goddess-like creature on the porch, the faceless woman with the scornful voice. Who was she?

The stag lowered its head and took several quick steps towards the porch and away from me. I felt a shudder of fear as I realised that it wanted to attack the woman, to charge her. The stag's voice trembled with anger and contempt.

"What do you hope to achieve with this madness, this treason?" I looked from the woman to the mystical beast as they continued to engage each other in increasingly bizarre conversation, seemingly oblivious to my presence. I had no idea what they were talking about, but had an unshakable feeling it was centralised around me. After all, it was *my* dream. The woman laughed without humour.

"You could never understand," she mocked, "but even restored to her status, I doubt she'd return." The woman sighed, tilting her head to one side, and I knew she was studying me. "Human living appears to compliment her."

"For now!" The stag growled as his hooves chomped up the gravel in anticipation of a fight. I ran the short distance between us, to be at his side again, and I placed my hand on the muscle of his neck in the hope of calming him. I understood, somehow, that if they hurt each other, it would hurt me too. I don't know why; I just knew I couldn't bear to see that happen.

He turned his head and looked me directly in the eyes, for the first time since this peculiar dream had begun. The beast was in the prime of his youth, but in contradiction, his eyes were ancient and heavy with weariness.

"Who is she?" I whispered. I watched, waiting, as his eyes studied my face.

"A problem," he sighed eventually. He seemed so sad that it pained me. I let my hand fall from his neck to drape over his shoulders. We stood like that for a short moment, until a terrible ear-ripping sound of snarling snapped my attention back to the porch.

Arwan's giant dogs had appeared out of nowhere. But they were not like I'd ever seen them before. They weren't themselves. They were almost...demonic. Their hackles stuck up like poisoned iron spikes down their backs, as they spat and snapped at the woman in crimson. I stared in horror and disbelief, my eyes wide with fear, every hair on my body on end, as they stalked up the steps to the porch, headed to where she floated just feet from their foaming angry snouts. They were going to tear her apart.

"No!" I cried. "You'll kill her!" I ran forward, but just as I reached the first step, the dogs lunged for the woman, flying several feet in the air from opposite directions. I screamed, turning my head away, cowering into myself, unable to accept what had just happened. She wouldn't stand a chance. I waited to hear the sounds of flesh and fabric being torn to pieces, but realised after a moment that there was nothing, nothing but silence and the sound of my frantic breathing.

I turned slowly back to face the porch and looked up the steps, then exhaled with relief in an audible gush. The woman was gone, disappeared into thin air. The dogs sniffed around the area she had vacated, whining and agitated that their hunt had eluded them. I felt suddenly light-headed as the terror slowly began to subside. I wondered distantly how I managed to stay asleep through the whole ordeal, everything seemed so real.

"Brook." My eyes focused past the dogs at the sound of my name and at the familiar voice that spoke it. Arwan stood in the doorframe of Avallon House. Even in my dreams, I felt instantly drawn to him. The pull in my core, at the centre of my being, was just as strong and compelling as when I was in his company for real.

I smiled up at him, instantly comforted by his sudden presence in the mayhem of my dream.

"Come inside; there is something you need to see," he said. The moon shone directly on his handsome face, and I saw that his eyes were desperate despite his gentle, coaxing tone. I automatically placed my bare foot on the bottom step, with the intent of ascending to join him, when the shrilling sound of my alarm cut through my dream and yanked me out, back to reality.

I sat upright in my bed, like a coiled spring, and glared down at my alarm clock as it flashed impatiently at me whilst beeping in its own particularly irritating way. I reached over and slammed my hand down on the snooze button, then let myself slowly and thoughtfully drop back down to the pillow.

As I walked up the High Street, still pondering my dream, the rain started. I opened up my brolly and carried on like everybody else. I loved that about Scotland. Unless it absolutely poured, people just carried on with life, be it washing the car or gossiping outside the newsagent. I guessed, in a place where it rained as much as it did here, what choice did you have?

It was Saturday morning, but Ruth had said I could use her office to make some calls. I was planning to take the residents to Ross Cove on Wednesday afternoon, and had to make the necessary arrangements.

As it turned out, Saturday was a pretty busy day at The Shades, with lots of relatives only able to visit at the weekends. It was lunchtime, and visitors and residents alike were eating together in the outdated dining room. The hum of cheerful chatting that I heard as I walked by made me smile.

I went straight to Ruth's office and opened the door. I flicked the lights on and sighed, as I was instantly faced with the leaning towers of paper that dominated so much of the room. As I negotiated my way around the precarious stacks, to the chair behind the desk, I wondered if Ruth would think it were cheeky of me if I offered to help with some of her filing.

I made a couple of phone calls to tie up various arrangements, and half an hour or so later, wandered back down the corridor to the dining room, to have a quick word with Cook about the pack lunches we would need.

After talking with Cook, I weaved my way back through the tables of the dining room. I was greeted by several of the residents still finishing up their lunches.

"Lass?" I turned to see Edith gesturing for me to come and join her. I noticed that she wasn't alone; her arm was linked to that of a much younger man whom I had seen once or twice around the village. There was something different about him today, something that I couldn't quite place. I walked over to their table as they stood to meet me.

"I just wanted to introduce you to my grandson, Alex," Edith said, touching the man's arm. I extended my hand to Edith's grandson and smiled.

"Hi, Alex. I'm Brook."

"Hi, how are...," he began, when Edith cut across him.

"Alex is the policeman here in the village," she said, proudly beaming up at her grandson.

"One of them," he interjected. "There are two of us, remember, Nan?" I noticed that his cheeks were flushing. Edith shrugged her shoulders dismissively.

"He cuts a fine picture in his uniform, Brook."

"Thanks, Nan," Alex muttered, rolling his eyes to the ceiling in mortification. That last comment hadn't helped his blush either. It suddenly dawned on me why he looked different today. The couple of times I had passed him in the street, he would of course have been in his police uniform, as opposed to the casual attire of jeans and green flannel shirt that he wore today.

"Oh, I thought I recognised you," I said, suppressing a smile at Edith's unashamed boasting.

"Yeah, I've seen you about the High Street too. How do you like Claremont?" he asked, swiftly moving the subject on. I noticed for the first time how much he looked like his grandmother. He was lucky enough to have inherited her cheekbones and full mouth, but his eyes were warm brown as opposed to blue.

"I like it very much, thank you. Everybody has been very welcoming," I answered truthfully.

"Oh, look at the time," said Edith suddenly, studying her watch in an exaggerated movement. "I'm going to be late for my card game with Doreen. You stay and chat to the lass," she said, patting Alex's arm again. "I'll see you next week." Alex put his arm round his grandmother's shoulders and kissed her on the cheek. The gesture was unashamedly affectionate. Edith turned to me.

"Are we still set for the trip to Ross Cove Wednesday?"

"Yes Edith, weather pending. I've just been making the final arrangements." The forecast for Wednesday was clear, but you could take nothing for granted.

"See you both later, then," she said, dividing up a devilish look between her grandson and me, before turning and shuffling out the dining room. I groaned inwardly as suspicion dawned. Was Edith playing cupid? Alex turned and watched his Nan's back retreating down the corridor, shaking his head incredulously. I was pleased to see that he looked about as mortified as I felt. He turned back to me after a moment, rubbing his shaved head in circular motions as if attempting to stir up something to say.

"So...um," inspiration hit his features like lightning from the sky. "So you're off to Ross Cove next week?"

"That's right. Morag and I thought it would be nice to get everybody out for the day, if the weather's nice," I explained.

"Morag Fraser?"

"Yes, do you know her? She works here too."

"I went to school with her younger brother." Of course, everybody knew everybody in Claremont. "It's my day off Wednesday. Maybe I could come along and help out?" he said eagerly.

"Okay, great." His eyes shone at me in the way I noticed some men's did, and I wondered if Edith's plan was coming together, on one side of the arrangement, anyway. If Edith's plan was to try to matchmake me with her grandson, she was going to find me more than a little recalcitrant. After years in an unhappy marriage, I was actually enjoying life as a young single woman, and I wasn't at all in a rush to give that status up. I couldn't deny that it would be handy to have an extra pair of youthful hands around on Wednesday afternoon, though.

"Great," he said. "I'll see you Wednesday, then."

"The bus leaves at 10:00 a.m. sharp," I advised, doing my best to ignore the cheeky schoolboy grin that had spread across his face.

"Sure, no problem; have you been out there before?"

"No, next week will be my first time," I answered.

"It's *stunning*," he grinned again, before turning and heading out of the dining room.

chapter

SIX

I sensed his presence before I actually saw him. My skin tingled in response to the increasingly familiar adjustment from somewhere deep within.

I turned to find him casually leaning in the door, arms and athletic legs crossed as he appraised me, a curious expression on the perfectly cut features of his face. He continued to watch me for longer than was comfortable. I stood there returning his gaze, cloth in one hand, furniture polish in the other. I could feel my cheeks beginning to flame. I began wondering whether he had any intention of actually saying something, or if he just wanted to stare to give me some sort of complex, in which case, mission accomplished. Then the silence broke.

"I think you should take lunch with me from now on, here in the dining room." His deep voice was smooth and strong, and held no hint that this suggestion was open to debate.

My eyebrows shot up in surprise. That was a shock. I quite clearly made him furious every time he spoke to me, and now he wanted to have lunch. I hadn't seen that one coming. I must have looked as astonished as I felt, because a smirk creased his beautiful, arrogant face in response.

My surprise swiftly turned to apprehension when it dawned on me that if I had to sit down to lunch with Arwan on a regular basis, he would have ample opportunity to bombard me with probing questions that I really didn't want to answer, but felt it nearly impossible not to! How did he do that?

What worried me more, however, was that if I was being honest with myself, I would like nothing more than to spend time with this curious man; every part of me seemed pulled in his direction. That aside, I had plenty of questions of my own, but it was just too dangerous. I could not allow him to tap into my past any more than he already had. The police had been adamant that nobody in my new life should ever know about my involvement with Adam Fleming, and until now I had never had any intention of saying the man's name out loud again. But Arwan seemed to have an uncanny knack of knowing the most probing of questions to ask. I just couldn't put myself in such a vulnerable position.

He stood upright then, readying to leave, deciding to take my lack of response as agreement.

"I wouldn't want to intrude," I began in a rush of words, "and besides, I'm quite happy to continue having my sandwich in the kitchen, but thank you, it was thoughtful of you to ask." I hoped I sounded firm yet polite, in my refusal of his offer. It was definitely not a good idea to have too much alone time with this man, no matter how much the idea might have its appeal.

My tone obviously didn't quite meet my requirements, because his responding light laugh sent a bolt of anger right through me. Anger wasn't an emotion that was particularly familiar to me, and I didn't like the way it was suddenly simmering at the edges of my self-control.

"I'll see you back here," he said. His tanzanite eyes seemed to literally shine with amusement. "At one o'clock," he added, before turning to leave. I thought my blood might actually be boiling. Who did he think he was?

"Mr Jones." I could hear the anger in my voice, but was glad of it now. This man merited it. He turned back to me, smirk still intact, arrogant head cocked to one side.

"Please, call me Arwan."

I ignored him. "Mr Jones, did you not hear what I said? I will not be having lunch with you today, or for that matter, on any day."

"Oh Brook, don't be difficult. I just want to get to know you better. Would it really be so unpleasant to join me for lunch?" The smile was gone from his face, but amusement still glowed from his lovely eyes, one black eyebrow arched in question.

My eyes escaped the constraints of my self-control and roved over his cheek bones, jaw, and chin. Well, I was only human after all, and he really was beyond attractive. Could one lunch break with him hurt? I couldn't believe I was actually contemplating agreeing to dine even once with him. The man was more volatile than Mount Etna. Where was the bubble and boil of my anger now? And why was he so difficult to say no to? I felt like I was being bewitched!

"I'll have lunch with you today," I said, feigning resignation, "but as a one-off. I wouldn't want anything you may have prepared to go to waste." To my annoyance, he continued to look amused as I carried on. "I feel it would be breaking our professional relationship to have lunch every day."

"Your work ethics are to be commended, but I'm all for breaking our professional relationship, Brook." All traces of his earlier humour had disappeared; his face and tone were unreadable to me. Was he trying to unnerve me with this sudden intensity? I was grateful to have the cloth and polish in my hands, as I fought an urgent desire to touch his face and to feel the warmth of his honey skin on my finger tips. I realised with humiliation that I was trembling.

"I look forward to our lunch date," he said finally, and then turned and left the room.

The moment I was released from his gaze, I inhaled a long, deep breath in attempt to clear my head and restart my heart. It was several minutes later before I felt steady enough to resume polishing his priceless antiques.

I thought I was the last person Arwan would want to sit down to lunch with, and yet wasn't that what he had just asked of me? Things were getting more confusing by the minute.

I made my way nervously to the dining room at one o'clock. The cartilage in my knees had turned to sponge, making my legs wobble as I walked. I had absolutely no idea what to expect. He must have heard me coming along the hall, because he was waiting for me as I entered, a satisfied smile on his face as he greeted me.

"Delighted you decided to make it. I wasn't at all sure that you wouldn't stand me up."

"It was a consideration," I muttered under my breath, and a smile twitched at the corner of his mouth. He pulled out a chair for me at the top of the table, a table that could easily have sat twelve people. The rich green and cream drapes that hung from the ceiling to floor at the large bay window were tied back, flooding the room with bright sunlight. Like all of Arwan's rooms, it was exquisitely decorated in Renaissance style with a modern twist. There was no denying his taste. Several of Arwan's own paintings adorned the walls, as well as others by various famous artists of the fifteenth, sixteenth, and seventeenth centuries, no doubt priceless.

I wondered if I was the only person ever to have joined him here for lunch. I don't know why, but I thought maybe I was. It seemed wrong that magnificence on this scale not be shared. There had never even been a visitor to his house in the whole time I'd worked here. Arwan was undoubtedly a very private man. Surely he must get lonely from time to time, with nothing other than two dogs for company. I hoped again that I might get some of my own questions answered before our lunch was over. I sat as he tucked my chair in behind me. Arwan was certainly a gentleman, and I grudgingly admitted to myself that this was a very attractive quality in a man.

I watched as he casually walked to his chair at the end of the table. He had changed, prior to lunch, into a pair of black, slim fit trousers and a pale pink shirt, which suited his honey skin and black hair perfectly. I struggled again not to stare at his face and become fixated on the sheer beauty of it. I wondered if he knew how handsome he was. I guessed that he did. There didn't seem to be much he wasn't aware of. I suddenly felt hugely self-conscious in my faded blue jeans and red jumper, looking completely under-dressed in comparison.

Thoughts of my clothing, however, were quickly waylaid when I noticed, for the first time, the food that was spread before me. The table seemed to display all of my favourite foods: lobster, prawns, crab, a whole sea bass, salads of every description, and several different kinds of bread, as well as a selection of cakes and tarts. It went on and on, quite clearly too much for two people to consume. In the middle of the long table, acting as a centrepiece, were the largest, most delicious looking apples and oranges I had ever seen, piled high in a large silver fruit bowl. If it weren't for the tangy citrus fragrance filling the air, I would have seriously doubted they were real. I inhaled deeply, sighing as visions of warm summer days filled my mind.

"Please," Arwan said gently, indicating with a wave of his hand that we should begin. I didn't know where to start, so opted for what was nearest to hand, the fish.

"How do you enjoy your work at the retirement home?" he asked after a moment.

I was pleased at his chosen line of questioning. I could answer truthfully. I had taken it for granted that he was aware of my other position; presumably either the agency or somebody in the village had told him. I was, however, curious as to why he was interested. I swallowed my mouthful of food.

"I enjoy it very much. I like being with the residents; it's comforting to me, for some reason. I'm not sure why." I hesitated, then continued in a quieter voice, "I teach them to sculpt. The residents seem to enjoy the feel of clay in their hands as much as I do. I think maybe it connects them with the earth. I think that would be important after a long life." I dropped my eyes from his penetrating stare to my plate, feeling suddenly vulnerable after my frankness.

"Is that how it makes you feel?" Arwan asked, his voice quiet, matching my own.

"Yes," I answered simply, looking back up to meet his steady gaze. "I feel in harmony with everything and everyone when I work with clay. Time explodes. You must know how that feels?" I asked, indicating one of his paintings hanging on the wall. He ignored my question.

"What do you like to sculpt?"

I frowned, thinking before answering, feeling even more vulnerable. My sculpting was my life; it felt fragile in his hands. I felt fragile. I took a deep breath and decided to put his interest down to that of a fellow artist simply showing respect for another art lover. His face had become impatient as he watched me trying to pull myself together to give him an answer, and when I opened my mouth to talk, it took a moment for the words to come.

"Anything beautiful," I finally managed. "Anything in nature that catches my eye, especially trees, and...I like old people's faces."

"You find old people beautiful?" He asked, seeming surprised.

"Very," I replied, a little defensively. "I love their lines. I can almost read them, like little personal maps of a person's life." I waited for him to say something, but he just continued to stare, his mesmerising eyes seemingly frustrated, perhaps seeking answers in my own eyes that my tongue hadn't provided. I couldn't understand what he was looking for. I was answering him honestly, too honestly, probably, but I sensed that he wasn't satisfied.

I decided to take the sudden break in conversation to ask a question or two of my own and deflect it from myself. "I have wondered why you live in this big house all on your own. Don't you get lonely?" The words rushed out before he could continue his probing, and I was instantly embarrassed by my bluntness. I was relieved, however, to see that the directness of my question seemed to amuse him as a smile spread across his face, exposing perfect white teeth, dispelling any sign of his earlier seriousness. He was so angelic when he smiled that it completely disarmed me.

"My mood recently has not been fit for the company of others." You got that right, I thought. He placed his elbows on the table, resting his chin on folded hands, and continued, his purplish gaze unwavering.

"I prefer the company of my books and antiquities. They're much more interesting, generally." His deep voice was casual. "Although it has to be said," he continued, "I am beginning to take pleasure in certain company." Despite his tone, his eyes were intense, but with an unfamiliar warmness in deep contrast to their colour.

I tried to look away from him and ignore his insinuation, but I was locked in, unable pull away. I was literally burning up as something scorched to life from somewhere in my chest. The heat spread out, firing through every vein in my body, as I remained unable to drop my eyes. I was vaguely aware, on some level, that he was enjoying my internal meltdown, as he was grinning at me again. I mentally cursed myself for being so damn readable, causing another wave of heat.

He rose from his chair, suddenly breaking his hold on me, and walked down the left side of the table, pausing as he reached to pluck one of the delicious looking oranges from the fruit pyramid in the centre of the table.

"Do you like oranges?" he asked, as he moved down the length of the table to where I sat. I watched as he pulled out the nearest chair to me and sat down. He held the sumptuous looking orange in strong hands for a moment, his eyes intent on my face, then began to peel.

I watched in a kind of trance as he pulled the thick bright rind easily from the slightly paler flesh within. Juice ran down his fingers as he peeled, his eyes never leaving my face. The fragrance of citrus was almost overwhelming. I didn't know oranges could smell so intensely. My mouth watered as I imagined how wonderful something that smelt that good would taste. I realised, after a moment, that he was holding a segment out for me; my hand rose and took it before I could think about what I was doing. I raised the orange to my lips and bit into the flesh. The moment the sweet juice hit my mouth, my mind was transported to a place filled with vivid brightness, musical sounds, and harmonious feelings.

I was in an orchard of orange trees that stretched in every direction as far as the eye could see. The gentle air about me was heavy with the scent of citrus, making my head spin. I closed my eyes for a moment, letting my head fall back and the sun warm my face as I inhaled a deep breath that seemed to fill my very being with the delight of life. I opened my eyes to a clear, bright, gentian blue sky housing nothing save a burning orb of fire sending waves of heat down to me. I pulled my gaze from the sky, that reminded me so much of Arwan's eyes, and looked down to the soft earth under my bare feet. A long ivory cotton dress, like the one from my dream, swirled around my legs as I bent to my knees.

My fingers dug easily into the soft black earth that warmed my hands and sent a blanket of comfort about me. Something about the earth pulled at my soul, as if this place and I were one and the same. I sighed dreamily as the sound of a musical voice travelled to me on the warm gentle breeze. I concentrated my lazy brain for a moment, trying to make out the words as the wind picked up, rustling the leaves on the orange trees and blowing my hair back from my face. The word "Achren" breezed gently in my ear. The familiarity of the word startled me from the bubble of the daydream.

Arwan was still sitting on my left, scanning my face as I tried to orient myself. I wasn't really sure what had just happened. It was the most real and tangible daydream I had ever experienced. The only thing I had ever felt like it was the dream of several nights before. I could feel a tumour of hysteria taking root in my chest. I had no idea what was happening to me. Who were these strange beings I dreamt about, and where was this peculiar place that my mind had just transported itself to?

I shook my head and focused on Arwan. God only knew what he was thinking, probably, "*Oh, here she goes again, slipping into another stupor.*" Did I need medical help, like my mother always seemed to think? Was I losing my grip on reality? I would have to seriously think about that later.

"I'm sorry," I whispered. "I don't know what just happened. I think I'm tired, or something." I felt that he expected me to say something else, but what it was, I didn't know. Then his handsome features suddenly became resigned, and he sighed. He muttered something under his breath that I didn't catch. My eyebrows furrowed as I wondered again what he wanted from me. I could feel pools of tears taking form in my eyes, as my confusion threatened to overwhelm me.

I stood to leave, feeling humiliated by my seemingly uncontrollable behaviour. He rose with me and pulled my chair away.

I stared up into his face as he stared back into mine. Something I saw there seemed to settle me somehow, bringing me back to myself. I resolved there and then to get to the bottom of what lay between this man and me. What were we to each other? I didn't know, but I was going to find out.

"Thank you for lunch," I said, as I pulled my eyes reluctantly from his and walked slowly from the room. I could feel the burn of his gaze on my back as I went.

chapter

SEVEN

As it turned out, the Ross Cove day trippers didn't leave The Shades until 10:45 a.m. I hadn't anticipated what a complete nightmare it was going to be to load eight pensioners and the associated essential equipment on to a minibus.

Alex had shown up bright and cheerful at nine forty-five. I was surprised and happy to see how well he coped with the residents. He was patience itself, and his confident, calm manner made him an instant hit with everybody. Edith was delighted that her favourite grandson had volunteered to attend, and her face beamed with pride all the way out to the cove.

The rigmarole was worth it. The looks on their faces as they gazed round the cove said it all. I understood immediately what all the hype was about. Even from the car park, I could see that Ross Cove was rugged and barren, but undeniably spectacular. We weren't exactly in the cove, but on the cliffs that surrounded it. As they did everywhere in the vicinity of Claremont, the woods hugged the coastline, but there was a large grassed area just before the land disappeared into the waves.

When I got as close to the edge as I was comfortable with, Joe pointed out a tiny fishing village and several little jetties where people could anchor private vessels. As I followed the line of the rock, I could just make out a little port in the distance, where several fishing boats were sitting docked after a morning at sea.

"That's Ross," he said as I followed the line of his finger. The cliffs themselves resembled a giant's bite, as if a huge set of teeth had taken out the side of the rock, and the sharp ridges and points left behind were where they had chiselled violently through the granite. Signs every few metres or so warned of the danger of standing too close to the edge.

Alex and Morag helped the less mobile of the residents off the bus and got them seated around a bench and table on the grassed area, looking out over the Irish Sea. The weather forecast hadn't let me down. It was crisp, but clear and bright, and the view out over the grey-green ocean was unobstructed as far as the eye could see. We couldn't have picked a better day. Morag had bought her camera with her, and proceeded to snap a few photos of everyone against the beautiful backdrop. Sometime later, Alex rolled out a rug, over one of the more grassy areas a few metres from the bench where the residents sat chatting and munching through their pack lunches, for the three of us to sit on and have our own.

"What do you think, Brook?" asked Alex, waving his hand in the direction of the sea.

"Awesome," I nodded, my eyes following the wave of his hand. I turned to look at Morag, and caught her smirking at Alex. I quickly brought my eyes back to my sandwich.

"It was good of you to come and help us, Alex," Morag said. I thought I saw her winking at him in my peripheral vision. I sighed inwardly. Not Morag too! I'd had about all the matchmaking I could handle from Edith on the bus, insisting that Alex and I sit together. What I was most uncomfortable about, however, was just how obliging he had appeared. He didn't seem in the least uncomfortable or awkward about what his Nan was so blatantly up to. I sighed and bit into my cheese and pickle sandwich.

"How's Daniel doing?" Alex asked Morag. I looked over at him, and he met my gaze with an apologetic smile. Perhaps he hadn't been as oblivious to my discomfort, after all.

"It's funny you should ask," she said, in a tone that instantly compelled our complete attention. To my surprise, she hesitated, then shrugged her slight shoulders. Her sea-green eyes fell slightly as she avoided our gazes, keeping her eyes glued to the tartan rug beneath her.

"Morag, what's the matter?" I asked, made anxious by her unusually troubled aura. In the time I'd known her, I'd never encountered her on a down day. Seeing her face cast in a worried expression was instantly unsettling.

"I'm a little worried about him, actually," she said finally, lifting her eyes to meet mine and then Alex's.

For a moment, I thought of what I knew of Daniel, her son. Physically, he was a typical fourteen-year-old boy, gangly, spotty, and awkward in his own skin. I had met him many times when he had joined his mum and me for dinner. He seemed like a nice kid, and appeared to have a really close relationship with his mum, which I found touching. I wondered what was going on, to cause Morag to look so worried.

"What's the little sod been up to?" said Alex, in jest. I guessed he was trying to ease Morag in some way. He really was a very decent man.

"It's just that he's become...," she frowned, thinking, "...distant somehow. We don't talk as much as we used to. You know, about any old stuff." She shook her head, swishing her blonde bob around her face.

"Maybe it's just his age," I said encouragingly. "He *is* a teenager. You know what they're like." We waited as Morag sipped cautiously at some hot tea from a thermos cup.

"He's started hanging around with a couple of older boys. The fact that they're older isn't really the problem. It's the boys themselves; there's something nasty about them."

"What do you mean, *nasty*?" Alex asked, seeming to suddenly have his professional hat on. His face had taken on an altogether serious expression.

"It's the way they look at me and speak to me. They're polite enough, but it isn't genuine." Her eyes narrowed as she continued, "I feel as if they're mocking me, sharing some joke at my expense. I know no good is going to come to Daniel from being friends with these guys." She looked down to her lap again. "You know about the Owen boy from the estate and that other poor laddie?"

As soon as she uttered those words, I understood immediately why she was worried. The headline of the local newspaper from several weeks ago flashed into my mind: "A Second Local Youth Dies Using Contaminated Heroin".

Jeremy Owen and another young boy, Michael Wells, had died shooting up contaminated heroin. According to the paper, neither was an addict, nor did either have a history of drug abuse. The tragedy had rocked the community. Jeremy Owen had only been fourteen. I had seen his mother amongst the mourners coming out of the church after the boy's service, just a few days after I arrived in Claremont. I had never seen grief on that scale before. She was white, lifeless, like a ghost, almost not there. It was painful to see.

"You don't think he's into drugs, do you?" I asked. I just couldn't imagine the healthy boy I had come to know over the last few months using heroin, but I also wasn't naive enough to think that it couldn't happen. Kids like to experiment, do reckless things.

"No, I don't think he's taking drugs, not yet," Morag replied, "but I can't help worrying. I remember what peer pressure is like."

"Daniel is a good lad, Morag," Alex said.

"So was Jeremy Owen!" she retorted, her tone sharp. She took a deep breath and smiled slightly. "Sorry, I know you guys are doing your best."

Alex grimaced, his tone suddenly chagrined. "We've interviewed dozens of kids, but if they know anything, which of course somebody must, they're giving up nothing." He leaned further into our little formation on the blanket, despite the fact that the sound of the sea would swallow our voices long before it hit the others sitting at the bench. "There was anthrax in the heroin that killed those boys."

"Anthrax," I echoed, stunned. The papers failed to mention what exactly the drug had been contaminated with.

"Aye, it's lethal, and I shouldn't probably be telling you this, but I've heard down the grapevine that there may be a bit of problem across the country. There have been similar deaths elsewhere."

"Good god," Morag muttered.

"The dealers don't care, do they?" I said, more to myself, though Alex answered.

"All they care about is money." He was practically scowling. "Every village, town, and city in the country has a drug problem of some sort that's unavoidable, but what's odd about what seems to be happening in the last few months is that neither of these kids were junkies. As far as we know, it was the first time either boy had ever touched any sort of drugs, let alone heroin. Kids generally at that age maybe have a couple of pulls on a joint, but that's about it."

"Do you think these older boys are into drugs, Morag?" I asked.

"I don't know, doll, it's just a feeling I have about them, really, it's the way they make me feel."

"Can you stop him from seeing them?" I asked hopefully.

"He's too old for that. He'd see them behind my back, anyway. At least I can kind of keep an eye on them if they're in my house from time to time."

"He really is a good kid, Mo," I said, in attempt to ease her worry. "I'm sure he'll be okay. Daniel will probably fall out with them in a few weeks, and you'll never see them again." She smiled, and I was relieved to see that the smile touched her eyes.

"I see Daniel round the village all the time. I'll keep an eye on him," Alex promised. "But he's never been any trouble, as far as I know."

Seagulls suddenly sounded overhead, and I looked up to see several circling above in the hopes of joining us for lunch. Doreen threw the crust from her sandwich onto the grass a few feet away, and they nosedived for the ground like doomed fighter jets. It wasn't long before we were engulfed by the large birds and their frantic squawking.

We finished up our lunches and decided to take a gentle walk along the cliffs.

Edith linked her arm in mine, and we ambled along, gazing out to sea, watching the waves break against the granite like white foam fireworks.

I inhaled a deep, long breath, enjoying the salty smell of the sea that filled the air. Edith's pace was slow, and it wasn't long before the others were slightly further up the path from us. I wondered if she was okay. Of the eight residents that were able to make the trip, I would have said Edith was the fittest, despite being the oldest at ninety-three.

Edith had really warmed to me over the weeks. The hostility she showed on the first day never resurfaced, and we rubbed along together quite well. She was a shrewd, witty woman, and actually a lot of fun to be around. Only that morning, she had us all in stitches when she informed the entire minibus that Paolo Nutini had a voice that made you want to "drop your drawers", and if only she was "sixty years younger"...She was a handsome woman with lovely high cheekbones, which were what had prompted me to sculpt her. Edith would have been a very attractive woman in her day; she still was.

"How are you, Edith?" I enquired. "You seem tired today. Are you feeling okay?" She didn't appear to have heard my questions.

"I heard you were working for Mr Jones, out in the woods?"

"Yes, I am," I agreed, wondering why she asked. "How do you know that?"

"Oh, everybody knows everything about everyone round here," she winked.

Small villages, I mused, really needed to get a life. For a woman with so many secrets, maybe a city with overcrowding issues might have been a better choice for a witness protection location.

Alex and Joe laughed heartily about something they shared between themselves, and the breeze carried the sound of their chuckling back to us. I noticed again how comfortable Alex seemed. I imagined that he would be confident and capable in almost any situation; he was definitely suited to the profession of policing. Edith's voice brought my attention back to her.

"I met his great grandfather once," she said, almost wistfully. "His name was also Arwan Jones." My acute interest was suddenly triggered. I told myself it was nothing to do with being infatuated by his grandson, of course. I was just interested in my employer and his family. There was nothing unusual about that, was there?

"It was only the once," she continued, as something adjusted in her countenance. "I've never forgotten him." She crossed her padded coat over her chest, as if chilled, then began her story.

"I was only nine years old. My mother and father were poor, dirt poor, as were most in those days. I was lucky to be one of the few girls in my class who always had shoes. My daddy made them, you see?" she said, suddenly bringing her focus back to me. I nodded in understanding, and she continued on. "My friend and I had decided to go into the woods early one morning and search for chantarelle mushrooms. On the occasions we'd been lucky enough to find some, the wealthy in the village had paid us well for them. A delicacy of sorts, I believe. Although the mornings were getting lighter with summer on the way, this particular morning was overcast and wet, so it was still dark amongst the trees. I remember thinking how the forest seemed reluctant to wake up, as if it wanted to cling to its cloak of darkness." Edith sighed. "Anyway, we split up, thinking we'd be able to cover more ground that way."

I was so completely wrapped up in Edith's story that I didn't notice we'd stopped walking and that the others were moving steadily further away along the edge of the cliffs. "I didn't hear him approach. I was deep in the woods; why didn't I hear him coming?" Although she looked at me, the question was for herself only.

"Who, Edith...who didn't you hear coming?" I asked gently.

"It didn't occur to me to think that he'd followed us," she continued quietly, the sound of waves exploding on granite almost drowning her out. "Or that he would have any ill intent. I knew him, you see? His name was Simon McAlister; my father knew him, drank with him sometimes. He lived on our street. He was nice at first, offering me sweets. I was so hungry that I didn't think twice about taking them, penny wheels, they were my favourite. I'd only had them once before. My young, naive mind never considered there'd be conditions, but of course you rarely get anything for nothing, do ye?" I realised with a jolt of horror where Edith's story was leading.

"I saw the moment when he decided that the niceties, as far as I was concerned, were about to stop; I saw as it flashed across his features. That's when it dawned on me that his presence was no coincidence. I had been so trusting of him, unsuspecting. He was a friend of the family; why wouldn't I trust him? He moved quickly then, roughly, pushing me to the ground, fumbling with my skirts with one hand and using the other to cover my mouth. I bit his hand!" she said, and triumph briefly crossed her features, before the sadness returned. "Of course, that just made him mad," she said, in that same quiet voice that I wasn't used to hearing from her lips.

"Edith, I'm so sorry," I murmured. She smiled at me absently.

"One moment he was all over me, his hands, and his alcoholic's breath, then in the next, he was gone. I remember lying there for a moment with my eyes squeezed shut, wondering if he'd killed me and I just hadn't realised. Why else would everything stop? I had been certain he would kill me. He couldn't have risked my daddy finding out, you see, he'd have been a dead man." Edith sighed, then her face took on a faraway expression.

"But when I opened my eyes, I knew I wasn't dead...I'd been saved. I'd seen him in the village once before, coming out of the bank. He was the finest looking man I'd ever seen, and here he was in the middle of the woods, saving my life."

"Arwan's great grandfather?" I whispered. "Arwan's great grandfather rescued you?" Edith nodded slowly.

"Lifted the bastard clean off me and held him by the neck with one hand. Simon McAlister's boots dangled in the air not a foot from my face. Mr Jones asked me if I was hurt, but I couldn't speak to answer him. He wasted not a word on Simon McAlister, but flung him into a nearby tree with some force, knocked him flat out. Then Mr Jones scooped me up into his arms and carried me back through the woods. He spoke to me all the way, making me smile and giggle. So much so that I almost forgot about the horror he had just rescued me from. It was so delightfully strange, but as he walked with me, everything seemed to come to life about us." Edith eyes glazed over. She spoke as if remembering a dream. "Warm sunlight broke the canopy of the woods as the birds came to life and chased each other from branch to branch, seeming to follow us as we went. Before I knew it, the chill had vanished from my little bones, and with it, all my fright. I know it's ridiculous now, but my child's mind believed he brought the sun out for me that morning, broke it through the dark clouds, just to comfort *me*." She sighed. "How could something so sickening and horrendous suddenly transform into the most staggeringly wonderful moment of my life? He carried me straight to my mother's door. I had no idea he even knew where we lived. Lucky for Simon McAlister, my father had left for work by the time we arrived. My mother notified the police, and Mr Jones told them where they'd find him, unconscious but not dead. My mother was so grateful, she cried hysterically as she thanked him. I can't remember what he said in return; I was too caught up, staring into his face. His eyes, I've never seen another pair to match them. Like violets, beautiful." I gasped. Arwan must have inherited his eyes from his great grandfather. I knew exactly what Edith was talking about; they were just like violets.

"I fell in love that morning," she said, "but I never saw him again." Her eyes shone with the moisture of threatening tears.

"He saved my life."

"You were so lucky, Edith. I can't imagine what would have happened if, well, if he hadn't been there."

"I was very lucky indeed, lass," she said, pulling a tissue from somewhere inside her coat and dabbing gently at the corners of her eyes. A moment later, a small smile returned to her face.

"Of course it wasn't just me he saved. If it weren't for Mr Jones, Claremont wouldn't exist as it does today."

"He saved Claremont?" I asked, not understanding her meaning.

"Aye, lass, developers from the city were looking to mine this whole area in the early twentieth century. The soil is rich in coal and other minerals. It would have meant the whole vicinity flattened, altered irreversibly," she explained. "The fat cats had plans, but Mr

Jones put a stop to it all. Nobody was sure exactly how he managed it, but presumably a lot of money changed hands somewhere along the line. Mr Jones purchased all the land that surrounds Claremont for quite some miles, and gifted it back to the village, to the people. The land here can never be touched. He gifted it to the people of Claremont."

"He sounds like he was quite a man," I said, awed.

"Aye, quite a man indeed." Edith cleared her throat. "Speaking of good men...," she said, grinning suddenly as her line of sight found her nephew's silhouette in the distance. "You could do a lot worse, you know."

"You're relentless, Edith," I laughed, as we resumed walking.

And Edith was right. Alex did seem a good man. I could see that about him almost immediately. But that didn't change my situation. I wasn't ready to go on a date with Alex. I was just finding myself, making a place for myself in the world, even if it was only the world of Claremont. I wasn't ready to trust anybody yet. I didn't trust myself to make the right decisions for me. Look at Adam. How could I have not seen the man that he was? When I looked back, it should have been obvious. No, I wasn't ready for a relationship, with anybody.

On the bus trip home, my mind was preoccupied with Edith's account of all those years ago. She'd been so lucky. What if Arwan's great grandfather hadn't have been there? I shuddered at the thought. I was so glad that Edith had a saviour that day. Arwan's great grandfather certainly sounded as intriguing a character as his great grandson. Buying a village and the surrounding area and then gifting it back to the people was no small gesture. What would drive a man to do that? Good will alone? It was possible.

I glanced over at Edith, sitting across the aisle. Alex sat by the window next to her, and she had let her head fall to his shoulder. She looked tired, and for the first time since I'd known her, she looked the full ninety-three years of her age.

Morag was chatting away with Joe on the seat behind me, and I found the rhythm of their voices and the gentle rocking of the bus comforting. I must have shut my eyes at some point and nodded off myself, because the next thing I knew, the bus had arrived back at The Shades.

We got everybody back inside much more quickly, thankfully, than we had gotten them out. I unpacked the bus with Alex as Morag got them settled.

"Everybody had a great time today," he said as he lifted the picnic hamper from the boot of the bus.

"Yes, I think they did," I agreed. "Thanks for your help. You're good with them, patient." I meant it too. Alex had been a great help. I was glad he came along. I liked him. He was impossible not to like.

Alex stood for a moment, watching me with the hamper in his arms. "Do you think you'll stay in Claremont long?"

"I haven't got any plans to leave," I said, puzzled by his question. "Why do you ask?" I waited as he put his answer together.

"There's something transitory about you. It's like you're just passing through, or something. I wouldn't be surprised if I woke up one day and heard you were gone." We stared at one another for a moment.

"You're a bit odd, aren't you?" I smiled. I wasn't planning on going anywhere.

"You've noticed." He grinned like a madman, making me laugh, then said, "Do you fancy going for some dinner tomorrow night?" I felt the smile slide off my face.

"I'm sorry, Alex, I don't date."

Alex looked surprised and dubious at the same time. "You don't date?"

"Nope."

He pursed his lips, thinking. "Well, it won't be a date then; we'll go strictly as friends."

"I don't think that's a good idea."

"Oh, come on. You have dinner with friends, right?"

I sighed. "Yes," I admitted, thinking of the many meals I had enjoyed with Morag.

"Well, it's a date then!" His eyes widened as he realised his error. "I mean, it's two friends going to Logan Mills for something to eat. What do you say?" I looked into his eyes and saw that they were sincere, if somewhat hopeful. I sighed inwardly.

"Okay." I managed a smile. I could do friends. In fact, I could happily do friends with Alex, if that's what he was offering. I just hoped he would stick to our agreement; I could do without the complications. But God help me if Edith found out. Somehow I couldn't see her swallowing the 'friends having dinner' thing.

It was three o'clock when I finally left The Shades. I didn't really feel like going straight home, and so had lingered, chatting with the residents.

I was just passing the library on the High Street when *'Achren'* popped into my head out of nowhere. I found myself saying it out loud again, "Achren." Yes, it was definitely strange, yet familiar. It annoyed me immensely, not being able to place it. I exhaled deeply. This was the perfect opportunity to do some investigating.

"Hi Brook, are you looking to join?" a man behind a counter asked, when he noticed me idling just inside the entrance of the library. He was completely bald, his head covered in nothing but countless brown freckles. What he lacked by way of hair on his head however, he made up on his face. A thick, bushy brown beard hid all his features from the nose down, until a smile parted the fuzz and revealed crooked teeth.

A couple of months ago, I'd have been shocked at a complete stranger knowing who I was, but that's just how it was in Claremont. I didn't bother to comment. After all, his name badge told me his name was Lachlan, so we were on a level footing.

"That would be great. I think I just need to use the Internet," I explained.

"Oh, that's a shame," he said, looking at me over half-rimmed spectacles. "Our only computer is on the blink at the moment." He pointed off to his left, where I turned to see an ancient looking PC on a desk, with a piece of paper stuck to the monitor explaining it was 'Out of Order!'

"Oh." Well, people used to cope without the Internet, and I was in a library; I'd have to do things the old-fashioned way. "That's okay. I'll join and see if I can find what I'm looking for on the shelves."

The library was actually pretty well-stocked for a small village, and was virtually empty, so I had it all to myself. Lachlan turned out to be very helpful, and gave me a quick guided tour of all the sections.

"I've worked here for twenty-odd years, so if you can't find anything and we've got it, I'll know," he informed me proudly.

"Thanks for your help," I smiled.

"You're welcome." I thought he was about to walk away, but he hesitated as if debating whether to say something else. He studied me over his glasses for a moment. "I actually just wanted to say thank-you for doing such a great job up at the home. Dorothy is my mother," he explained. "She was a very independent lady at one time and was really rather upset when she first had to be moved to The Shades, but I've seen such a difference in her since you started. It's as if she's taking pleasure in her life again."

I was so touched by his thanks that I could barely respond. I thought the residents were getting something out of our sessions together, but it was overwhelming to hear just how much.

"I'm enjoying myself too," was all I could manage.

A moment later he was gone, and I was left to scan the shelves.

What was I looking for? Achren. What actually was Achren? It was hard to know where to start. Morag had thought it was the Celtic word for "Other-World". I moved without consciously making the decision to the small religion section.

After a moment, I found a couple of books on Celtic mythology and carried them over to a large table in the centre of the library. Lachlan was back behind the counter, and he looked up when I emerged from the shelves with my books.

"Find what you were looking for?"

"Possibly," I said, as I sat down at the table. My hand trembled as I opened the first book, *Scottish & Celtic Legends*, and went straight to the index at the back. I ran my finger down the list of words at the top of the *A*s, but there was nothing, no mention of Achren or of anything similar. I closed the book and moved it to one side. I picked up the second, entitled *Other-Worlds of Celtic Myth.* Again I flicked directly to the index. It was the fifth listing: "Achren" jumped out at me from the page, making me gasp. My heart raced and my trembling intensified as I turned to page 212 and began to read...

"The immortal warrior King of Achren, the land of plenty, watches over the gateway between worlds.

"In the myths and legends of the Celtic world, it is believed that gateways provide access from the mortal world to the world of immortals and vice versa. The warrior King and his omnipotent warriors keep vigil, hindering soul thieves and other creatures looking to plunder in the land of mortals.

"For centuries, mortal believers have searched the Celtic landscapes of Ireland, Scotland, Wales, and Cornwall, looking for the gateways and the chance to enter Achren, where there is said to be no thirst or hunger, no poverty or sickness.

"Some believe access lies in the waterways and rivers, others in rocks or even the earth itself."

I took a sharp intake of breath as I read the next paragraph, and the memory of my first morning in Claremont came to the forefront of my mind.

'Seekers of the gateways believe white stags, although extremely rare, are messengers from Achren. The Celts believed the mystic creatures carry the very essence of Achren within their hearts, which thus enables them to pass between the worlds at will. Any mortal lucky enough to sight one, and follow, may be led to the secret gateways.'

I finished the passage and closed the book. Morag had been right; Achren was another world, or so the ancient Celts believed. What was happening here? What did Achren mean to me? I had no clue. I didn't for a second believe that other worlds existed within our world, but I couldn't deny that there appeared to be some sort of force at work that was trying to point me in that direction.

I returned the books to the shelves without bothering to check them out; I'd found what I'd come for. I thanked Lachlan for his help and left the library.

When I got home, my newly installed telephone answering machine flashed at me with my first message. I pressed the play button and waited...

"Hello, it's Ruth. Um...I didn't get a chance to tell you before you left this afternoon but, um...there will be a brief meeting in the dining room for all staff tomorrow morning. I, um, er...well, I hope to see you there." After she hung up, I hit the erase button, thinking how distracted she had sounded, as if something was troubling her. Or maybe, like me, she just hated talking into answering machines. I hadn't seen her around The Shades a lot lately; she'd been spending most of her time shut up in her chaotic office. I wondered what the meeting could be about. Staff meetings weren't really regular practice at The Shades.

After a long, hot shower and an hour of mindless telly, I headed down the corridor to bed. I wasn't particularly tired, but didn't really know what else to do with myself. I had been rendered incapable of concentrating on anything in particular, with my mind continuously returning to what I had discovered in the library that afternoon.

Okay, so I had discovered that Achren was indeed considered by some to be another realm of reality, another world. That was fascinating, but it didn't help a bit. My mind switched to Arwan, the very heart of it all, I was sure. I couldn't help feeling that if I could find out what Achren meant to me, I would find out what Arwan meant to me, or vice versa.

As I lay there in the dim light, staring up at a blank ceiling, I decided that the unavoidable time had come when I had to consider the fact that I was potentially having a nervous breakdown or something similar. I couldn't deny that the last year of my life had been the most stressful period I had ever experienced, and I only had to think back to the black jeep episode to realise just how easily freaked out I was. Could all this be in my head, a reaction to all the drama, stress, and fear of the last year? Now that likelihood, unlike other-worlds, was certainly not out of the realms of possibility. I tried to think objectively, as if I was another person, a rational, normal person. Would that person think I was insane? Morag didn't seem to think so, although I hadn't told Morag about Arwan appearing out of thin air to save me from an early grave, nor had I told her about the abnormally vivid daydream I had experienced whilst lunching with him. Perhaps I didn't tell her because I knew what she would think, and I didn't want to see the look on her face that I had seen so many times on my parents' faces when I was growing up. It still pained me to think of it.

I couldn't remember falling asleep, but I must have at some point, because my alarm woke me from my dreamless slumber at seven fifteen. I had remembered to set my alarm slightly early, so I could arrive promptly at The Shades for the staff meeting Ruth had called. I had a tiny inkling that whatever had prompted it, wasn't going to be good news.

After a piece of toast and a strong cup of coffee, I threw on a pair of white jeans and a pink jersey top. My hair was the usual wayward mess, so I ran a comb through it as best I could, then tied it up, out the way. I grabbed my handbag from the sofa in the lounge and headed for the front door. I walked past a mirror I had recently hung in the hall, and then backstepped several paces and paused to examine myself. I spent a moment fussing with lose curls and tucking my top into the waistband of my jeans, only to pull it all out again a moment later. I clamped my hands on my hips and sighed. For the first time in weeks, I was reluctant to leave the house.

I felt burdened as I headed along the High Street to The Shades. I walked past the bakery, and the sound of Duncan Buckie's voice trailed from the open door along with the smell of freshly baked bread. I acknowledged the irony in the coupling of the senses, a scent that lured and a sound that repelled. I turned to glance in the window. There he was, leaning his great bulk up against the pastry counter, laughing with the serving girls behind. It was such an unnatural sound, a lie on his lips. He seemed to sense eyes on him, as he suddenly straightened and turned to meet my gaze. I snapped my head back to the street ahead, but not before I saw the smile freeze on his face and something hard creep into his eyes.

I quickened my pace instinctively, wanting to put some distance between me and the man in the bakery. I would endeavour to do my best to avoid Duncan Buckie at all costs in future; however, that would be easier said than done in a village with a population lucky to max out at two thousand.

When I arrived at The Shades, staff had already begun to congregate in the dining room, but as yet, there was no sign of Ruth.

I said a general hello and sat down next to Clive, who was swigging away at a cup of coffee.

Of all the rooms at The Shades, the dining room was the most in need of updating. The yellow paint was peeling and chipped in many places, revealing its predecessor colour, brown, and the blue carpet was worn away to the underlay in various places. I wondered if it would ever get done up, when Ruth pushed through the doors. I noticed immediately how frazzled she appeared, her red hair unusually erratic. A long, thin ladder ran up the stocking of one of her legs, as if her stockings had been yanked on in a hurry. Purplish smudges hung like crescent moons under her eyes. Ruth clearly hadn't slept last night. I groaned inwardly; no, this definitely wasn't going to be good news.

The staff of The Shades sat around two pushed-together tables, as Ruth walked over and stood directly in front of us. Morag suddenly surged into the room, apologising for being late. She found a seat across the table and met my eye, pulling a face that said, '*What's this all about, then?*' I shrugged my shoulders and shook my head.

"I'm very sorry to have to inform you of some bad news," Ruth began. That was no surprise to me; it was etched all over her face, but the rest of the group muttered amongst themselves until she began to explain.

"Last week I had a phone call from the council head office in Glasgow. Apparently, they're making cutbacks and trying to generate revenue." Ruth paused, pursed her lips, and shut her eyes, taking a moment before she could continue. "It seems they have decided to sell The Shades." Several staff gasped, and confused voices erupted around the table. This was not the news anybody had been expecting. I glanced at Morag. Her face was as surprised as I imagined my own was.

"I hoped I wouldn't have to call this meeting," Ruth continued, raising her voice slightly, to be heard over the confusion. "I've been desperately trying to negotiate with the Council, but..." Her voice broke as she continued, and I could see she was fighting back the tears. "They don't seem willing to compromise in any way." Clive spoke up next to me.

"Won't the new owner want to continue running The Shades as a retirement home?"

"That's very unlikely," Ruth croaked. "I believe the building will likely be developed, turned into flats for residential sale."

"How long have we got?" Clive asked. Ruth looked very pale, as if all the blood had abandoned her cheeks.

"The Shades goes on the market on Monday." The table erupted again. The word "Monday" was echoed over and over again in disbelief. Several people had pulled mobile phones from pockets and were already sharing the news with loved ones.

"When The Shades is sold, I will have to begin transferring the residents to other homes in the surrounding areas. Head office has promised to try and transfer as many staff as possible, but I have been told to expect redundancies." She sniffed loudly as she looked around the table. "I'm so sorry to have to tell you like this, but I had little choice in the matter. The residents do not know as of yet, but I will inform them on Saturday."

Clive stood up and brought his fists down on the table, making his coffee mug bounce almost comically in defiance of the situation.

"How can they sell The Shades just like that? What about my bairns, Ruth? I've got three mouths to feed, ye ken!"

My heart went out to Clive and the others, and what about the residents? Some of these people had been here for years; a move to another home would be too traumatic. It could cost lives. I thought of Edith and of how tired she had looked yesterday at Ross Cove. How would she feel, having to move at this stage of her life to who knew where? And then there was Doreen, who had only so recently become happy here. What would happen to her, another move? I dreaded to think. This was terrible news for the people of Claremont. In two days' time, the residents of The Shades would be told that their home would soon be no more.

I didn't know what to do with myself when I got home. I began pacing my little living room floor, racking my brains for some sort of solution to the imminent sale of The Shades. Although I felt terribly for all the staff, my heart was breaking for the residents. I found myself muttering about Councils and their seemingly idiotic decisions, as I continued to pound the carpet.

I had completely forgotten about dinner with Alex until my doorbell rang promptly at seven. I paused in my tracks. Oh crap!

I opened the door sheepishly.

"Alex, I'm really sorry, I completely forgot. Stuff happened at work today, and I haven't thought about anything else since."

"Hey, that's okay, I heard. It's all over Claremont."

I sighed. I just hoped the news hadn't leaked back to the residents yet; they would be hurt, hearing the news secondhand. I forced myself to focus on Alex.

"I don't know if dinner is such a great idea tonight."

He'd clearly made an effort for our "just friends" dinner. He wore grey trousers and an immaculately pressed white shirt, and the whiff of aftershave that greeted me as I opened the door tingled at my nose. I noticed that there were little patches of moisture on his shoulders where the rain had found him on his way to the doorstep.

He moved to walk by me through the door, but instead of walking into the hall, he stopped and wrapped his arms around me. I let my head fall to his shoulder for a moment, then moved away from him. Even as upset as I was, I couldn't forget the signals that he might interpret incorrectly.

"Look," he said, sliding his hands into his pockets in a show of restraint. "I think we should still go for dinner. You look like you could do with it." His eyes flashed wide. "I did not mean that the way it sounded. I mean you look good, I just thought you might like to get out of Claremont for the night, that's all." I couldn't help but smile. It didn't look like I was getting out of it. I looked down at myself. I still had the same white jeans and pink jumper on that I'd worn to work. As if reading my thoughts, he said, "You look great, Brook. You always do. Come on." He extended his hand to me, and after a moment, I accepted it.

chapter

EIGHT

It was a wet, dark night, the bright weather of the day before a distant memory.

In an attempt to avoid a drenching, we ran to Alex's car, parked up on the street. Then we cruised out of Claremont in a slightly awkward silence.

The road that ran out to Logan Mills was the one and only road into and out of Claremont. It was narrow and in a pretty bad state of disrepair. Potholes were a common feature, and that, combined with torrential rain and the fact that there was no lighting to speak, of made it a hazardous drive.

Alex broke the silence.

"You'll miss them all when The Shades sells." It wasn't a question, but a statement of fact. I nodded.

Silence.

"So is my Nan driving you nuts, or what?"

"Or what," I answered. "I love Edith."

"She is a little crazy, though," he said affectionately.

"I don't think so; she's amazing for her age."

"Really?" he sounded dubious. "She must like you. My grandmother can be one prickly customer."

I laughed. "In the beginning, she was a little hostile, but I spent some time with her, just chatting and getting to know her. I think she appreciated it. We get along great now. Sometimes elderly people just want somebody to listen to them. I've noticed most people treat them like they're already ghosts." I realised he was staring at me, at the expense of the road. "Alex, the road?"

"Oh aye, sorry!" he said, snapping his eyes back to the windscreen.

"The two of you seem very close," I pointed out, as we carried on our way through the black night. I fixated my eyes on the lines in the middle of the road, as they blurred into one continuous white line.

"She raised me." That was news to me. I turned to look at his profile.

"I didn't realise."

"Aye, my parents were killed in a car crash when I was three; she took me and my brother in," he explained matter-of-factly.

"I'm sorry about your parents." He shrugged his shoulders.

"Thanks, but I don't really remember much about them. I was too young when they died." He paused, pursing his lips in thought, in the way I had noticed he sometimes did. "Actually, I was probably the right age." He glanced at me sideways. "I mean, if something like that's going to happen to a bairn, I guess it's best if it happens when they're young, so they don't know any different. Do you know what I mean?" I nodded thoughtfully.

"I know what you mean," I said, then after a moment, added, "They'd be proud of you, you know?" Any parent would be proud of Alex, a fine young man in many respects.

"You say that like they can see me," he said, glancing at me sideways, a teasing smile on his lips.

"How do you know they don't?"

He raised his eyebrows, contemplating, then nodded at the possibility. "I don't," he said finally. "I'm glad you came to live in

Claremont. Even if The Shades sells, I think you've done people a lot of good here. We're lucky to have you." He kept his eyes on the road, but I didn't miss the intensity of his voice. I smiled.

"I don't know about that," I said quietly "but I'm glad I moved here too." It was the truth, I really was glad.

"Oh, c'mon!"

"What's the matter?" I asked, startled by his sudden outburst.

"You're having a laugh, not tonight!"

"Alex?"

"I've lost power, there's no acceleration," he answered through gritted teeth. I noticed lights flashing on his dash and his right foot viciously pumping the accelerator to no avail. We were slowing down rather rapidly, and an incline in the road wasn't helping.

"Are you any good with cars?" I asked hopefully as we came to a stop.

"Nope, but I've got it covered," he said, flashing a little yellow business card at me. At least he seemed to have cheered himself up. I presumed that he was resigned to the fact that our evening was not quite going to plan.

Alex phoned the emergency breakdown number on his mobile, as I gazed out into the night. At least his phone was in network coverage. I hoped we weren't going to be stuck long; it was pretty chilly, and I hadn't lifted my coat on the way out.

"About an hour, I'm afraid," he said, hanging up. His voice was apologetic, but I noted that his expression didn't seem to mirror it. Could he actually be pleased about this sudden turn of events? Alex and I stuck in a small space, together, alone in the dark for the next hour at least. Could this get any more awkward? Just the kind of situation I had wanted to avoid.

"Are you cold?" he asked.

"No, I'm fine," I said, a little harshly, wrapping my arms around myself. The warm air from the heater was dispersing rapidly with no power to keep it going.

"I could put my arm around you, if you think it might warm you up?" If it weren't for the laughter in his voice, I would have got out the car and walked back to Claremont, torrential rain or not.

"Just friends, remember?" I said, with a touch of frost.

"I thought you had a sense of humour," he laughed.

"I do, but something funny has to have been said to trigger it," I retorted, but couldn't help smiling.

We hadn't seen a single car since we had broken down, so my heart lifted at the glare of high beams in the rear window, and it soared when a car pulled in behind us.

"Looks like they're early," Alex mumbled, clearly peeved that our stranded status was about to be remedied. "I'll be back in a minute." He got out the car, letting in the rain and a cold gust of wind as he opened the door and went to meet the mechanic.

Less than thirty seconds later, the driver door flung open again, and a wild looking Alex flumped back down in his seat.

"Is everything okay?" I asked, intrigued by his annoyed expression. He was soaked through, his white shirt now a dull grey. All the earlier humour had disappeared from his face. I wondered if we were here for the duration.

"It's not the mechanic," he grumbled. I swivelled in my seat to look out the rear window. The car was still there, its high beams flooding Alex's car with bright light, making me squint. I looked back at him, confused.

"It's Arwan Jones," he spat. Butterflies rose in my stomach, and I felt my heart stutter.

"What does he want?" I asked, trying to keep my tone casual.

Alex hesitated. "You, it would appear."

"Me?"

"He says it's too cold a night for you to be stranded out here, and that he'll drive you home." He glared out the windscreen, not meeting my eye.

"Is that so," I said. "Well, how very thoughtful of him!" I was a little annoyed myself. It was typical of a man like Arwan to assume that I would abandon Alex. "There's no way I'm leaving you out here on your own."

What was he doing here anyway, I wondered. Was he following me? I didn't seem to be able to get away from him. First enforced lunches, and now this!

"You should accept his lift." Alex said.

"No way!" I snapped.

"He's right; you shouldn't be stuck out here on a night like tonight. The mechanic will be here soon anyway and this is just too awkward."

"What do you mean?" I asked.

"He's waiting." Alex's eyes suddenly narrowed as they looked past me out the window. I turned to follow his gaze, and there was Arwan, waiting under a black umbrella for me to join him, clearly not intending on taking no for an answer. Even in the dark, I could see his white teeth smiling their disarming smile. I wasn't sure whether it was for my benefit or Alex's, but as the minutes ticked by, and Arwan remained waiting by my door I realised he wasn't going to go anywhere until I joined him. The last thing I wanted was for Alex to feel uncomfortable. If my leaving with Arwan would put an end to it, I would have to go with him, whether I liked it or not. I sighed.

"I'm really sorry about tonight, Alex. Will you phone me later and let me know you got home okay?"

"Huh!" he exclaimed. "It's *you* that should be phoning me," he said, grimacing in Arwan's direction. I gave Alex an apologetic smile, shrugged my shoulders in defeat, and stepped out into the night.

As I stepped out of Alex's car, Arwan's free arm was immediately around my waist, and I felt the resulting wave of heat explode through me. I wished he didn't have that affect on me. I didn't know what to do with it, how to handle it. Nobody I had ever known had made me feel like Arwan Jones did. Just one touch sent more emotions and sensations searing through me than seven years of marriage to Adam had achieved, and that was quite clearly a dangerous thing for me.

If I let Arwan get to me, I was in for a lifetime of pain, I just knew it. My head was telling me to run as far away as possible, that he was no good for me in any capacity. I had some sort of strange intuition that he could hurt me, not physically but emotionally. I had to try to break the hold he had over me and control the erratic way he affected me, before I was in too deep and the worst could happen. I couldn't fathom what games he was playing, or why he was playing them, but I was going to have to find a way to put a stop to them.

He was still smiling as he opened the passenger door of the Audi. Once I was inside the car, I watched as he strolled, despite the weather, round to the driver's side, opened the door, closed the umbrella, and gracefully slid into the driver's seat. A heartbeat later, he was turning the car in the road and we were heading back in the direction of Claremont, leaving Alex far behind.

"Well, that was a spot of good fortune. I would hate the thoughts of you stuck out here all night with Alex Mcleod," he said jovially.

"How did you know I was out here?" I demanded. I felt guilty enough about leaving Alex without Arwan rubbing it in. I watched his face as he expertly manoeuvred the car on the country road, and waited for him to answer me. I felt annoyed, despite the fact that I would soon be home in the warmth. Why was he being so damn cocky? "Are you keeping tabs on me or something?" It was difficult to see his expression clearly in the dark, but I was sure he was smirking.

"I was merely returning from Glasgow on business, and there you were. It would have been thoughtless of me to drive by without stopping to see if I could assist in some way." His voice was all innocence as he glanced at me, his eyes leaving the road for a little longer than was safe. I was too annoyed to register the fact that he had materialised from the opposite direction to Glasgow.

"I'd have thought you would be pleased to be rescued?" he said, arching an eyebrow. God, he was sexy. I fought to focus on my anger.

"I don't need rescuing! I was perfectly safe with Alex, and now he's stuck out in the middle of nowhere on his own for God knows how long, and I feel rubbish for abandoning him!" His eyes were on me again, but I refused to meet his gaze, knowing that the arrogance I would see would only increase my anger. I could feel his eyes on my face, staring for just that second longer than was strictly comfortable, making my nerve endings tingle and dance around, and forcing shivers to run up and down my spine—shivers that had nothing to do with the cold. I was crazy. I should have stayed with Alex.

I was suddenly aware that we had turned off the road back to Claremont and were heading along an off road in the direction of who knew where.

"Where are we going?" I demanded, concerned by the unfamiliar route we were now taking.

"You're frightened," he stated, shooting me a mocking sidelong glance. I could tell by the way his eyes shone in the dark that he was enjoying himself.

"Not in the least!" I retorted. "Why would I be?"

He laughed loudly at my bravado; then his expression turned thoughtful. "There's something I want to show you. I thought it might be inspiring in some way to your sculpting." I could detect no humour in his tone, so assumed he wasn't joking.

"Really?" I asked dubiously, intrigue beginning to replace my anger. He added nothing more, but the smile never left the planes of his handsome face.

The weather appeared to have taken a freakish U-turn. The rain had stopped, and the clouds had all but disappeared. The moon shone brightly, completely transforming the night from windy and wet to bright and silvery. When did that happen? The weather was so unpredictable in this part of the country.

We stopped, a few moments later, when the dirt road came to a dead end. My eyes scanned the night outside, but we were completely surrounded by dense woodland. What could he mean to show me out here? Arwan was opening my door and helping me out the Audi before I could ask what on earth was going on. He grabbed my hand casually, sending a fresh surge of heat through me, and led the way up a tiny path that I would never have found during the day, let alone at night. Thanks to the sudden appearance of the moon, it was not at all difficult to negotiate the narrow path, and although the ground felt a little juicy underfoot, it was certainly not as waterlogged as I would have expected. The air around us had warmed somewhat, making the evening almost balmy, in extreme contrast to the earlier chilly wind, and a light mist buffeted the air around our feet as we progressed deeper into the trees.

I glanced up at his face as we walked. Even in the dark, I could see it was tense with excitement and anticipation, his eyes bright with delight at the suspense of unveiling his surprise. I stumbled slightly on a piece of uneven ground, too caught up in watching his lovely, strong profile instead of watching where I was going. He stopped suddenly, and looked down at me.

"Are you all right?"

"I'm fine," I whispered. "A little intrigued, though." He smiled again and resumed walking. I hadn't noticed that all my worries of earlier in the day had left me. Thoughts of The Shades had all but disappeared the moment Arwan was in my presence.

The trees about us started to thin out, and I realised that the ground had begun to decline, as if we were coming down a hill. Eventually the ground levelled out, and we were standing in a beautiful glen. The air felt warmer still, and the mist was thickening about our feet.

"There," Arwan whispered, pointing to a large tree some distance away. I walked slowly towards it. Our hands were still joined, but I was leading now.

It was much larger than I first thought, and as we got nearer, I noticed more and more about it. It was an ancient oak, its massive trunk twisted into bends and turns that headed up to the night sky before turning into strong arms reaching up to touch the moon with leafy fingertips. What was truly breathtaking was the way the moonlight played tricks on the trunk and roots, which ran some way along the ground before disappearing underneath the earth. Shadows fell on the twisted wood, creating an eerie impression of spirit nymphs interwoven with the ancient bark. My eyes saw the swell of a breast or the curve of a waist, feminine lines that melted into the tree.

It was truly breathtaking, a gift from Mother Nature to fuel the imagination. The tree would undoubtedly be incredible in its own right during the day, but clothed in the pale blue light of the moon as it was now, it was truly other-worldly. Arwan was right. I knew my hands would be desperately trying to recreate the magic before me as soon as they touched clay. I was in complete awe of its ancient beauty and grace.

My eyes swept up and down from roots to leaf tips over and over again.

"Do you like it?" Arwan whispered as he pulled me round to face him, his eyes searching my face. I was speechless. It wasn't just the tree and its supernatural beauty that had left my throat paralysed, though it was certainly a factor. It was hard not to connect the strength and mysterious presence of the great oak to that of the man before me. Somehow they were akin to one another.

Arwan's expression became concerned when I didn't answer, unable to do more than stare at his face, opening and closing my mouth in an attempt to force something out. Arwan dropped my hand then, and raised both of his, to gently hold my face. I gasped. It didn't seem to matter how often he touched me; the affect of it on every molecule of my being never wavered. I stared up at him through lashes which seemed suddenly weighted and lazy. I felt my teeth bite down into the flesh of my lower lip. Arwan radiated masculinity, from the way he looked and walked to his very presence, which in turn seemed to trigger feelings within me of total femininity. I had never felt more of a woman than I did at that moment. It was like we were two ends of the spectrum, perfect opposites designed to fit together to create just the right balance. He stepped closer, closer than he'd ever been before, his face just inches from mine. My stomach flipped and my heart raced at the feel of his breath on my skin. If he were not holding my face, I was sure my legs would give way, sending me to the ground in a boneless heap.

I wondered, then, if I was lost to him, if nothing else mattered except being with him. What would that mean to me? My life had already been thrown into turmoil as a result of my involvement with one man, and I couldn't shake the fear from within that this man could hurt me so much more than Adam ever could.

It was then that my inner survivor kicked in, yelling at me to step away from him. I began to desperately fight the overwhelming sensations he gave me, physically and mentally. It wasn't a one-sided fight. There was another equally powerful part of me that was desperate, desperate for him.

I realised he meant to kiss me as he lowered his face to mine, his purplish blue eyes strong and sure, seeming to cut through the dark as they bored into mine. I stepped away from him. I don't know how I managed to do it, but I broke free of his spell and free of his hands. I had escaped him before it was too late. I just knew that if I'd let him kiss me, he'd have won. I would only want to exist if I could be with him. I couldn't allow myself to feel that way, not after everything I had been through. The strength I had found to stand against Adam, to leave one life to start another, would all have been for nothing if I were to let another man have the same control over me.

We pulled up out the front of my house. Even though he had taken my hand as he led me back through the woods, we hadn't spoken a word since, and I felt awkward and unsure of what to say. I didn't want to hurt his feelings in the same way I didn't want to hurt Alex's, but it was hard to compare the two. Although Alex was a confident, capable man, his strength seemed so much more fragile when compared to the strength of the man seated next to me.

Arwan switched the engine off and placed both hands lightly on the steering wheel as he stared out into the night, his expression contemplative. A hint of a smile lurked at the corners of his mouth.

"Well," he said, after a moment, "if it's a chase you want, I can accommodate." I turned in my seat, blinking owlishly at him as I digested his words.

"A chase!" I echoed, astounded. "I don't want you to chase me; I want you to leave me alone!" I was suddenly furious.

"I don't think that's true."

"How would you know? You can't read my thoughts!"

"No, but everything you think and *feel* shows on your face," he replied smoothly.

"If you're so good at reading my expressions, then I'm surprised you didn't pick up on the brush off I gave you a few minutes ago in the glen. Perhaps next time a knee somewhere soft might be easier for you to interpret!" I felt a pang of guilt at the harshness of my words, which quickly evaporated as his chuckling filled the car.

"I don't think you're the violent type, Brook." He arched a black brow whilst firing his annoyingly disarming smile at me. We sat for a moment, staring at each other. I hated to hear how ragged my breathing was as a result of our exchange, and it was beyond frustrating for me to see him sitting there, all nonchalance and arrogance.

Then unexpectedly he reached a hand over and traced warm fingers down the length of my jaw. I sucked in a breath as something akin to an electric shock jolted through me. The look of tenderness now in his eyes completely floored me.

"You are the most rapturous creature I ever saw," he murmured. I felt instantly paralysed. A smile spread across his face as he slowly withdrew his hand.

"Damn," I muttered, shaking my head as the anger seeped back in. How did he do that? I moved to get out of the car, thinking escape was my only chance, but a hand on my arm restrained me. Having no choice, I turned back to face him.

"You know if you arrange more dinner dates with Alex it will only hurt his feelings when he realises you only have eyes for me." I was momentarily too stunned to respond. This man took cocky to new heights. "I would be delighted to take you out to dinner every night if you wish?" he added, suddenly grinning.

"Who do you think you are, and how the hell did you know I was having dinner with him? I never told you that, and besides, you can't tell me who I can and can't have dinner with." I said angrily. We stared at each other for a moment; well, he stared and I glared. His expression was completely riling in its dismissal of anything I had said.

I turned back towards the door and managed to get it open and get myself out in one fairly swift movement. I swung the car door shut as forcefully as I could, and headed for the sanctuary of the house.

The sound of his car door opening had me looking round to find him leaning against the bonnet of the Audi, arms folded. Under the glow of the street light I could see the glitter of his eyes, and every plane of his perfectly cut features suddenly set like cold stone.

"Alex Mcleod, or, for that matter, any man alive, will never touch a hand to you again. I promise you that." In the next breath, he was back behind the wheel of the car and zooming off down the road.

I unlocked the front door and shoved it open with such force that it bounced off the hall wall and nearly whacked me in the face as I stepped over the threshold.

chapter

NINE

After shutting the door on my infuriating exchange with Arwan, I stood in the hall, panting with emotion, wondering what in hell he was all about.

When had he decided he didn't hate me but instead wanted to date me? That must be one of the biggest U-turns in the history of relations between a man and a woman!

The phone rang from the living room. I felt a surge of guilt. Alex. My god, I'd forgotten all about him.

I ran the short distance to the living room and picked up the receiver. "Hi, Alex."

"You made it home, then." He sounded peeved, but about his car or about my disappearance with Arwan, I wasn't sure yet.

"Yes, I'm fine. How about you; were you waiting long?"

"Not really."

"Well, that's good." Silence set in. "I'm really sorry about tonight, Alex," I said finally.

"It wasn't your fault," he replied, a little sulkily, I thought. He didn't mention Arwan, but I sensed that had to be what was on his mind.

"Well, good night, then," I said quietly.

"Night, Brook."

I sighed as I hung up the receiver. I really didn't want to hurt Alex's feelings. I felt guilty, but knew I shouldn't. I had been honest with Alex. I had told him I didn't want to date anyone. Why couldn't we just be friends? I would be a good friend to him, if only he would let himself see me in that way.

I wandered through to the kitchen and slumped down at the table. My eyes rested on the new packet of clay I had picked up on my trip to Logan Mills. I reached for it without thinking and tore open the silver packaging. The heady smell of earth rose up to greet me.

It was easy to take my mind back to the glen, to conjure the memory of that majestic oak tree. I began absently to warm the cool clay between my fingers, kneading it and rolling it, bringing it to life with the heat of my hands. All thoughts vacated my mind. I was no longer a burdened woman, but much more simply, a vessel with a sole purpose to recreate the astonishing grace and beauty of that oak tree.

My hands moved with no doubt or uncertainty as they began to mould and shape the almost feminine curves and twists of the tree that was so firmly embedded in my memory, my gift from Arwan.

I don't know how long I worked like that, in a trance of creativity, but at some point, although I only vaguely remembered doing so, I headed to my bedroom and found slumber.

The sound of my doorbell woke me abruptly. I drew back the duvet reluctantly, still drowsy with sleep, and got up and hunted around for my dressing gown. I finally found it hanging up on the back of the bathroom door.

My visitor was getting impatient. The door bell rang for a second time. I looked at my watch, eight o'clock, a little early for visitors. I realised I must have forgotten to set my alarm when I went to bed the night before.

I walked down the hall to the door and, vigilant as ever, stuck the chain on and opened the door a crack.

"Daniel!" I exclaimed. Morag's teenage son stood on my doorstep. I slipped the chain off and opened the door wide.

"Hi, Brook." I noted that he looked more awkward than usual, dressed in his slightly too-large school uniform. His shirt was tucked in on one side and hanging out on the other. A blue and white tie knotted at his neck had been pulled loose with what looked like some force. I'd guessed he'd been immaculate on leaving his mother's. Teenage boys were amazing.

"What's going on?" I asked, smiling. The pained look on his face told me he was here under duress.

"My mum reckons you're not eating properly." He looked down at his black polished shoes, not meeting my eye. "She made you some pancakes," he continued, pointing to a picnic basket at his feet. "I wasn't allowed to eat at home; mum wants me to eat with you, so I can tell her I saw you have breakfast."

I wondered if I should have been angry at Morag's assumption that I wasn't feeding myself, but I wasn't, because she was right.

Despite dinner plans of the night before taking an unexpected turn, I hadn't bothered to feed myself before I started sculpting. I couldn't actually remember when my last meal had been. I'd barely eaten properly for months. I hadn't weighed myself, but I knew I'd been losing weight; I could feel it in my clothes.

Daniel looked from his shoes to my face, waiting for my response.

"She's a piece of work," I grinned.

"Tell me about it."

"Come on in," I encouraged. I was actually pleased to have company. It meant I didn't have to think about what had transpired between me and Arwan the night before. I knew I wouldn't be able to put it off forever; sooner or later I was going to have to think about how to handle things, but for now, it could wait.

We sat down at my tiny kitchen table together, and I opened the basket Daniel had placed there, to see what Morag had sent over. It housed a tasty stash of fresh pancakes, lemon wedges, sugar, and maple syrup, all in separate plastic containers. I lifted out the last of the supplies and noticed that there was something else at the bottom of the basket.

"What's this?" I asked Daniel, lifting out a very old looking book.

"Oh yeah, mum says she found that for you last night. I was to tell you there might be some stuff about Arcross or something in there."

"Achren," I corrected.

"Yeah, that was it. I think it belonged to my great aunt, and she left it for my mum when she died."

I turned what appeared to be a journal over in my hands. It was old, and there was a stag's antler gilded in gold on the dark brown cover. I ran my hand gently over it and could feel the slight raise of the gild under my skin. I flicked briefly through the pages, and saw that there were handwritten entries within.

"Are we going to eat?" I'd forgotten Daniel was there.

"Sure," I said, putting the journal down on the table and bringing my attention back to my guest. I would have plenty of time that night to look at it.

"Let's get your mum's pancakes back in the pan," I said, flicking on the hotplate.

A few minutes later, Daniel and I were munching companionably.

"How's school?" I asked casually, thinking maybe I could sound him out a little about his new friends Morag was so worried about. I tried to keep how keenly interested I was out of the tone of my voice.

"Boring." A classic teenage response. I didn't let it put me off. I chewed and then swallowed a mouthful of pancake.

"I bet you've got plenty of friends, though...at school, I mean?"

He stopped chewing for a moment and looked me directly in the eye. "Mum's been talking to you," he stated, with an incredulous shake of his head.

I decided to come clean, subtlety clearly not my strong point. "She's just worried. She's a mother; she wouldn't be doing her job if she didn't."

He sighed. "Aye, I get that, but there's nothing for her to worry about. She's cramping my style, wanting to ken what I'm doing every second of the day."

I struggled not to giggle. Morag was definitely worried about these new friends of Daniel's, but I wondered if she was letting the line between policing and parenting blur somewhat.

I watched thoughtfully as Daniel forked the last piece of pancake on his plate into his mouth and sat back in the chair. He raised his hands to his hair and gently patted, checking that every dishevelled sandy strand was still in its not so apparently random place. He eyed my plate, where a final pancake lay rolled and smothered in sugar and lemon. I'd been nudging it with my fork for the last few minutes.

"You going to eat that?"

"Nope, it's yours." I shovelled it onto his plate. "But don't tell your mother, okay?"

"Deal," he snickered.

Daniel left after eating his fill, and I got showered and dressed, putting on a pair of black jeans and a lime green fitted jumper that I thought somehow complimented my dark eyes and hair. I couldn't help myself. I was making an effort to look nice, despite the conscious effort I was making not to think about Arwan. It was fruitless. I always thought about him, always. I had from the moment I saw him on that stormy afternoon. He consumed me nearly all of the time. I knew that and tried to fight against it, but there was no point in denying it; I was drawn to him.

The man was so damn unpredictable, though. I could arrive at Avallon House today, and he might completely ignore me. Though I somehow thought that was unlikely. Something had changed in his perception of me, how he reacted to me. Would he want to lunch with me today? I thought I knew the answer to that as well. Did I have the strength to put a stop to it? I thought perhaps I should, that I must, in the interests of self-preservation.

I arrived at Avallon House and noticed that Arwan didn't appear to be home. I couldn't help but wonder if he'd changed his mind about me, had decided to let me get on with housekeeping his home rather than engaging me in whatever it was he was trying to engage me in. Well, at least it would spare me the task, I mused, attempting to cover the empty feeling that swamped me.

I had been adamant on the way over that I would have to put him straight on how things were going to be between us. But perhaps that conversation wasn't going to be necessary after all.

I spent the first hour of the morning in the library, dusting and vacuuming every nook and cranny. The roar of the hoover had been comforting in a strange kind of way. The noise somehow superseded the relentless voice in my head, with all its questions and worries, allowing me to get on with the job at hand in an almost dreamlike state. All only temporary, of course. One thing I'd learned, you can't keep what gnaws at you at bay for long.

I walked across the reception hall, followed by the clicking of eight paws on the wooden floor, and pushed through the door to the kitchen.

The first thing that hit me was bright golden light, followed by a warm gentle breeze coming from the open patio doors. I was astounded; just over an hour ago, the weather had been typically dreary for the time of year, and yet in the time I had been working away in the library, the sun had forced its way through the opaque sky and produced a glorious afternoon in the middle of autumn.

I walked, mesmerised, through the open doors, and stepped out into brilliant clarity. It had to be at least twenty-three degrees, a hot day for Scotland, even in the height of summer.

I stared up into the blue in disbelief, shielding my eyes from the sun with my hands. I turned around slowly, eyes trained to the sky, following a thick rim of grey cloud in the distance, from which I could see rain falling in wispy tendrils to the earth. The large hole in the canopy of cloud gave way to scorching sunshine seemingly just over his land. Freaky.

The sweet scents and sounds of life all around me pulled my eyes back to my immediate surroundings; fat bumblebees buzzed about the garden in a hypnotic drone, alighting occasionally on the several varieties of flower that bloomed unexpectedly in the sunshine.

How was this possible? We were closer to winter than to summer. Birds twittered exuberantly from treetops in an excited little chorus, seemingly as confused about the sudden climate change as I was. The garden was literally alive with activity in every direction. I inhaled deeply as I watched two large orange and black butterflies playing and circling one another in a lovers' dance around the garden.

"Glorious day, isn't it?" I felt dizzy at the very sound of him, and pulled in the direction of his voice like the earth to the sun.

He was seated at a table on a raised wooden deck. Under the warm rays, he was truly something to behold. His skin belonged to the sun, turning his honey tones a beautiful soft gold that took my breath away. He held his dark head to one side, his finely cut features relaxed, but it was his eyes that I was drawn to the most. They were so bright and brilliant, they were almost luminous. He was dressed casually but immaculately in jeans and designer t-shirt. I suppressed a sigh at the sight of strong forearms basking in the unscheduled sunshine, and couldn't help wondering what the rest of him must look like beneath the clothes. I'd guess, like his arms, that he was muscled and sculpted all over, hard and taught. There was nothing soft about Arwan Jones.

"Indeed it is," I murmured.

Before him lay another decadent spread of food, our lunch, presumably. He was up and out of his chair in a blink of an eye, and had the other chair pulled out as he looked over to me expectantly, a black brow raised in invitation. I realised that he was testing me, daring me to object. I made my way over as casually as possible, unwilling to let him see how his sudden presence affected me.

The dogs had stretched themselves out lazily on the grass at the foot of the decking steps, white bellies worshipping the sun as I walked by.

Arwan tucked my chair in behind me. I was acutely aware of how close he was, and felt my blood quicken in response. He murmured something into my hair as I sat, but I didn't catch it.

"Would you allow me to serve you, Brook?" he asked, lifting the plate in front of me.

"Sure, okay," I mumbled. The fact that he had already started loading my plate rendered my answer inconsequential.

I watched as he selected all my favourite foods, fish, salad, and freshly baked bread, which he took the time to spread with butter. He placed the plate down in front of me, then lifted a jug and filled a glass with iced water.

"Thank you," I croaked, as he placed the glass next to my plate. I found his gesture unexplainably moving. I was touched by it, by the very fact that he had wanted to serve me lunch. It was one of the most simple but intimate things anybody had ever done for me. He played unfair, that was for sure, I mused. No woman stood a chance against this kind of charm. It was flawless in its execution, a relentless assault.

After indicating that I should start, he found his seat and went about filling his own plate.

We ate in a strained kind of silence for a while, although it only appeared strained to me; Arwan was his usual mixture of casual and nonchalance. It was hard to imagine him ever feeling anything other than complete confidence. That in itself was intimidating; most of the time I felt anything but sure of myself.

"Were you close to your parents as a child?"

I groaned inwardly; more probing questions. I thought a while before I answered, swallowing the remainders of crusty loaf.

"Not really. They divorced when I was young, met new partners, and remarried. I never really felt I belonged with either of them. I wasn't the priority growing up. They weren't neglectful, as such, just indifferent." A shadow fell across his face, and I looked to the sky, wondering if the vortex of sunshine were about to disappear. But there were no clouds anywhere nearby.

"You have no brothers or sisters?"

I brought my eyes back to him. "No," I said, contemplatively. I had always wondered when one or other set of parents would make a happy announcement with their respective new partners, but it never came. I shouldn't have been surprised. I don't think they ever really meant to have me. Some people just weren't great with kids, and that doesn't always change just because one comes along one day and demands that you look after it.

"It would have been nice to have a sister," I admitted. I had been very lonely at times, as a kid. I noticed that Arwan seemed annoyed or frustrated by something, his face turning grim. I wondered what I'd said to annoy him. It intrigued me immensely that my life seemed to arouse such varying emotions in him. I decided that was enough about me, so I flipped the conversation.

"What about you? Do you have a good relationship with your parents?"

"I haven't seen my parents for a long time." Interesting. I sensed that he didn't want to elaborate. A family feud, I wondered? That would explain why I'd never seen a relative at Avallon House.

I plucked an olive from my plate and popped it into my mouth, chewing and quickly swallowing as I thought about how to continue. "Do you have siblings?" I asked, wondering if he'd thought I was overstepping the mark.

"I have a brother."

"Oh, are the two of you close?"

"No."

Okay, then. I studied his face, but he was giving nothing away, his features impassive, eyes like purple glass.

"I understand your great grandfather purchased and gave the land around here to the people of Claremont. That was an incredible act of generosity," I offered, hoping to somehow break through his armour.

"The land here is, ah...special," he replied, watching me intently. I nodded in agreement, wondering if he was going to add anything, but it seemed he'd said all he was prepared to on the matter.

I cleared my plate and placed my knife and fork together, and after a moment Arwan did the same.

"I should like to see some of your sculptures sometime." My heart practically seized up in my chest. The last person I would want to show my art to was Arwan. How could what I do ever compare to his talent?

"Sure," I replied, with a dismissive wave of my hand. "I'll bring something by." Or not.

"I'd like to see the oak tree," he said, his purplish eyes shining from across the table.

A rush of memories of the night before came flooding back, scorching a crimson glow up my neck to my cheeks, as I involuntarily thought about the way he had looked at me in the silver light, held me in his arms.

I cleared my throat nosily as I struggled to bring myself back. I had intended to maintain an aura of peevishness about the night before, in a desperate attempt to keep him at arm's length. But all of that had seemed to dissipate the moment I'd heard his voice in the garden. I was going to have to try a lot harder, that was clear. No time like the present.

"About last night," I began. "I just wanted us both to be clear on the way things are." I wondered if he heard the slight quiver to my words.

"Oh, I'm crystal clear, Brook, but I'd be happy for you to elaborate if you think it would help," he purred.

"I think it would," I said, nodding adamantly. Arwan smiled.

"Then please." He leaned back into his chair, crossing his arms over his chest as I bit my lip and sucked in a deep breath. How I was going to make this sound convincing with him sitting there, looking like, well quite frankly like some sort of a god, I didn't know.

"I work for you; you are my boss. Agreed?" I paused until he inclined his dark head slightly. I took another deep breath. "I think it's best if that's how things stay." I paused again, this time paying particular attention to his face. He showed no emotion, just continued to watch with his ice eyes. I couldn't gauge his reaction, but a slight shifting in the atmosphere between us made the skin prickle on my arms. I rubbed at them absently, and forced myself to continue.

"I don't want things to be awkward between us."

Who was I kidding? Things couldn't really get more awkward as far as I was concerned, but I had started, so it was best to bash on. I had a feeling it was now or never.

"I'm your housekeeper, and I think that's how it should stay." My closing statement sounded borderline hysterical. I digested his stony expression, his cool eyes. As the silence stretched out around us, I found his lack of response extremely unsettling. What he wasn't saying hung in the air with an almost bloody violence. I cleared my throat awkwardly. I wanted to drop my gaze from his, but couldn't. He wouldn't let me go.

"So we're crystal about everything?" I said, attempting to ease the tension I could feel rapidly building.

"You belong with me," he said, darkly. I felt my jaw drop.

"I don't *belong* with anyone."

"You're wrong."

I stood up abruptly. "Look, I think it's best if I get back to what you're paying me to do." I turned from the table with the intent of descending the decking steps, when I felt his iron grip on my arm, pulling me round to face him. I gasped. How did he do that? I didn't see him stand, let alone move to where I was.

"You're fighting a battle you can't win." His eyes bored into mine as he pulled me closer into the circle of his arms. I felt the heat of him instantly. The core of my resolve began to melt, at the intensity of his voice and the unexpected close proximity of his lips and his warm breath on my neck. I fought to orient myself, not wanting to feel the almost undeniable gravitational pull I always felt in his direction, the need to merge with him, kicking up a gear.

After a moment he released me with what I thought was reluctance, and indicated my recently vacated chair.

"Please, sit down," he said gently, in his most compelling voice. I obeyed. The tension lifted immediately as Arwan returned to his seat. But one thing was clear; he wasn't about to take no for an answer.

I raised my shoulders and looked him directly in the eye as he sat opposite me. His face was relaxed again. Not for long; I was determined to prove more of a challenge than Arwan Jones could think possible. If this was a battle, I had to bring out the heavy artillery. A grin threatened at the corners of his lips, as if he had somehow registered my thoughts.

"No more lunches, Arwan. I mean it; this cannot happen again, or I won't be able to continue my position here." I hoped he wouldn't hear the lie in my words. He poured ice water into his glass before responding. I sensed a change of tact.

"Try all you like, but I think you will find it quite difficult to avoid me. In fact, I'm fairly confident in saying that it would be virtually impossible." He grinned openly now as he met my eye before taking a sip from his glass.

"You might be surprised how evasive a girl can be when she puts her mind to it!" I said hotly. His eyes glittered, sending my pulse racing in my throat.

"If I thought that were possible, you would never leave my sight again...but even so," he continued, "I wouldn't make idle threats. You might not like the consequences." He grinned again, baring perfect white teeth. "On second thoughts, attempt your evasive plan. I could live with the consequences quite happily." His eyes suddenly smouldered, with some wicked thought, and my temperature soared in response.

I struggled with several different emotions, bewilderment, vulnerability, and desire, and then settled on indignation.

"Who do you think you are? You don't own me, Arwan, I barely know you! I'll leave here right now and never come back." Lie! "You're so used to getting what you want that you think you can have anything or anyone, like some sort of spoilt cave man. People aren't possessions; you can't just snap your fingers and claim somebody's life like one of your antiques!"

I stood to leave for the second time, but was once again restrained by his hand, an iron grip on my wrist. My bones felt small and fragile under his fingers, like sea shells he could crush at leisure. He'd done it again, moved to my side without my seeing.

"You are absolutely right; I am used to getting what I want," he murmured darkly into the nape of my neck, "and you are mine."

The dogs had found their feet and whined to each other softly as they observed us. I angled my head so I could look up at his face, and saw that his black brows were furrowed in a frown above eyes that returned my gaze in a purple blaze. After a long moment, he sighed, and I thought how incredibly sad he looked.

"I'm sorry, Brook, forgive me?" His tone was suddenly gentle, coaxing. He lessened his grip on my arms, but continued to hold me to him. "Don't look at me like that; I would never hurt you." My terror subsided as his tones lulled the fear from my blood. "You were frightened of your husband, weren't you?" I wondered what he saw in my expression. Adam had never physically hurt me, but the threat of it never seemed too far away. I knew he was capable of it, so I did everything in my power never to provoke that side of him. Complete compliance. It was humiliating to remember the way things were in my old life. Arwan was wrong, though. My fear didn't stem from any threat I felt physically; I knew he would never hurt me like that. What frightened me was what he could do to my heart. I felt emotionally vulnerable to him, wide open to anguish, and I understood that that had to change.

"Forgive me," he repeated in the same soft, hypnotic tone. "Please sit with me. It is not my intention to upset you. I just need you to understand what you mean to me. I can't tolerate any sort of vision without you in it. It would drive me eternally insane if you were to leave me." It was hard to stay angry with him when the sincerity of his words radiated in his eyes as he spoke. Despite my resolution to keep my distance from him, the feeling of being drawn to him seemed to surge with renewed vigour, with every word he uttered. I felt the sudden urge to touch his face, to try ease his distress, but I knew I must not.

I fell back into my seat and took a sip of the cool water before letting my eyes fall shut with a sigh. I wanted a moment free from his eyes, to feel the sun on my face and to listen to the sounds of summer in his garden, and to pretend that this man had no hold over me. A man, I mused, a man who could move faster than my eyes could follow!

I opened my eyes to see him lounging casually in his chair as he waited for me to come back to him.

"I want you to tell me how you move the way you do. How you manage to be in one place, and I blink and you're in another. How do you do that?"

He smirked. "I work out."

I pinched my brow between my thumb and forefinger in frustration, before taking a deep breath and meeting his gaze again. The smirk lingered on his features, and all I could do to stop myself screaming like a petulant child was to knock back the last of the water in my glass. I wiped my mouth with a napkin.

"You're being deliberately evasive. Why?" I demanded.

"The answers are there for you Brook, all of them. Things will be much clearer for you, in time." I sighed. What the hell was that supposed to mean? Could I not get one straight answer out of the man?

A bumblebee hovered inquisitively over the contents of the table, bouncing from plate to plate before deciding there was nothing of interest and flying off with a disgruntled buzz.

I shook my head. "You're speaking in riddles. Why can't you give me a straight answer?"

He ran a hand through coal hair, making the air catch in my lungs at the sight. Like so many things about him, the gesture seemed familiar to me, like I'd watched him do it a thousand times. He eyed me levelly.

"You really want to know?"

I nodded eagerly at the prospect of finally getting some answers. "Yes, yes I do."

My mobile suddenly shrilled out from the pocket of my jeans. I ignored it and continued to hold his gaze in expectation.

"Shouldn't you answer that?"

Damn it! I yanked the mobile from my pocket. It was a voicemail; lack of cellular signal at the mansion meant sometimes my phone clicked straight to answer phone. I dialled up the answer service, quietly simmering at the intrusion. It was Morag. I froze as I heard the anxiety in her voice. Edith was very ill and desperate to see me. "If you can, Brook, get here as quick as you can," she pleaded. "She's adamant she must see you, and I don't know how long...just get here when you can."

I flipped my phone shut, standing up abruptly. I could feel my entire body trembling.

"Arwan, you'll have to excuse me, one of my friends at the home is ill. I have to get to her. I'm sorry, can I finish up tomorrow?" The distress in my tone was blatant.

"Forget that." he said. "Will you allow me to drive you?"

I hesitated for a moment, taken aback by the concern suddenly clouding his lovely purple eyes.

"Okay," I agreed.

Moments later, we were driving under the rim of thick grey cloud that I had seen from the garden. The afternoon was instantly darker, and rain spattered on the windscreen in blustery bursts, the bliss of the surprise summer's day in Arwan's garden left behind.

When we arrived at the home, Morag was waiting for me at the front door, blonde brows shooting up in surprise as she saw Arwan.

"Morag, this is Arwan, Arwan this is Morag," I said, introducing them. Arwan nodded politely and Morag smiled, curiosity and open appreciation replacing her anxious expression for an instant.

"What's going on, Morag?"

"The doctor says she's had a series of heart attacks through the night, several small ones, but one major. He doesn't think she will make it beyond a few hours; she's very weak. We've made her as comfortable as possible, and the doctor has ensured she's not in any pain. She's refusing to be moved to hospital. Perhaps you could try and convince her it would be for the best." I nodded grimly.

"Where's Alex?" I asked, worrying about how Edith's state would be affecting him. She'd been like a mother to him and his brother.

"He's gone home for a shower. He sat with her all night."

The atmosphere was heavy with expectation in Edith's room, as if the inevitable had been accepted and the waiting had begun. I had never been in her room before, and noticed it was full of photographs of a young Alex and another boy, presumably his brother. One frame, slightly larger than all the others, showed Alex as a dazzling fresh recruit to the police, embracing his proud Nan with blatant love and affection. Every wall held a Scottish landscape, and I was touched to see several familiar pots and sculptures on her dressing table.

A machine beeped quietly, unobtrusively, representing Edith's heartbeat. Other than that, the room was silent. I had never realised silence could be so loud until that moment, that silence could scream death in a way sound could not. Edith was not alone; she was obscured by Hector Armstrong, the local GP, leaning over and checking the drip in his patient's arm.

As the doctor straightened and moved away from the bed, I saw Edith properly for the first time. She was hooked up to the heart monitor with various wires, and a thin tube ran from her nose to an oxygen tank by the bed. Her eyes were closed, and had it not been for the subdued beeping representing her tired heart, I would have thought her already dead.

The atmosphere of expectation in the room found materialisation in the middle-aged doctor's kind face, as well as in his barely concealable grief. My heart went out to him as I realised he must know Edith well.

"She's been waiting for you," he said, and with a parting whispered word to Arwan, he left us alone with Edith.

I pulled a seat over to her bed and placed her small wrinkled hand in mine. Arwan hung back in the doorframe, handsome face unreadable but watching, always watching.

"Edith, sorry I took so long getting here," I said gently. Her eyes flickered open at the sound of my voice and rested on my face. Where was the woman I had grown to care so much about? She was so pale, so tired, but her eyes seemed to focus as she ran them over my face.

"Brook?" she said, in a dry whisper. "Thank-you for coming to see me, lass."

"Of course I came, Edith." She smiled, faintly.

"You're a good lassie." I lifted a glass of water from her side table and supported her head as she took a sip.

"Hello, Edith."

My eyes flickered to Arwan in the doorway, as did Edith's.

"Mr Jones?" I turned back to Edith in the bed, and was immediately dumbstruck by her reaction to Arwan. Her eyes were wide with wonder, her mouth slack with disbelief.

"It's been a long time, hasn't it?" he said, smiling kindly as he moved closer to the bed. He pulled over another chair and sat down beside me.

"Too long," she replied in a faraway whisper. A single tear fell from each eye and traced down her cheeks.

It seemed that in her semiconscious state, her eyes believed they were looking at Arwan's great grandfather, Arwan Jones Snr, who had saved her young life in the woods around Claremont, all those years ago.

I stood up gently, releasing Edith's hand, and indicated that Arwan should swap seats with me. He did so, placing his hand in hers. The moment his skin touched hers, an exuberant smile found her lips before her features settled into those of a shy little girl. I couldn't believe what I was seeing, but it was such an overwhelming relief to see some life and colour in her cheeks again that I was deliriously happy to go along with it.

"I always hoped you'd come back to see me one day," she simpered, her watery eyes glued to his face.

"You're just as pretty as ever," he returned. She giggled, then a moment passed in silence.

"I waited for you," she whispered. Arwan smiled at her again. "Will you stay long?" she asked, with desperate hope in her eyes.

"This isn't my home," Arwan said, gently stroking her hand. I thought she was going to weep again as her face briefly crumpled, before she pulled it back to a faint smile and nodded with a realisation I didn't understand.

"I know that," she whispered, "and it isn't the lass's either." Edith's eyes flickered briefly to me, then were drawn back to Arwan. I wasn't sure what she meant by that, but she clearly wasn't quite herself.

I listened as Arwan and Edith settled in to a quiet conversation, seemingly in a little bubble all of their own. I shivered at the sheer goodness radiating from Arwan. He must have known that Edith had mistaken him for his grandfather, and yet there he sat, engaging her in the only way I could ever dream possible that would have brought the life back to her eyes. This incredible gesture left me utterly speechless.

Edith seemed to be getting perkier by the moment, and with Arwan's aid, had even raised herself up slightly, almost to a sitting position, as they chatted away together, seemingly oblivious to my presence, about the old days in Claremont.

I sat by them as unobtrusively as I could, my eyes switching between them in state of complete wonder. Arwan was like no other man, or human, I had ever known.

An hour passed before Edith finally agreed to let go of Arwan's hand, under the promise that he would return and visit her soon.

Arwan opened the passenger door of the Audi, and closed it again after I was comfortably seated inside. He drove carefully through the village centre, the car's tires humming noisily on the cobbles.

It was just after three o'clock, and the school had emptied for the day. The street was teeming with gum-flapping school kids laughing and joking, carefree and boisterous to boot, as they headed for their homes, oblivious to the rain.

I studied Arwan's profile for a moment, my mind reeling with what I'd just witnessed.

"What you did back there, for Edith, that was..." Words failed me. My awestruck brain was giving me nothing. I didn't have words to describe what he had done or the gratitude I felt. The Edith who had met us when we first arrived at The Shades that afternoon, and the one who waved us off heartily only moments ago, were two completely different people. It was like he had lulled her back from the brink.

He shrugged his shoulders dismissively.

"No, don't do that!" I pleaded. "You must have seen what you did back there? You brought her to life!" Okay, that was definitely an exaggeration, but not a million miles away from what had happened. Doctor Armstrong's legs had virtually buckled beneath him when he came to check on his patient as we were leaving.

Arwan looked at me sidelong. "Do you have faith, Brook?"

My eyes widened briefly at the question. Was he asking me if I believed in God? I looked out my window, but saw nothing as we drove past the last of the school kids and began the short journey out of Claremont back to Avallon House.

"I believe in the power of faith," I said eventually. "I think that to believe in something resolutely would be a wonderful thing." I'd just witnessed the proof of my words. Edith clearly had believed Arwan to be his great grandfather, and that belief had seemingly done something no medicine had managed to do. That was the power of faith. It didn't matter how tenuous the foundations of faith were, as long as it was believed. The truth was irrelevant. If you had unwavering faith, the magic was there, and *stuff* could happen.

"But you don't have a faith?" he said, pulling me from my reverie. I thought for a moment.

"No, perhaps not in the conventional sense, but I know I'm made up of energy and matter, just like everything else in the universe. It's like we're all connected, we break down to the same thing, essentially, everything and everyone. We're all one and the same; that knowledge is deeply spiritual to me."

"It is to me too," he murmured. Then he reached over a hand and tucked an escaped curl behind my ear, making my pulse quicken. I turned to him and thought how tired he seemed to suddenly look, his eyes weary, old beyond their years.

"There's no greater comfort than that, is there?" he said. I shook my head slowly.

"I don't think so," I whispered.

Arwan parked next to my little car when we arrived back at Avallon House, but seemed in no hurry to move from the warmth of the cab. The sky was once again one continuous ceiling of opaque grey, and despite being mid-afternoon, it was already beginning to darken. It wasn't quite raining, but Scotch mist was substituting until the heavens were ready to open again.

I glanced over at Arwan, somewhat apprehensively, feeling unsure of how to say goodbye. After a moment, I unbuckled my seat belt and turned in my seat to face him. I breathed deeply, and attempted to regulate my heartbeat. I wanted to concentrate on what I needed to say to him rather than on the affect that his presence, even his smell, was having on me in such close proximity. He let his hands relax on the wheel and turned to meet my gaze. He was so incredibly beautiful that I lost the ability to formulate words. I knew what I wanted to say, and what I should say, but I was momentarily rendered useless by the sheer presence of him; the perfect angles of his face, the line of his straight nose, and his eyes, always the eyes.

I moistened my own lips unconsciously as my gaze found the red of his mouth, a lovely mouth, flawless, like everything about him.

"Is something the matter?" The sound of his voice pulled me up. I felt my cheeks heat up. I had been staring at him, again. I sighed. I didn't know how not to look at him.

"Nothing," I mumbled, dropping my gaze to my lap.

A moment passed in silence. I was frightened to look up at him, but I could feel that he was looking at me. I cleared my throat.

"Thanks for what you did today," I said to my jeans, before reluctantly looking up at him through my lashes.

The purple eyes that looked back at me were impassioned. "I would do anything for you."

I tried unsuccessfully to swallow the lump in my throat that was my erratic pulse. I had to get out of there before I did something stupid, like kiss him.

chapter

TEN

As soon as I got home, I went straight to the phone and called The Shades. Morag assured me that Edith was doing miraculously well.

"She's sitting up, watching *Taggart* and munching on a packet of crisps," Morag informed me. "I don't know what you two said to her, but the doctor reckons he's never seen anything like it in twenty-five years."

I hung up the phone and sank onto the sofa. Edith appeared to be recuperating, but what would happen to her fragile recovery once she heard about the sale of what had been her home for the last ten years? My relief was short-lived.

The following morning, my movements were slow and thoughtful. Although I was desperate to see Edith, I was in no hurry to get to work.

When I did finally arrive at The Shades, the atmosphere was heavy with the sadness and worry of the staff. Even though the residents weren't being told about the sale of their home until the following day, I'd be surprised if the men in suits wandering around the building with clipboards and measuring equipment had gone unnoticed. Couldn't they have at least waited until the residents knew what was going on? Where was the thought or compassion?

I made my way straight to the recreation room.

How was I going to get through the morning with my friends and not tell them what I knew?

I paused at the door, taking a deep breath. I tried an experimental smile on my mouth, but it felt forced and unnatural. They'd see right through it.

"Hi everyone," I said, resting my eyes on no one in particular, when I finally veered round the corner. Other than Edith, all of The Shades residents were sitting, chatting amongst themselves and waiting for me to arrive.

"Hello, lass," I heard Joe say amongst other greetings. "Doesn't she look bonny today?" Consent broke out through the room.

"You're too smooth, Joe," I smiled, and he grinned in return.

"Always was, always will be!" he replied.

"Aye, just like the top of your head!" Doreen interjected, much to the hilarity of some of the others.

I couldn't help but laugh along. I waited till the room settled down.

"I thought I'd let you guys decide what you want to do today," I offered. A strange silence fell over the group, and several residents glanced briefly at one another, but after a moment, Joe spoke up.

"I think we'd like to sculpt."

"Brook?" It was Ruth. Well, her head anyway, peering round the door frame. I put my scalpel down, got up, and went over to her hovering cranium.

"Is everything okay, Ruth?" I whispered. She seemed pumped about something; her eyes were round and bright.

"Can I have a word with you for a minute?" she almost pleaded. "In my office?"

"Um, sure." I was instantly curious.

I followed her out into the corridor and down the end of the hall to her office. She beckoned me inside in a manner that suggested that whatever she had to say was bursting to escape the confines of her lips. Ruth was clearly very excited about something. I had barely sat down when she exploded.

"I have some news!"

"What kind of news?" I asked, feeling the slightest lift in my internal tensions.

"We've been saved! We've been saved!" My jaw dropped, and I watched excitement and relief roll off Ruth in waves as she told me all about it.

"The Council just phoned. The Shades has been bought already." I frowned slightly, wondering how exactly that was good news.

"The investor," Ruth continued in answer to my confused expression, while simultaneously bouncing up and down on her swivel chair, "is going to continue to run the building as a retirement home; other than redecorating, they don't want to change a single thing!" Now it was my turn to jump up.

"Ruth, that's great!"

She flew from behind her desk and seemed to find me in one large step through the piles of paper, pulling me in for a big hug. After a moment of joint celebration, we found our seats again. Ruth patted at her wayward red hair, as if calming it would somehow calm her heart.

"Do the others know yet?" I asked eagerly.

"I'm going to call another meeting this afternoon and tell everybody," she explained. I thought about what a huge relief it would be to Clive, Morag, and the rest of the staff. Nobody was going to be out of a job, and the residents weren't being flung out of their home. Yes, this really was wonderful news, and best of all, Edith could continue to recover in the sanctity of The Shades, surrounded by the people she knew and loved. I laughed out loud at the realisation.

"I want to throw a party here tomorrow night, to thank the investor that's saved us all and," Ruth hesitated, smiling a little apologetically, "I wondered if perhaps you would offer him one of your magnificent sculptures as a heartfelt thank you from all of us?"

I nodded. “It would be my pleasure.” I knew instantly which sculpture to give. The best I had done yet.

When I arrived home that afternoon, I was so full of hypertension that I could barely sit down. As I flung my coat over a chair in the kitchen, my stomach growled, reminding me that I hadn’t eaten anything since breakfast. I opened the fridge, still smiling to myself, and grabbed the necessities for a cheese and tomato sandwich.

I was just dabbing the last crumb from my plate, when my eyes rested on Morag’s Aunt Rudy’s journal. I shoved my plate to the side and replaced it slowly with the old brown diary.

For reasons I didn’t know, I felt reluctant to open it. Something told me that when I did, there would be no going back, but going back from what? I ran my hand over the gold gilt for the second time, hesitating, debating whether to proceed. I breathed deeply, then opened to the first page.

Most of the entries didn’t make much sense. They seemed to be written in some sort of shorthand that only the author would understand. I could make out bits and pieces. It appeared that Rudy and her friends were quite the pagans, and had spent a substantial amount of their time carrying out various rituals and spells, the latter of which were detailed. There were spells for luck, love, fertility, prosperity, warding off evil, encouraging good, and many more. Different coloured candles seemed to feature regularly, as did twigs from various trees, willow, elm, and oak in particular.

I also managed to pick up that Rudy and her friends, as Morag had mentioned in the Balmoral, believed that somewhere in the general Claremont vicinity, there was the existence of a gateway to another world. From what I could gather from the almost illegible scribble and shorthand, Rudy had scoured the local area, paying particular attention to the River Byron, which ran through Claremont not particularly far from my house, as well as to the cliffs out at Ross Cove. I had deduced that their searches were basically fruitless, until I turned to the last entry. For reasons known only to Morag’s aunt, her final journal entry was written in clear, bold longhand. Was it because she was so excited about what she’d discovered that she couldn't risk losing anything in translation? My pulse throbbed in the hollow of my neck as I continued to read...

'Exciting breakthrough today; whilst doing my usual research work, I stumbled across an account of a witch trial which took place in Claremont in 1694. A young woman by the name of Jade McEwen was tried and executed for allegedly practising witchcraft. According to the trial manuscripts, which provided a surprising amount of detail, Jade McEwen was witnessed by several villagers appearing through an oak tree. The witnesses claimed that the accused had not been in the area previously, but had actually been seen literally emerging from the trunk of a giant oak tree somewhere here in Claremont. The exact location was not provided in the account, but we begin our search for the tree tomorrow. I believe the tree mentioned in Jade McEwen's trial of 1694 is the gateway to the Other-world we have been searching for.'

I shut the journal, stood up, and walked slowly over to the kitchen counter where my sculpture of the night before lay resting under a moist blue and white check tea towel. Could it be the same one? Could the oak tree that Arwan had shown me be the same oak tree that Jade McEwen was seen materialising from, way back in 1694? I raised my arm, feeling strangely detached from my body, and gently pulled the towel away. I took a sharp intake of breath as the sculpture bought the majesty of the oak back to me, and I thought that perhaps the answer was yes.

My mind went into overdrive. Could I find the oak in the woods again? I wasn't sure, but I had to try.

I picked up my coat from the chair and grabbed my car keys from their hook, then rushed out the front door.

It was just after five o'clock, but the night was clear, and it was still light, just. I had that in my favour.

I headed out of Claremont, keeping my eyes alert, looking for the road that Arwan had taken the other night. If I could find it, then surely I would find the path through the woods, which in turn led to the glen where the oak tree stood.

I was wired, hyped up. The blood coursed through my veins in excitement and anticipation. Answers lay round the corner, I could feel it. If I could just find the damn road!

I tapped the steering wheel with my hand in agitation.

"It must be somewhere near here," I muttered, scanning the line of trees. I tried to remember how long it had taken Arwan to drive me home from when we left the tree that night. Ten, maybe fifteen minutes? I couldn't be sure. I'd had a lot on my mind. I slammed on the breaks, lucky there was no one behind me, and then groaned. It was a track, but it was on the wrong side of the road and far too narrow for a car, let alone Arwan's Audi. I drove on.

After twenty minutes, I knew I must have missed the little road I was looking for. The light was beginning to fade. I would never find it now. I felt the adrenalin leave my system like helium from a balloon.

I flicked on my headlights and made a U-turn in the road, then headed back to Claremont. I would try again tomorrow morning. I could park up somewhere and walk, and then there would be no missing anything. I considered the idea of asking Arwan how to find the tree, but quickly dismissed it. For some reason, I didn't want him to know I was trying to find it again without him.

I was suddenly pulled from my plans for the following day by the sight of Daniel Fraser, Morag's son, with two older looking guys. They were walking up the narrow break in the line of trees that I had just moments ago mistaken for the one I had been looking for. Under most circumstances, I would not have found this scenario odd at all. The woodland around Claremont was popular with all ages for camping or trekking, but there had been something unsettling about Daniel's face. I only saw it briefly as my headlights illuminated the trio, but I could have sworn he looked frightened. The two bigger boys were flanking him on either side, almost as if to stop him running away. In fact, I was fairly sure that that was exactly what they were doing. I thought of what Morag had said earlier in the week at Ross Cove: "There's something nasty about them. They're not good kids."

I wondered if those were the two boys Morag was so concerned about. The look I'd seen on Daniel's face, and something about the body language of all three, made me anxious, very anxious.

With no further thought, I stuck my indicator on and parked up on the side of the road. What exactly I was planning on doing when I caught up with them, I didn't know, but I had to at least see that Daniel was okay.

I locked the car and jogged over to the break in the trees where the boys had disappeared, and I looked up the narrow path. It didn't extend in a straight line, and already the boys were out of sight. The sun was well into its westerly retreat by now, and I hoped I could catch them up before it vanished completely. I didn't particularly fancy trekking around the woods in the dark. I consoled myself with the fact that they couldn't have gotten far. It had been only moments since I'd seen them from the road. At least they wouldn't turn around and see me clambering up the hill behind them.

The air outside the car was crisp, and I wished I had my thicker jacket. I took a deep breath for courage, pulled my hands up into my thin sleeves, and began up the path. Thankfully the weather was in between showers, but I was shivering, and I could feel my heart racing. I told myself that it was due to the cold and to walking up the incline, but I knew that the hill wasn't really the problem. The woods around me seemed full of rustling shapes and shadows ghosting about in the half light, always slightly ahead of my darting eyes. I shuddered in between shivers and tried to pull my thoughts from the woods and back to the reality of the matter at hand. I mentally chastised myself for allowing my imagination to run amuck rather than focussing on the very real and potentially dangerous situation I was actually heading into. I hadn't seen much of the two guys with Daniel, other than the fact that one was dark and the other blonde, but I did notice that they were both relatively big for adolescent boys, certainly substantially bigger than either Daniel or me. I groaned inwardly, but urged myself to continue walking up the uneven path.

I walked at a good pace for some time, but found no sight or sound of the three boys. I had expected to hear them, if not see them, fairly quickly, but they had managed to get further than I would have thought possible in such a short space of time. I could still hear the occasional passing of traffic from the road, but it didn't feel so close or reassuring as it did when I started out. The sun had all but disappeared below the tree line; only a blaze of red remained. I felt like the last of my nerves were disappearing with it.

What the hell was I going to say when I eventually managed to catch them up? I hadn't thought that far ahead yet. "*Excuse me, boys, would you mind telling me what you think you're doing out here in the dark and cold? Now get home for your dinner.*" Daniel would never forgive me if I'd jumped to the wrong conclusion and ended up embarrassing him in front of his friends, but I couldn't worry about that now. I had to see him for myself. If he was okay, then I would turn back for the car, feeling a little foolish, but happy in the knowledge that all was well. I was hopeful indeed that that would be the case.

As the noise from the road fell even further away, the sound of my passage up the path picked up the gap with the snap and crunch of every leaf or twig my feet met. No matter how carefully I trod, or how quiet I tried to be, the noise of my progress felt deafening in comparison to the sounds of the woods, which seemed to have become eerily quiet. Combining the feet crunching with my chattering teeth, I imagined I sounded like a drunk in charge of a jackhammer rather than like the nimble footed cat I was trying to be.

My heart, already thudding rapidly, kicked up a notch when I finally heard the sounds of male voices up ahead. I stopped in my tracks and listened. I was still too far away to make out what they were saying. I hesitated, not knowing how to proceed. Okay, this was a public path, why not just pretend you're out on an evening stroll and that you just happen upon them? I clearly wasn't dressed for an evening stroll on a cold autumn night, but hopefully they wouldn't notice that particular fact. How observant were teenage boys? I prayed not very. I would just casually say hello, have a good look at Daniel, and then proceed from there as I deemed necessary.

Deciding that was probably the best I was going to come up with, I continued up the path. I ignored the fact that I was shaking almost violently now as the voices became louder.

"Look Daniel, I'm tellin ye, you'll ha the best night of ya life!" It was a harsh voice I could hear that was trying unsuccessfully to be light. What were they talking about? I heard Daniel next.

"I'm not interested in that stuff, Doogie. Can't we just have the beers?" I realised with horror that he was pleading. It was a fraction of a second before my horror turned to anger, giving me the final boost of courage I needed to round the corner.

I had been expecting to walk right into them on the path, and was surprised to see them in the woods, slightly off the track. Daniel was sitting on a log, and another, the dark haired one, who I presumed was Doogie, sat next to him with his arm about Daniel's shoulders. The gesture at a glance might have appeared friendly, but the boy's knuckles were white with force as they gripped the shoulder. Both older boys appeared dressed for the cold weather, in big bomber style jackets. The blonde one was now wearing a black beanie against the chill, and was busying gathering bits of wood from the ground around him, presumably to feed the dismal camp fire that was fighting for life not far from the log. Daniel was dressed only in a thin grey hoodie, and appeared to be shivering as violently as I was. This had clearly been an unplanned evening woodland trip for him. I held my nerve and prepared to do some acting.

"Daniel?" I tried to sound casual, but the chilly wind and my anxiety levels betrayed me. All three heads snapped round in my direction with startled expressions. Somehow I managed to hold myself together to continue.

"Daniel, is that you in there?" I narrowed my eyes as if trying to secure his identity. The boy called Doogie quickly regained his composure at my surprise intrusion.

"Well then, who do we have here?" he said, keeping his arm tightly around Daniel.

"Hi," I said, ignoring his question and the appreciative leer on his face. I continued to address Daniel only. "Do you need a lift home?" I said encouragingly. The boy looked terrified, and I was instantly glad I had followed. What I was going to do, however, if this Doogie character and his mate weren't prepared to let him go, I didn't know.

"Daniel doesnae need a lift anywhere, princess, he's hangin oot with me and Stu the now. Yer welcome to join us?" Doogie drawled in his thick raspy accent.

He threw a sly grin in the direction of the other boy. Daniel didn't move, his eyes trained to my face. I knew with certainty that he didn't want me to leave without him.

"Daniel?" I said, continuing to ignore his self-appointed spokesman. I took a step in his direction and indicated with my hand that he should stand to join me. He started to rise, but Doogie forced his hand on his shoulder, putting him back down on the log with a thump.

I wondered how old the two boys were. They looked a lot older than Daniel, seventeen, eighteen maybe. More men than boys, I decided, too old to be hanging around with Daniel. Both faces lacked the honest and open appeal of Daniel's, but it was Doogie's hard face and eyes that worried me the most. His skin was pale in the twilight; more so than the other boy, he appeared almost ghoulish. No wonder Morag had been so distressed by them.

I tried to focus myself on how I was going to get both of us out of there. Either one of them could overpower me, that was obvious; they were double my size. The blonde guy, Stuart, had stopped what he was doing and appeared to be watching events with mild amusement. He came and stood near Doogie, still sitting on the log, and blocked Daniel from my sight.

That was when I first noticed the upside down lunchbox functioning as a makeshift table, a foot or so from the boys, by the campfire. Even in the lacklustre light of the fire, and with the distance between us, I could see what lay on top: syringe, bent silver spoon, lighter, and a little clear plastic money bag bulging with brown powder. Heroin. Morag was right. From what I had overheard before the boys had been aware of my presence, it didn't sound like I was too late. I had to get Daniel out of there.

Doogie rose from the log, releasing Daniel, and briefly glanced down to the upturned lunchbox before moving his eyes back to me. A smile spread across his face as he realised that I had registered his plans for the evening. Underneath the smile, the backdrop of his face had taken on a new act entirely. The mocking, polite charade he had played out initially had all but disappeared, replaced by unchecked menace. I forced my eyes away from his, and took a step sideways, so as to see Daniel.

"Daniel, let's go right now." I was grateful to hear the ring of authority in my tone. Daniel bit his lip nervously for a moment, his eyes darting back and forth between me and the backs of the two older boys. I nodded encouragingly at him, and to my relief, he slowly began to rise off the log.

"Sit doon!" Doogie roared. I grimaced as the thunder in his tone left me under no illusions; Daniel and I weren't just going to be able to walk away from this. Heightened panic surged through me. What if I'd made this situation worse for Daniel?

Doogie and I glared at each other for a moment, each sizing the other up and deciding the best way to proceed. He was clearly in charge of this double act; the other boy seemed to be on the periphery of proceedings with only half interested amusement. I didn't think he looked overly bright, definitely not a candidate for a discussion on the likelihood of life on Mars. Doogie, however, didn't appear to suffer from the same affliction; his cunning eyes darted all over the place as he considered his next move.

The red aftermath of the sun had disappeared entirely, the forest now silvery. I noticed distantly that it seemed unusually quiet, as if every woodland inhabitant were silently watching this peculiar human performance unfold in their habitat, from the safety of foliage and shadows. I didn't know how this particular production was going to end, but one thing I did know was that I wasn't going anywhere without Daniel.

I drew a deep breath and bit the bullet. I marched off the track into the trees with the intention of grabbing Daniel by the arm and yanking him off the log to follow me back down to the car. I got to around two feet in front of a very surprised looking Daniel, when Doogie stood directly in my path, grabbing me forcibly by both arms.

"Wha de ye think you're doing, darlin?" he jeered. "Are ye wanting to join the party after all?" The other boy, Stuart, laughed nervously. I had a feeling that events were taking an unscheduled turn, as far as he was concerned, and that he wasn't entirely comfortable about it. I had caught a strong blast of whisky on Doogie's breath as he spoke. I thought he was probably drunk. Close up, I could see by the light of the moon that his eyes were blurry, and he swayed ever so slightly as he grasped my arms.

"Look," I said, trying to maintain something of my earlier authoritarian tone. I could feel my arms bruising painfully under the force of his fingers. "What you two boys do is up to you, but Daniel is coming home with me. So I suggest you get your hands off me right now and let us go!"

"Let her go, Doogie," Daniel said quietly, speaking for the first time. He was very frightened. "I'll stay here if that's what you want, but let her go."

"Be quiet, Daniel!" I snapped. "I'm not going anywhere without you."

"Step aside *'Doogie',*" I said, making a mock at his name. The next thing I was aware of was a hissing noise, like air escaping from a tyre. I realised with a terrifying jolt of disbelief that the noise was coming from no tyre, but from me. Doogie had landed a right hook into the pit of my stomach. I buckled over, taking several steps back, only just managing to hold my feet. After the shock came the pain. Ridiculing his name had been a mistake.

For a long moment, it felt like I couldn't breathe. I'd been winded, the air knocked clean out of my lungs. Tears clouded my bulging eyes with the effort of trying to heave in a much-needed breath. I continued to produce strange gasping noises from somewhere in my chest, as my lungs fought to return to function. Finally my airways began to open again, and night air filled my chest. It still hurt to breathe, but after a minute, I managed to straighten up and look into Doogie's eyes to see if there was any sign of guilt in their depths for having punched a woman of slight build in the stomach. No, of course there wasn't.

"Daniel, stand up," I croaked. My throat felt raw, the words rasped their way out, but there was an undeniable resolve despite it all. He obeyed, and this time Doogie made no move to stop him. I yanked my car keys from my jeans. "My car's parked down on the road. Lock yourself in. I'll be down in a minute." I extended the keys to him while Doogie and Stuart watched on, as if in disbelief. I wondered if they'd expected the cheap shot to my stomach to floor me, to knock the courage out of me along with the air. Daniel lunged for my keys.

A shadow of rage fell over Doogie's face. "Yer gonna have to pay for that, ye little interfering bitch."

I perfectly understood what he was saying; he held nothing in check, showed no restraint, but I exhaled with relief as Daniel ran down the track and round the corner, out of sight and into the night. At least he was safe. I swayed then with shock and fear, as I registered what was going to happen now; the look on Doogie's face left me in no doubt. I could expect no help from the other, I realised; he was as frightened of Doogie as I was. He kept his gaze on the ground, never meeting my eyes. Maybe he'd witnessed this kind of thing before. I guessed he wasn't happy about the way their evening had panned out, but he wasn't going to risk the wrath of Doogie in an attempt to stop it.

I don't know why I thought of him then, but the beautiful image of Arwan's face swam in front of my eyes, and with it came a fleeting moment of calmness, abruptly snatched away as Doogie took a step towards me, his face intent. I turned in an attempt to run, but he caught my arm and yanked me violently back to him. His hands were tearing at my jacket, trying feverishly to pull it from me. I drew in a breath and screamed as loud as I could in his ear, and in return he punched me in the face, bringing white dots to my eyes.

I realised that screaming, like the name mockery, had been another not so great idea. After all, there was nobody around to hear me. What had been the point? All I had achieved was to anger my attacker further. He was rougher now in his pursuit, furious at my attempt to hinder him. My face throbbed painfully, but strangely the sensation acted as a distraction to what his hands were doing. It burnt and tingled, as fluid charged to the damaged skin around my left cheek and eye. I put my hand to my face and felt the hot sticky moisture of blood. He had somehow got my jacket off and was making to push me to the ground. I staggered, taking a step backwards. The backs of my knees met with something hard.

At that moment, several things happened. Doogie had completely let go of me. I felt relieved on some level, but whatever I had backed into, presumably the fallen log, had caused me to lose balance and sent me flying backwards. As I fell, clutching desperately at the air for something to hold on to, two separate incandescent white flashes appeared from somewhere behind me, lighting up the entire woods like a nuclear bomb. As I continued my descent, I had time to register the petrified expression on Doogie's face as the white engulfed him, but before my brain could begin to try and make sense of what I'd seen, my head met forcibly with the solid ground, and everything went black.

chapter ELEVEN

My conscious mind had begun to consider the prospect of waking up, at the sound of murmured voices coming from somewhere nearby. I wanted to ignore the whisperings, but they seemed to be getting louder by the moment. I knew something bad had happened, but I wasn't quite ready to think about what that was yet. I was somewhere warm, soft, and comfortable, and that's just how I wanted to stay.

"I think she should be in a hospital," said a curt, familiar voice that my tired brain, despite my best efforts not to, tried to place. That same part of my brain tried to pry my eyes open in the hope of seeing who had spoken, but my lids weren't ready to cooperate.

"I have examined Ms Davenport, and she's in perfect health. As you saw, she's merely tired and sleeping after a traumatic evening." I was stunned into alertness at the sound of Arwan's voice, and with the alertness came the memory of the dark woods and of Doogie's mean eyes.

My heart hammered in my ribs as the night's events came flooding back. I remembered the punch to the stomach and the blow he'd delivered my face after I'd screamed in his ear. I winced in reflex, but when I tried to focus my brain on where I thought his knuckles had met my skin, I could feel no pain. That was decidedly odd. Surely I would still be feeling that? That blow had nearly knocked me clean out, in itself. I thought of Daniel's frightened face as Doogie held him on the log. Daniel had got away though, hadn't he? I was sure I remembered the sight of him disappearing into the darkness.

It was definitely time to wake up. My eyes fluttered open, to discover that I was in an unfamiliar room. I wasn't ready to move, but allowed my eyes to quickly sweep across it. The decor and opulence left me in little doubt as to where I was. I lay in a huge bed covered in the most ludicrously decadent bedding of scarlet velvet and black silk. A stunning mirror, its great frame a mass of gilded flowers and foliage, dominated one of the walls, and threw back the image of my astonished face. Something struck me as odd about my reflection, but I didn't have time to ponder over it, with other more important things to think about.

How did I get in Arwan's house? Was I actually in his bed?

The room was dimly lit by a lamp on a sideboard, which also held a glass jug of water and several glasses on an intricate tray. I could see the shadows of Arwan and the other person stretching into the bedroom from just along the corridor.

"I'm not happy about leaving her here," was the other's eventual sulky response.

"Well, Constable Mcleod, there's not really a whole lot you can do about that, is there? Ms Davenport will be staying here until I decide otherwise." It was Alex's voice I could hear with Arwan. I was about to cough to alert them of my recent consciousness, when Alex spoke again.

"Those two kids are petrified, a pair of dribbling vegetables rambling about white lights and demons." I sprang into a sitting position at the turn in conversation.

"What the hell happened in those woods tonight?" Alex continued. "I'm not defending that pair of scumbags, God knows that, but I need some answers from you, Mr Jones; something doesn't add up here."

I wondered how absurdly superior Arwan's expression was, to match his tone as he replied. "I understand that hallucinations are a common side effect to a cocktail of drink and drugs. I wouldn't pay too much heed to what Douglas McDonald has to say. I'm just relieved that I happened to be walking my dogs in that particular area tonight."

Why was I suddenly thinking the white lights I had seen before I'd lost consciousness were Arwan's dogs? As if my thoughts had summoned them, both dogs whined as they stood up from the floor beside the bed. I hadn't realised they were there. At the sound, Alex rushed into the room. I noticed instantly how tired he looked. My heart broke for him; he would have been so worried about Edith, and now me and Daniel. Arwan entered a moment later, but stayed back, leaning nonchalantly in the doorframe, face impassive.

"Brook, you're awake, are you okay?"

"I'm fine," I answered quickly and dismissively. I wanted to know the answer to more pertinent questions. "How's Daniel? Did he get away?"

"He's back home with Morag, shaken, but otherwise fine." He paused for a moment, seemingly struggling with some emotion. Then anxiety broke through his features. "What the hell were you thinking, following those boys into the woods like that?"

"I had to see if Daniel was okay," I said softly, not rising to his anger. I knew it only stemmed from worry for me. "You know Morag was concerned about those older boys, and it looks like she was right to be. I heard them trying to bully Daniel into shooting up heroin, Alex. What if it was contaminated like the stuff those two poor boys took?"

"You should have called me," he said, his tone becoming gentle. I glanced over at Arwan, still poised in the doorframe, watching our exchange with cold eyes.

"I think you should get checked out at the hospital," Alex said, bringing my eyes back to him.

"I actually feel fine, just a little tired," I said, genuinely surprised. I should by rights have had a banging headache and a swollen, throbbing eye socket, but strangely, all I felt was exhaustion. Alex sighed, resigned.

"I'll have to talk to you again in the morning. I'll need an official statement from you. It'll wait till tomorrow, though; you really do look tired." He paused then, eyes full of worry and tenderness. He raised a hand, which hovered by my brow as if about to brush a few strands of hair from my cheek. My eyes flickered to Arwan; his face gave nothing away, but I felt the atmosphere in the room charge. Alex's hand lingered in hesitation, then dropped back down to his side as he sighed. I wondered if he noticed the static tension in the air.

"Thanks, Alex, I appreciate it," I said. Alex glanced over his shoulder at Arwan before turning back to me.

"I could take you home to your own bed if you like?" he said in a whisper. The look on his face was painfully hopeful.

"That won't be necessary, Constable. I think you should go now, and leave Brook to her rest. I will bring her along to the station in the morning." I was glad Arwan answered for me. I didn't want to be directly responsible for the look on Alex's face at that moment, but I wasn't going anywhere, not tonight. I had to speak to Arwan, alone.

"You saved me?" I demanded, the moment he returned from seeing Alex out.

"Of course." He stood in the door, arms crossed, eyes watching, his athlete's body practically filling the frame. He wore a purplish blue fitted jumper almost identical to the colour of his eyes, and it hugged his chest, clearly defining his muscular physique. "I make it my business to know where you are."

"I don't understand," I said, confused. "Why?"

"You should know why."

I frowned. Why was he talking in riddles and avoiding my questions? "You're not making any sense. How could I possibly know why?"

He walked from the doorframe into the bedroom and sat on a Chippendale chair by the bed, about three feet away from me. Temptingly close. If I reached out, I could touch him. I wanted to.

I wanted him to touch me, everywhere. Snap out of it, lady! I shook my head, attempting to focus. I touched my cheek, which should have been swollen and painful. It suddenly dawned on me what was odd about my reflection. I should have been black and blue. My head snapped back to the mirror, which reflected my puzzled face back at me for a second time, and then I slowly turned back to Arwan.

"I was knocked out, and punched in the eye and stomach, and yet I feel nothing but tired, and I don't have a single mark on my face. How can that be?" I demanded.

His handsome face grimaced at my frank appraisal of the night's events.

"I think you did something," I whispered.

"Clearly you're a fast healer." I glared at him, waiting for another answer; sarcasm was not going to wash with me tonight. But no other came. "Your policeman friend was right about one thing, though," he said, breaking the silence. "You should not have followed those boys into the woods by yourself, but of course you would, whether it put you in danger or not."

"I had to," I said, pulling back the covers and swinging my legs down from the bed. I hadn't thought about what I was or wasn't wearing, until I slipped off the bed and padded past him. Luckily, I still wore my jeans and top. I walked over to the side table with the glasses and jug, and poured myself some water. I felt his eyes move with me as I did so. I turned back to face him, watching him carefully as I sipped. I put the glass back on the table and moved to stand directly in front of the mirror.

It wasn't a trick of the half light; my face was completely bruise-, graze-, cut-, and anything else-free that should have been there after what I'd experienced. I turned back to face him.

"Are you going to tell me what happened tonight? How you just happened to be there? I don't have a mark on me, and trust me, I should." He moved with such speed that my eyes lost the focus of him, as he was suddenly just inches from where I stood. I felt the heat of him instantly. I should have demanded again how he managed to move like that, so quickly, unnaturally, but with his beautiful face looking down into mine, rational thought was rendered impossible. My stomach flew into a flurry of butterflies.

"You have no idea what it would do to me to lose you after..." His words, thick with emotion, trailed off, but his hands had found my shoulders, holding me with almost brutal force. The way he looked at me, with a mixture of pain and possessiveness, played havoc with my equilibrium.

"After what?" I asked. "I don't understand." I was pleading; I could hear it in my voice. "Please," I whispered, "tell me what's happening here." Tears hit my cheeks. The terrifying event of the night, combined with the sheer frustration at feeling so confused about the man before me, finally took its toll. I felt exhausted, but sleep would be impossible, with my mind working on overdrive trying to derive some sense out of the strange things that seemed to be happening to me in this place, with this man. The answers lay with Arwan, I was sure of it.

The next sensation I felt was his arms wrapped tight around me, his hand stroking my hair and face, his voice murmuring words of comfort. I was suddenly bathing in light, and he was the conductor. After a moment, he gathered me up effortlessly and carried me back to the bed.

"All will be as it should be, I promise. You should rest now." At the very suggestion of sleep from his lips, combined with his most lulling tone, my eyelids became burdened with weight. I tried half-heartedly to fight against their closure, but couldn't. I understood that I needed to sleep. He lay me down with great gentleness, like I was precious to him, and tucked me under the covers. My eyes were closed, but I sensed him standing over me as I drifted off to sleep.

On some conscious level, I realised that none of my questions had been answered, and that the mystery that surrounded him and the connection he had to me still seemed impenetrable. But I was too exhausted; I just needed to sleep.

The white stag led me to my dreams that night. We ambled together through an old wood at daybreak. The sun was just beginning to rise in the east, turning to bronze the sky occasionally glimpsed through the canopy of trees. The breeze was warm and gentle and, just like in the other dream, I wore a long, flowing ivory gown. My hand lay across the stag's broad back as we walked among ancient oaks covered in ivy and mistletoe. My feet were bare, and the soft green grass below them felt plush and soothing, like the richest velvet.

Eventually the wood gave way to a pool of water. I realised absently that it was the setting of my favourite painting of Arwan's. I broke from the stag and ran delighted over to the gently rippling water and submerged a toe. The water was neither hot nor cold, but the perfect temperature. I sighed with pleasure.

I realised after a moment that we were not alone.

A figure stood watching from the edge of the wood, but the glare from the rising sun cutting through the trees made it impossible to see who it was. I took several steps towards the figure, unafraid, but eager to see who watched me. Then I saw him. My breath caught in my lungs as I broke into a run. The stag had wandered off to graze, unconcerned with my sudden preoccupation. My feet pushed into the velvet grass, I had to get to him. I had to get to Arwan. A moment later, I was leaping up into his outstretched arms as he caught me easily, gathering me up to him. His expression was one of such overwhelming love that I thought I would die by the very force of it.

After a moment, he set me gently down on my feet, arms still wrapped about my waist. I looked up into his glorious face. I didn't think it would be possible, but he was even more spellbinding to me here, in this place of magic. His hair seemed blacker, like the richest silt from the oldest riverbed. The colour of his skin was the sun itself, and his strength was the force that shaped the earth's mountains, his very breath my life.

"Morgen," he said, looking down into my face, "My One."

I wanted to stay there with him forever. I knew it was a dream, but if staying asleep for eternity was what it would take to be with him, I would happily sleep my life away. Then suddenly I was distracted by a noise coming from the surrounding woods. My eyes followed the sound for the source, and I was startled to see, standing amongst the trees, the same jewel veiled, red-haired woman I'd dreamt of before. Who was she, and what was she doing in my dreams? I opened my mouth to speak but she beat me to it.

"Wake up!" she shrieked. The sheer shrill of her voice warped my dreamscape, a second before it shattered into a million pieces.

I sat bolt upright in the huge bed, my heart pounding from being prematurely yanked from a deep sleep. I remembered my dream with clarity, which had frankly been going great up until the point my dream stalker showed up. I winced, hearing in my mind once more the horrible shrill sound of her voice. But I didn't have long to ponder over it, because I suddenly registered another sound altogether, though it was as equally distressing, and this time I wasn't dreaming. I looked to the open door and listened trying to identify the source of the strange noise. Then it came to me, it was the sound of an animal whining in distress.

I jumped down to the floor with a thump. But I had moved too fast, too soon, and had to steady myself, leaning heavily on the bed for a moment. The whining continued. It sounded like one or both of Arwan's dogs were in pain. The sound was distinctly distressing, a cry of pain, yet it was muffled slightly, as if it reached me from behind a door, somewhere not too far away. I let go of the bed and straightened. After a couple of small experimental steps in the direction of the doorway told me that I was no longer sleep dizzy, I ran out into the hall.

I had never been upstairs at Avallon House, in the entire time I had worked for Arwan, so I had no idea where I was. I looked to my left down the corridor. There was an open door a short distance away, which looked like it headed to the staircase and down to the reception hall. I was fairly sure that the sound wasn't coming from that direction. I turned my head to the right, towards a long length of corridor, where I could see many doors leading into other rooms. I was relieved that several lamps lit its length and that it wasn't darkened. I took a deep breath and, spurred on by the agony in the whine, headed down the corridor.

I was too on edge to really notice the corridor walls, hung in fine, embroidered, emerald silk, or to see the portrait paintings that decorated them.

I came to a stop outside a door that looked solid and heavy, but which was carved with an intricate and delicate floral pattern. I tried the door handle—locked. I moved on to the next door, pulled down the corridor by the incessant whining of an animal somewhere in agony.

I had every intention of yanking the next door open and discovering what lay behind it. The whining was escalating; somehow, one of Arwan's dogs had gotten trapped in that room and had possibly hurt itself, and I had to go in and rescue it. I was aware, however, that it wasn't just the noise that pulled me to the door. Yes, that was what brought me here, but something else was now driving me to see what lay within that room. Something was in there that I needed to see. I just knew it.

My hand tightened on the door handle and turned. I let out an audible breath; unlike the first door, it wasn't locked. I placed my free hand on the face of the oak door and began to push it open.

"I trust you slept well?"

I shrieked and spun on my feet. Arwan stood no more than three feet away, flanked on either side by his dogs. The whining from behind the door had ceased, like it never was. I suddenly felt like I'd been caught with my hand in the till. How would this look to Arwan? Like I'd just been caught snooping around his house, that was how! A bright red glow burned up my neck to my face.

I looked wide-eyed from one dog to the other and then back to Arwan.

"I...I, er...I heard one of the dogs whining from behind this door." I tapped the door in question lightly with my knuckle, but kept my eyes trained on Arwan. "I thought perhaps they were trapped inside." My explanation seemed hollow, with both dogs grinning at me from his side. I shook my head. "I don't understand. I heard whining. I came to help." I felt the eyes of the portraits, heavy with accusation in their stern expressions, as I waited for him to say something. Arwan looked slowly and pointedly to the door and back to me.

"Go ahead," he said, "look inside."

I realised that I was still holding tightly to the handle. Even caught as I was, I felt almost overwhelmingly reluctant to let go of it, and for a fleeting moment I almost did as he said, but seeing with my own eyes that the dogs were fine had robbed me of my valid reason in doing so. I would just look downright nosey.

It boiled down to humiliation in the end. I was being foolish, clearly. The dogs were fine. Who knew what I had heard? It could have been anything in a house that old, a door in need of oil, an open window, simple as that. And my desire to see what was in that room, yeah, that was just pure nosiness too. I wasn't generally a nosey person, but who was I kidding? Anything that involved Arwan intrigued me, including his house. I realised that my stomach was clenched like my hand on the door. I forced both to relax. Then, after one last, longing glance at the oak door, I sighed and walked slowly past Arwan, keeping my eyes averted but letting my hand stroke the head of the nearest dog on my way.

When I made it back to my temporary bedroom, I saw that Arwan had laid clothes out on the bed for me. Naturally, they were exquisite, brand new, and in exactly my size. Next to the clothes was a plump white bath towel. I grabbed it off the bed and headed for a little door off my room, which I assumed was an en suite, and after pushing it open, I discovered that that was exactly what it was.

I felt better after a hot power shower. I got dressed in the clothes Arwan had provided, and was just buttoning up the last button on the red blouse when he appeared in the doorway. I jumped, not having heard his approach.

"I really wish you'd cough or something!" I snapped. My reprimand seemed lost on him, and I realised that he was preoccupied with something. "What is it?" I asked.

"Your skin," he remarked softly. My hands instinctively flew to my face. What was wrong with my skin? "It's flushed from the shower. Beautiful doesn't begin..." His murmur trailed off.

I felt a shiver run through me, as I let my now trembling hands fall back to my sides. He really didn't play fair. He moved from the frame into the room, closer. I gulped, and then cleared my throat. I didn't know what he was planning on doing or saying, but I suspected an interception might be in order. I realised that I hadn't thanked him for saving my life for the second time.

"I meant to thank you for coming to my rescue again last night. I seem to be making a habit of getting into scrapes lately. I don't know what would have happened if you hadn't shown up when you did." He smiled slightly and inclined his head. I swallowed hard, watching as he moved around the room, pacing almost catlike. There was something distinctly predatory about his movements, slow and calculated. I felt my heart rate kick up a notch as I backed up slightly, finding the back of the bed.

"Mortality is an interesting thing isn't it?"

I watched him carefully as he continued to pace the room, seeming to be moving always that bit closer. "How so?" I asked, not taking my eyes off him.

"Fleeting, I guess, is what I mean. Here one moment, gone the next. Would you like to live forever, Brook?"

"No!" I answered quickly, surprised by the resolution in my tone, as I continued to watch him move about the room.

"An unappealing idea to you, then?" he said evenly, his eyes suddenly cool glass.

"It's impossible, so why entertain such an idea?"

"Nothing that can be conceived is impossible."

I pondered that for a moment. "Would you want to live for eternity?" I asked.

He stopped in his tracks. He'd managed to get within feet of me. I felt trapped by him as I looked up into his face.

"There would be one condition, one necessity, for me to live a happy eternal existence," he said slowly, as if carefully weighing his words.

I realised that the breath had ceased to move about my lungs. "What, what would you need to live forever?" I asked.

He held my gaze, his incomparable eyes incarcerating me. A long moment passed between us, where time seemed to stand still. His unique rose petal fragrance found my senses; he was so close, and had me wanting to inhale deeply, but I seemed to have lost the ability to breathe. I'd never known strength like his; not only did I believe he was physically capable of most things, but his very presence was enough to floor me, to render me useless for anything but to be absorbed by him. My brain yelled danger, danger! My heart yelled something else entirely. I'd never felt anything like it before. I desired him, but it was more than that, I craved him. A vivid image of what all that toned, virile manliness might be like under the sheets flashed in my mind.

"We have to go."

"Huh?" I said absently, totally absorbed in my "naked Arwan fantasy". I ran my fingers through my hair and took a moment to redirect my brain to what he'd said. "Where?" I didn't want to go anywhere at that particular moment in time, and it hadn't gone unnoticed that he hadn't answered my question.

"To the station; your policeman friend is expecting us to make official statements regarding last night."

"Oh yes, of course." I'd momentarily forgotten all about last night, let alone making statements, but the way he kept referring to Alex as my "policeman friend", and the tone he had adopted, hadn't been lost on me.

chapter

TWELVE

"The next thing I knew, I was waking up at Avallon House," I said, leaning back into my chair at the table where Alex had been taking my statement. I had just reached the end of my account of the night before. Reliving the events had been draining, and I raised my hands to gently massage my throbbing temples.

I glanced around the small office while I waited, as Alex wrote the last details of my statement.

It was more like a holiday cottage than a police station, I thought, although Alex had explained that there was a small cell towards the back of the building. I didn't imagine it had seen much use over the years, bar the odd drunk. That all had changed last night, of course, when Doogie and Stuart had found themselves residing there briefly before being transferred to larger accommodations in Glasgow earlier that morning. There was a distinctly feminine air to the whole place. I guessed that Alex's partner's wife probably spent quite a bit of time fussing around back here. There were vases of freshly cut flowers along with perfectly plumped throw cushions on a black leather sofa. It was only Alex's uniform, combined with his austere mood, that reminded me of where we were. Arwan had been taken to a separate room by Alex's partner, and was giving his own account of the previous night's events.

After what felt like a long time, Alex finally put his pen down and looked up.

"Daniel says Doogie hit you really hard." It was more of an accusation than a question.

"I told you that, Alex; I told you he hit me in the stomach." I watched as he rubbed his chin thoughtfully. He hadn't shaved that morning, and a stubbly shadow was forming.

"I know," he nodded "You also told me he later hit you in the face."

"I did," I confirmed, wondering where he was leading the conversation.

"The boy, Stuart, said that Doogie punched you in the eye so hard, your cheek split from the force of it."

I bit my lip guiltily, my eyes looking anywhere but at Alex. I had left that little detail out. I'd had to. There was no explanation for the fact that there wasn't a mark on me. No explanation that was plausible, anyway. I cleared my throat.

"As you can see," I said, touching the cheek in question, "I'm not marked, and my cheek didn't split. It was enough to frighten me, but that was all." Apart from the fact that I was lying, I didn't understand why he was looking at me so dubiously. Surely, of the several accounts, mine would have been deemed the most reliable? I felt a bit miffed; I was the victim here.

Alex opened a drawer in the desk and removed a blue folder, putting it down on the table between us. He looked at me for a long moment, eyes considering. He opened the folder and pulled out what appeared to be another statement. He ran his finger down the left-hand side as if looking for something, then tapped the page lightly when he found it.

"First the wolves came, then the demon," he paused, looking up from the page, bringing his eyes back to mine, "a demon from hell." He quoted directly from the paper. I had a brief flashback to the night before, to the moment when the bright white lights had flashed past me, illuminating Doogie's terrified face as I fell and hit my head. A chill breezed down my spine. I couldn't argue with his description; the boy had seen something that rattled him, that was for sure. "Those were a few of the coherent words we actually managed to get out of Doogie McDonald. They're scared, Brook; I mean, shit scared." He shook his head slowly, his finger tapping the folder on the desk. "If those boys weren't so shook up about whatever happened out there last night, there's a chance they could have led us to their boss, the person providing them with the dirty gear." I squeezed my eyes shut for an instant as I thought of the two boys who hadn't been as lucky as Daniel. I didn't know, myself, what had happened after I blacked out last night, but I knew enough about Arwan to have a good guess.

"That's because you know he's not human." I jerked in my chair at the sound of Lugh's voice, the voice of the huge white stag from my dream. It had been so clear and strong that my first thought was that he was in the room with us, and my eyes swept about, looking for him. Then I realised that Alex hadn't heard anything and that he was looking at me like I was some sort of weirdo.

"Not human?" I muttered under my breath.

"What did you say? I didn't hear you." I looked up at Alex, but didn't see him. *Arwan Jones is not human.* Was that what my subconscious was trying to tell me?

"Brook, what's the matter?" Arwan is not human that's what! "Do you need some air or something, a glass of water?"

Distantly, I could hear Alex talking to me, anxiety creeping into his tone at my suddenly strange behaviour. Not human? Then what? A demon, like Doogie had said? I didn't notice Alex getting up out of his chair as my brain tried to make sense of this revelation. Surely not a demon; he seemed too good. I'd seen him do wonderful things with my own eyes, with Edith.

I laughed out loud. Since when did I believe in the existence of demons? I was completely unaware that I sounded hysterical, muttering under my breath and cackling like a madwoman. Yet I was willing to accept the possibility that he wasn't human, right? I realised then that Arwan had never tried to hide his unusualness from me. He had been showing me from the day I met him that he was different.

Somehow, Alex's voice finally managed to break through my bubble. "You're shaking like a leaf."

I realised he was right; my whole body was trembling with shock, trying to come to terms with the realisation that Arwan was more than different. The room suddenly lurched, quickly followed by my stomach. I pulled myself from the chair, nearly stumbling as the walls swam about me.

"I'm going to be sick!" I rushed for the door and found the bathroom down the hall just in time, as I violently emptied the contents of my stomach.

A moment later, I straightened up, panting from the trauma, and went over to the washbasin. I cupped my hands and drank deeply, then splashed a couple of handfuls over my face. The feel of cold water seemed to help settle me. I grabbed some paper towels from a dispenser by the mirror over the sink, and dried my face. I caught sight of my reflection. I was pale and drawn. All blood had vacated my cheeks. I raised my hand; it was nowhere near steady.

I was aware, distantly, that Alex was outside the door, asking if I was all right. He sounded worried. I knew I should answer him, but I wasn't quite ready to pretend everything was okay.

I took a couple of deep, long breaths, making myself feel the calming rise and fall of my chest.

"I'm serious; if you don't answer me, this door is coming down!" Alex's voice finally broke through to me. I sighed, and with a final deep breath, unlocked the door.

"I'm sorry; I didn't mean to press you so much. You've had a terrible time over the last twenty-four hours. I should have been a bit more understanding."

I sipped some cool water from a plastic cup Alex had given me after I'd somehow managed to convince him I was fine. "You're just doing what you have to. It's not your fault. The shock of last night was bound to catch up with me at some point. I'm just sorry you had to deal with it," I said, unable to meet his eyes for too long.

Of course I was shocked about what had happened last night, but the main thing was that Daniel got away unharmed; that was all I had really cared about. My own welfare, of course, was important, but the truth was that I had other things of a much greater magnitude to come to terms with, things that I couldn't possibly tell Alex about.

Alex tucked Doogie's statement back in the folder and returned it to his desk drawer. He sighed deeply.

"Look," he said, "the most important thing is that you're okay and Daniel's okay. My God, I've known Morag most of my life, and Daniel all of his, but something doesn't add up here."

I sympathised with Alex's situation. He didn't know just how weird things were, but I wasn't about to fill him in. I couldn't afford to spend the next few weeks with Doogie and Stuart in a mental institution. I had to find out what was going on, who Arwan was, or, more precisely, what Arwan was.

"I've told you everything I remember, Alex," I said, with what I hoped was the ring of finality. Alex was no fool; he knew I was lying, but there wasn't a whole lot he could do about it, and I was fairly sure he wasn't going to press me and risk tipping me over the edge again.

After a moment, he nodded, seemingly resigned for the time being, as he pushed my statement across the table and handed me his pen.

"I just need you to sign and date the bottom of each page."

When I put the pen down, it appeared that official business was over. Alex seemed much more relaxed.

"Are you feeling up to going to the party at The Shades tonight?" he asked. Was that tonight? Apparently so; I didn't know what day of the week it was, let alone what I was doing that night.

"Yes, I'll be there," I replied, as I tried to orient my brain to a subject that seemed relatively normal when compared to recent events. "What about you?" I enquired. His face seemed to beam at my interest. Not good.

"Sure, aye, I'll be there," he grinned.

"Is your Nan still sulking about her forced bed rest?" I asked.

"You bet. She can't believe she has to sit the party out on doctor's orders." He shook his head, his eyebrows raised above his brown eyes in disbelief. "I can't believe she *wants* to go. I didn't think she'd see the night through, Brook. I thought my Nan was a spent force."

I nodded in understanding. "I know," I agreed. Neither had I, until I had seen her eyes alight on Arwan.

Arwan was still giving his statement when I left the station. In a way, that was a relief; I needed time to come to terms with what I now believed about him. I had questions, lots of them, flying around my brain, that he was going to have to answer. I wondered how his version of events and Doogie and Stuart's were going to differ. Quite significantly, I would imagine. He would have frightened the hell out of those boys, I knew that, but Arwan was a volatile man. They were lucky to get away with their lives.

I parked up out front my little bungalow, to find Morag waiting for me. As soon as she saw my car pull up, she was up and out of her own.

"Hi Mo, I hope you haven't been waiting long?" I asked, still distracted with my own thoughts as we met at the bottom of the steps that led to my front door. Not surprisingly, she looked like she hadn't slept a wink, her face pale and her eyes bloodshot.

"A couple of hours," she said, as if it were inconsequential. She was carrying a large plastic container in her right arm. We climbed the steps together, our feet in sync.

"Come on in," I said, unlocking the front door and opening it wide for her to enter. I led her through to the kitchen and went straight to the sink to fill the kettle up. I had a suspicion we could both do with a fix of strong coffee. With one hand, I grabbed two mugs from the cupboard above the sink, making them clink together as I put them down on the counter.

"How's Daniel doing this morning?" I asked, turning back to her. Her hands flew to her face, and she burst into tears. "Mo? What is it? Is he okay?" I went to her side and wrapped an arm round her shoulders. "What is it?" I asked again, although I suppose I could have guessed. After a moment, she seemed to pull herself together. I released her and grabbed a tissue from the kitchen counter and offered it.

"Thanks," she croaked before loudly blowing her nose. Then she crossed the room and chucked the tissue in the bin before turning to look directly at me with her moist, reddened eyes. "I will never, ever, as long as I live, be able to thank you enough for what you did last night. For what you did for my only boy and for me, I will never have the words." She came over to where I stood leaning against the kitchen counter, and kissed me on the cheek. "Thank you," she whispered, her face taut with emotion. Then she went and sat at the kitchen table by the plastic container she'd bought with her. "I baked you cheesecake; you're looking too thin," she said, tapping the container. I grinned.

"You're turning into my 'feeder', Morag, do you know that?"

I poured the coffee, then cut each of us a generous slice of cake. We ate in silence for a moment, savouring the deliciousness of home baking.

"So what happened in the woods after Daniel got away?" Morag asked eventually. I chewed, then swallowed a mouthful of cake.

"Things kind of got a bit messy," I admitted "You were so right about those boys." I shuddered. "If Arwan hadn't come along, I don't know what would have happened."

Morag looked pained, and I instantly regretted being so frank. "But he did!" I added quickly. "And everybody's okay." Although that wasn't strictly true. As far as I was aware, Doogie and Stuart were far from okay.

I considered telling Morag what I suspected about Arwan, that he was different, but I couldn't bring myself to utter the words. It felt like a bridge too far for somebody even as open-minded and accepting as Morag. I could barely believe it myself, but too much had happened that couldn't be explained rationally. Like the way he moved and his moods that were tangible, affecting the atmosphere around him. He was strong too. I remembered how he had caught me in the library that morning, and had barely flinched under my weight as I freefell into his arms. Then there was the weather. Did he somehow control it? The climate in his garden and the rest of the country seemed to be located in two different hemispheres.

"Are things better between you and Arwan now?" Morag asked, breaking through my reverie. I sighed and rolled my eyes as I pondered her question.

"Yes and no," I said finally. She smiled.

"I'm sure the two of you will figure it out." Morag swallowed the last of her coffee and pushed herself up from the chair. "I have to go, but I'll see you tonight, won't I?" The party; I'd forgotten again.

"Oh crap!" With all the dramas of the last twenty-four hours, I hadn't gotten a chance to get my oak tree sculpture fired, ready for the presentation that night.

"What is it?"

"Nothing; I just need to do something, that's all." I would have to head out to Logan Mills straightaway, or there wouldn't be time.

I followed Morag out the door, armed with my sculpture.

chapter THIRTEEN

It being Saturday afternoon, the road into and out of Claremont was reasonably busy. The round trip to the potter's kiln in Logan Mills had taken the best part of the afternoon, but when I studied my finished fired product on the kitchen table, I felt a mixture of pride and satisfaction. I thought I had really done the tree justice, and I couldn't help wondering whether Arwan would approve. I felt a little regret at the fact that he would never get to see it.

I glanced at my watch: six-thirty. I just had time for a quick blast in the shower before the hunt for something to wear commenced.

Having showered and washed my hair, I finally settled on an olive green, off the shoulder jersey dress with a wide black belt and a pair of black open toe high heels. Miraculously, my hair seemed to have tamed into something that didn't look like I'd been dragged through the bush, after twenty minutes with the hairdryer, so I decided to leave it down. I puckered my lips in the mirror and applied a layer of lipstick. Three minutes later, after collecting my sculpture from the kitchen, I was heading out the door.

The night was crisp but clear, the sky above an abyss of unfathomable twinkling black. The Balmoral was heaving with young Saturday night clientele, and the sounds of people enjoying themselves escaped from the propped open door as I passed by. I realised in that moment that I loved Claremont. It was a strange way to feel about a place after such a short period of time, but that's how I felt. I was grateful to the village for having accepted me, unconditionally, when I was at my lowest ebb. Six months earlier, I would never have dreamed that such a thing could happen to me, and I would go through it all again, testifying, witness protection, the lot, just to be here with these people.

When I arrived at The Shades, I managed to slip past the arriving party guests and went straight to Ruth's office to drop my sculpture in for the presentation. The room was dark, and I guessed she was tied up entertaining those invited to celebrate the home's sudden change in fortune. I left the sculpture on her desk, and with one final glance at the twists and turns of its trunk, headed for the residents' lift to the next floor. I hadn't seen Edith for a while, and wanted to see how she was doing.

I raised my hand to knock on her door, when the wood pulled away from my knuckles and Alex suddenly emerged from within. I jumped a foot in the air at his surprise materialisation. He snickered as he closed the door gently behind him.

"Sorry I frightened you."

I rolled my eyes irritably. I didn't take well to being scared witless. "How's she doing?" I asked after taking a moment to recover my good humour and heart rate.

"Sleeping like a baby."

"That's good," I said, as I turned and we walked together back down the corridor.

"Aye, there's life in the old girl yet." Thanks to Arwan, I thought; he had saved Edith and me, twice, for that matter.

"Did Stuart or Doogie give up anything else today about the identity of their supplier?" I asked hopefully.

"All those lads are capable of for the time being is dribbling spit," he replied. "It's going to be a while before the city cops get anything more out of them, if ever."

I bit my lip guiltily. I felt responsible. Arwan would have been ruthless, but even despite that, I couldn't blame him. He would have wanted to kill them, but he didn't; he showed restraint. Alex didn't realise that he so easily could have been investigating a double murder. I felt Alex's eyes on my face as we reached the lift.

"You look great."

"Thanks," I muttered, embarrassed. The doors closed on the lift. I felt slightly awkward in the confined space, with Alex standing so close that our arms touched. I cleared my throat nervously, keeping my eyes trained to the floor count above the door, as Alex whistled cheerily, seemingly completely at ease at my side. The lift seemed to be taking forever to descend one floor.

Finally released from the lift, we followed the sound of a party in progress to the day room, which had completely transformed into something resembling a modest wedding reception venue. The furniture had been pushed to the edges of the room, creating a large central reservation in the middle for dancing, which several of the residents and guests were doing as we entered. The curtains were closed to the night outside, and multi-coloured party lights throbbed erratically around the room in classic disco fashion. A Dean Martin track crooned out from the DJ's speakers, set up just left of the entrance and acting as a sort of focal point. Two tables had been shoved together in one of the back corners and covered with beer, wine, and snack foods.

We wandered through the crowd, stopping to say hello to the various residents, as Alex introduced me to any locals I hadn't met before, while we headed to the table for a drink. As Alex poured me a glass of wine, I noticed Duncan Buckie joining the party. What was he doing here? Then it occurred to me that he would be just as keen to know who the new owner of The Shades was as anybody else, maybe more. Whoever it was clearly wouldn't be short of a pound or two. No doubt Buckie saw this as the perfect networking opportunity. I wondered how long it would take his pudgy hand to produce a business card.

Alex interrupted my thoughts, and I turned back to face him, accepting the glass he offered me. Then he leaned in over the music. "I'm sorry about the other night," he said, his tone apologetic, "not my ideal first date." I realised he was referring to the night we had broken down on our way to Logan Mills. The word "date" grated a little; he'd promised we were just friends, and now all of sudden we were dating.

"It wasn't your fault, Alex. These things happen," I said, blasé. I sipped my warm Chardonnay and scanned the crowd, hoping to see Morag and the potential of a rescue from an uncomfortable conversation.

"The strangest thing was that when the mechanic arrived, he couldn't see anything wrong with the car." He paused, studying my face for a moment, and then continued, a hard edge to his voice. "He asked me to try the engine, and it started right away."

"That is odd," I agreed, curiously. Alex grimaced.

"I wouldn't be surprised if Arwan Jones didn't sabotage my car just so he could get to you."

Something adjusted internally, at the mention of Arwan. The memory of his beautiful face in the moonlight just inches from mine flashed before my eyes. How could I have ever thought he was human? I knew I should tell Alex he was being ridiculous. How on earth would Arwan sabotage his car? But of course, I knew there was every possibility that he had. I believed wholly that Arwan could do anything he set his mind to.

"I think you're being a little paranoid, Alex," I managed. He made a grunting sound and glared over my shoulder to the back of the room.

"Speak about the devil and he appears," he muttered.

"What?" I asked, confused. He pointed behind me, and I spun round to face the door. There was Arwan, being ushered into the room by an overly eager and excited Ruth. The whole room seemed to stop and fall silent underneath the music, as the awareness of his presence flew round the room like a hurricane. For just an instant, every occupant in the room seemed under his spell, every woman sighing and every man admiring, entranced by this incredible figure of a man. And what a figure it was. He looked powerful, immaculate, and utterly urbane in a black fitted suit with an olive green shirt underneath, a colour that I realised perfectly matched my dress.

Everybody in Claremont was aware of the existence of Arwan Jones, but few in the community had ever before been in his presence. I noticed that his expression was polite, but detached. He didn't seem to be paying much attention to several people suddenly vying for his attention. Duncan Buckie materialised on cue and thrust a hand at Arwan to shake, but again he didn't seem to notice the gesture; his glorious eyes were preoccupied, scanning the surrounding groups of people, looking for somebody, presumably. Buckie withdrew his hand, clearly annoyed.

I watched Arwan's eyes as they swept the room, and felt a sharp intake of breath as they alighted on me and locked in. My legs fought to walk to his side, pulled by insides demanding to be near him, but I fought against the urge and somehow managed to stay put. I guessed immediately that he was the mystery buyer. Why else would he be here?

The DJ picked that moment to put his next record on, and Otis Redding's *These Arms of Mine* filled the room.

"Dance with me, Brook." It was Alex, breaking my link to Arwan, hand reached out to take mine. I hesitated, flustered for more than one reason. "Come on, Brook," he said with playful mockery, "unless you can't dance, of course?"

The surprise appearance of Arwan had forced an instant pull-myself-together moment on me, and I was about to tell Alex that I needed some fresh air when I absorbed the expression on his face. He looked so vulnerable and boyish that I found myself raising my hand to his...but it was another's hand that caught mine, sending a charge of heat through my veins.

"I made a promise to Ms Davenport that I have every intention of keeping." Arwan addressed Alex coolly, and I remembered his words of another evening: "No man will lay a hand on you again, I promise you that." I glared up at Arwan, and he wisely said no more to Alex. I was furious, and he knew it, but before I could protest he pulled me up against him. Then he placed my left hand around his neck, and held on to the other, while his free arm circled around my waist, drawing me closer still as he turned my back to Alex. Outrage bubbled up inside of me, but before I could protest, his glorious scent had found me.

I was suddenly oblivious to the faces around us, reflecting varying degrees of surprise and anger. It was just him and I, locked together. The crowded room had fallen away, my eyes seeing nothing but Arwan. I had no choice but to react to him; my hips swayed along with his to the sensual beat that enveloped us. I was surrounded by the strength of his arms as he leaned down and into me, making my head fall back and my hair sweep from my shoulders. I felt my mouth part and my teeth press deep down into my lower lip, as he proceeded to kiss along the line of my jaw and then my neck, sending a current of pleasure rushing to the peaks of my breasts as they pressed against his chest. I sighed as my hand entwined into the black of his hair, and I realised that every molecule of my being was fighting to merge with him, to connect with him, like we were two parts of the same thing. I felt his hand drop mine and reach in for the nape of my neck as he adjusted me to look directly into his eyes. Then he bent his head, as if seeking my mouth, and I closed my eyes in aroused expectation, lips pouting as I waited...and waited.

My eyes flashed open again when I realised he hadn't kissed me. The grin on his face snapped me out of my trance, and it dawned on me with embarrassment that the song had stopped and we had ceased dancing but remained in one another's arms.

Mortification quickly set in. What had I just done in front of twenty or so geriatrics and their families? Arwan chuckled in my ear, no doubt at the expression on my face. I peered reluctantly around his shoulder, and to my immense relief, the only faces looking our way were the face of Alex, drilling a death stare into Arwan's back, and that of one very excited looking Morag, who was at that very moment mouthing "Go girl!" The rest of the room congregated around the beverage table in what appeared to be almost a frenzy. I wondered what had everybody so excited, when Brenda, one of the residents, shuffled by with a large piece of fruit cake balanced on a tiny plate.

I exhaled. "Thank god for cake," I muttered. It took considerable effort, but I managed to unlock my arms from around Arwan, and a moment later, he did the same. I could feel my blood coursing through my veins, seeking the lost connection to him, my body aching with the absence of its link to his. I heard him groan over my shoulder, and turned to see what had captured his attention. Duncan Buckie was making a beeline for him through the dispersing cake crowd, armed with two loaded plates. I took the opportunity to make a break for it, desperately in need of a moment on my own.

"Thank you for the...dance," I said. To my complete humiliation, my voice came out in a tight squeak, and I found I couldn't meet his eye. I turned unsteadily and was about to walk away, when he caught my arm, turning me back to him. He lifted my chin so I had no choice but to look at him.

"Don't go far," he murmured, but I heard every word over the hum of the party. He released me, and I stumbled my way to Morag, who stood, mouth slack and green eyes wide, a few feet away. She linked her arm through mine, clearly thinking I needed the support, and marched me out into the hallway and into a darkened office opposite the staff tea room. The room wasn't regularly used, and housed several storage boxes and tall filing cabinets crammed with old records, but someone had managed to squeeze in a small sofa, and it was on this that we sat.

"Something you want to tell me?" she said excitedly. I could see the whites of her teeth as she grinned at me in the dark.

"Um, I don't know. Oh god, Mo, I really don't know what just happened!"

"Don't play coy with me, missy; Arwan Jones just danced with you and practically ravished you in public, that's what just happened!" she shrieked. "You were lucky the cake came out when it did, or there'd have been a jammed phone line to the cardiac department at the hospital!"

"I know," I cringed, embarrassed. I was glad it was dark, so Morag couldn't see just how inflamed my face was.

"Don't be embarrassed; it was incredible! The sexiest thing I've ever seen!" I cursed inwardly; the woman had the eyes of a feline. We fell silent for a moment as several people walked by the open office door, chatting and laughing as they went.

"I don't know what's happening to me, Morag," I whispered. "Whenever he's near me, I can't think straight. I just become transfixed with everything about him, and if he touches me, it's intensified a million times." I could feel tears building up with the weight of my confusion. Morag must have seen the shine in my eyes in the dark, because she wrapped a comforting arm about my shoulders.

"Look, doll, if you like him, which I think you do, why don't you just go for it? I think you probably deserve a break, more than most," she said, squeezing my shoulder lightly.

Morag didn't understand. This was no normal situation. There were things I had to know, questions that needed answering. I didn't really understand what Arwan was. All I knew with any certainty was that he was different, perhaps to the point of being nonhuman. I turned to look at her through the dark.

"I'm frightened..." was all I got out before the overhead strip light blinked twice, then exploded the room in artificial light, momentarily blinding us. I blinked at the silhouette in the doorway until my eyes adjusted. It was Ruth.

"There you two are. We're about to present Mr Jones with your lovely sculpture, Brook. Come on, you don't want to miss it." She was holding my sculpture of the ancient oak tree that Arwan had shown me a few nights earlier. My stomach clenched at the prospect of his scrutinising my work. Then I mentally shrugged, resigned. Maybe it was right that he should have it, after all. Perhaps, subconsciously, I'd sculpted it for him all along.

Mo pushed herself off the sofa and offered me her hand, which I took, allowing her to pull me up after her. Then, arms linked together, we followed Ruth back down the corridor to the day room.

Everybody was standing in a semicircle in front of the DJ setup. Several people stood chatting to Arwan at the centre. He looked relaxed and at ease, a smile playing at the corner of his lips. He was in mid-conversation, but as if sensing me, he turned and met my gaze, smiled with his eyes, nodded, and returned to his conversation. I noticed with dismay that there was no sign of Alex. To say he had looked hacked off when Arwan had intercepted our dance would be understating things. I didn't want to hurt him, but I had a feeling that I already had.

Ruth suddenly coughed dramatically, in a subtle attempt to quieten the buzz of a roomful of excited people. When that didn't work, Clive hollered from somewhere in the back, "Can we have everyone's attention at the front please?" It worked; the room fell quiet.

"Thank you, Clive," Ruth beamed. "Well I'll keep this short and sweet. Everybody knows why we're here tonight, to show our immense gratitude to the man that saved The Shades from closure. Mr Jones," she said, turning to face the man of the moment, "words can't express what you've done here for all the residents, not to mention the jobs you've saved, but we'd like to present you with a small token of our appreciation and to welcome you into The Shades family."

Arwan stepped forward and took Ruth's offered hand for a shake, then bent and kissed her on each cheek, to her obvious sheer delight. With the other hand he accepted my sculpture. Some cameras flashed behind me, and I turned to see a couple of journo types I hadn't noticed before, taking snaps. I guessed this would be pretty big news locally. "Claremont Millionaire Saves Residential Home from Closure." etcetera. Arwan was a hero to everyone in this village.

Ruth, still visibly delirious from her sudden close proximity to Arwan, with which I could wholeheartedly sympathize, somehow managed to lead the room into a loud round of applause as he accepted my sculpture. I gaped at him as he held it in his large hands like it were some priceless ancient relic, his eyes running over it again and again, just as mine had over the original subject. My heart thudded manically in my chest, as two recent pieces of the puzzle that was my life fell into place. Arwan was connected to that tree, to our tree, and in that moment, I knew with an unshakable certainty that it was the very tree that Morag's aunty had believed was a gateway to another world. Did Arwan, like Jade McEwan, emerge at some point from the tree he held so carefully in his powerful hands? The passage from Morag's Aunt Rudy's journal flashed before my eyes. 'Jade McEwen was witnessed by several villagers appearing through an oak tree. The witnesses claimed that the accused had not been in the area previously but had actually been seen literally emerging from the trunk of a giant oak tree somewhere here in Claremont.'

The applause died away, and then Arwan spoke, his voice smooth and strong, but his eyes seeming to see only me. "I will treasure it for my entire existence."

It was now or never. I quickly glanced around the room one final time, prior to my dash for the door. I could only see Arwan's profile, but he was apparently deep in conversation with a still rather giddy looking Ruth. There appeared to be a growing congregation of the room's variously aged females all gravitating towards Arwan in a simpering throng. That chaffed, but I had no right to feel that way. I pulled my eyes from him and looked around for Alex. There was still no sign of him. I was sure he was sulking. I hadn't seen him since *that* dance with Arwan. I sighed inwardly. I would have to speak to him and make sure he was okay, but for now I just needed to get out The Shades and into the sanctity of my home, to think things through. In my peripheral vision, I became aware of people heading my way, so with no further thought, I ducked out of the room before I could be waylaid, and bolted down the hall to the exit.

I pushed open the front door and was greeted immediately with the rejuvenating crisp night air. I closed my eyes and breathed deeply as I let the door close behind me. It was such a relief to be out of the confines of that crowded, noisy room. A moment later, I opened my eyes and made to head down the path, only to be pulled up abruptly. Something was blocking my way, something large, solid and white: Arwan's Audi. I yelped loudly, my heart instantly pounding erratically. I watched as the passenger door slowly swung open just inches from me, illuminating the interior. Arwan sat casually behind the wheel.

"What...how did you...I don't...," I stuttered, trying to unscramble my screwing mind to form a sentence that made any sort of sense.

"You need some answers."

It took me a moment to register what he'd actually said. I knew he could move impossibly fast, and I suspected almost beyond a doubt that he wasn't human, but I was still coming to terms with that realisation. I'd left him only moments ago, apparently absorbed in conversation, and now, somehow, here he was in front of me, behind the wheel of his car! But the prospect of finally getting some answers out of him was enough to push all that to one side for the moment. He waited patiently as I pieced a response together.

"Um, yes, yes I do," I nodded, and quickly climbed up into the car, pulling the door shut behind me. A second later, we were pulling away from The Shades.

"Where are we going?" I asked.

He gave me a scorching sidelong glance, a smile playing about his perfect mouth.

"Your place."

"My place?"

"I'd like to see where you live."

"Oh." I mentally ran through the interior of my house as I remembered last leaving it. I let out a silent breath. I was fairly sure it was tidy enough to avoid embarrassment, and was certain I had removed from the living room radiator and put away several pairs of knickers that morning. Phew!

We drove the short drive to my house in silence. I was petrified. I knew that if I spoke, my voice would give that away. I was going to get some answers, finally. No more riddles, but I couldn't help but wonder how having answers might potentially change the dynamics between him and me. What was he going to tell me, and would I be able to live with whatever it was? I didn't know, but I didn't have long to ponder over it; we were parking up out front of my house in what felt like seconds.

I was humiliated to realise that my legs visibly shook as we ascended the steps to my front door, and my hand trembled as it rose for the lock.

Leading Arwan down the corridor to my living room was a strange experience. I had never imagined him in my own home, surrounded by my simple things. And yet, after quietly examining my various pieces of artwork dotted about the place, and casually reclining on my sofa, apparently completely at ease, he somehow seemed to belong there.

"Can I get you something to drink?" I offered, my voice breathless with nerves.

"No, thank-you."

I had no choice, then, but to sit next to him on the sofa, which he'd managed to completely dwarf with his athlete's physique. We were so close that our sides touched, and the fragrance of him filled my senses, sending them into exhilaration mode. I cleared my throat and focused, looking at him sideways. Now was definitely not the time to get distracted by his gorgeousness.

"You're not human!" I blurted, and immediately realised how utterly insane that sounded. I shook my head. I was such an idiot sometimes. I waited for him to erupt into laughter and tell me I was off my head, but instead he shook his head slowly, cold eyes trained to my face.

"No, I am not."

A gasp escaped my lips. No matter what I'd come to believe over the last crazy twenty-four hours, there had always been a fear in the back of my mind that I was mad, and had lost my grip on reality after the strains of the last year. But to hear him confirm my suspicions felt something akin to a great weight being lifted from my shoulders. The fact that he was a nonhuman, for the smallest fraction of second, seemed almost by the by. I wasn't mad, a fear that I'd had most of my life, hooray!

I slipped my high heels off my feet and folded my legs beneath me in businesslike fashion, as I turned to face him more directly.

"You're from Achren," I whispered, "the Other-world. The place I've read about in the library exists, doesn't it?" I was excited now.

"You seem to have figured a lot of things out on your own." He sounded pleased. I supposed I had, but I thought again about the fact that he had never really tried to hide anything from me, not his speed, or his strength. Nothing, he had kept nothing back from me.

"What are you?" I asked, my voice quivering as the reality of what he had just confirmed began to sink in. He seemed to search my face before he answered.

"I am a warrior, first and foremost, an *immortal* warrior King." I gasped again as he watched me with his steady purple gaze. I took several deep breaths and attempted to pull myself together, as the questions continued to mount in my exploding mind. The word "immortal" fired around my brain.

"You can't die?" I asked, gobsmacked. He shook his head.

"My essence will always be connected with a physical form."

I realised that I'd stopped breathing, and forced myself to inhale deeply before I continued. "You can do things with the weather, can't you? You control it. Make the sun come out, the clouds disappear." I remembered the glorious sunshine I had experienced at Avallon House. I think I had always realised on some level that the difference in temperature in his garden to that in the rest of Claremont was way too dramatic to simply be some sort of freak weather phenomenon. He said nothing, but nodded, his eyes always intently watching my reaction to his affirmations of my beliefs about him.

"I knew it," I muttered under my breath. I took in another steadying breath and continued. "It was you in the woods with Edith. It was you who saved her as a child all those years ago, wasn't it?"

"It was."

"Does she know about you?"

"She suspects."

I nodded, remembering the way she had looked at him. "How are you so quick? And your eyes, they change colour." I was bombarding him with questions, but I figured I might not get another chance. I couldn't know how long he would stay in Claremont.

"I have complete control over all atoms of my makeup. I can split them, then merge them anywhere I want, at a speed that is unquantifiable by any current man-made technology." He smirked suddenly. "As you can imagine, it's quite a useful ability."

I shook my head and exhaled loudly in reverence. "Indeed." I don't know what I'd expected him to say, but it certainly wasn't that. "And your eyes?" I reminded him.

"My eyes flash green with fury."

I gulped. The sheer power that was boiling away inside Arwan was terrifying. I fought to compose myself so I could continue my questioning.

"How long have you..." I rephrased. "How old are you?"

"I'm not sure, exactly. Time used to mean nothing to me; it had no relevance until fairly recently." My entire body seemed to ripple with goose pimples.

"Are you some sort of god?" I croaked. He draped an arm along the sofa behind me before answering, the intimacy of the gesture sending a million butterflies fluttering wildly in my belly.

"There is divinity in my direct lineage; my grandfather is Camalus, god of the Sky, but I am simply a king to the people of Achren, a warrior." I could do nothing for a moment but stare at him, as everything in the background seemed to drain of colour, making Arwan even more startlingly beautiful to look at than usual. It was like seeing him in his magnificent entirety for just a moment. I let out a long, slow breath and forced myself to break away from his gaze. When I felt safe enough to look at him again, I asked another question.

"You said you're a warrior, and a warrior fights, right? Who do you fight?"

"I *protect*, and sometimes that ends in a fight." He answered with a wolf's grin that sent a chill down my spine. Arwan would be a formidable in a fight. I was under no illusions about that. I frowned as I continued to process what he was telling me.

"What are you protecting?"

"Humanity," he answered flatly. "There are many levels of reality, other-worlds, and there are gateways like the oak, which provide access. With the help of others, I watch the gate and protect the boundaries from the creatures that try to seep through. Those that watch the gateways are all that stand between earth and the annihilation of the human race."

Whoa, this was way too much for my brain to compute. I rubbed at my suddenly-pounding forehead as my mind turned into one huge pulsing knot. "Wait just a minute," I said, as the weight of his words continued to sink in. "Who wants to annihilate the human race?"

He arched a black brow. "You'd be surprised." I frowned again, biting down into my lip, letting my gaze fall to my lap, where I plucked a nonexistent fibre from my dress.

"Why are you telling me this?" I whispered, not meeting his gaze. "Why me? I don't understand." A moment passed, and I thought he meant not to answer me. I lifted my eyes to meet his, and saw that his handsome face was torn with emotion.

"You've had enough to absorb for one night," he finally said. I sighed in disappointment. Why leave me hanging with the most important question? "But I need you to swear you'll do something for me."

I didn't hesitate. "Of course, anything, what is it?" I would do anything for him. I'd probably Highland fling off a cliff if he asked me to. Actually, there was no probably about it.

"I have to go away for a while."

I felt myself slump. "Back to Achren?" He nodded.

"When will you be back?"

He smiled slightly, seemingly pleased with my concern. "As soon as I can," he murmured.

I tried not to acknowledge the look of tenderness that had flooded into his purple eyes, but my stuttering heartbeat betrayed me.

"So what is it?" I reminded him. "What do you want me to do?" I was curious. What could I possibly give a divine immortal?

"*Need,* Brook," he said quietly "I need you to promise me that you won't do anything *rash* while I'm away, that you will keep yourself perfectly safe." I felt tension radiating from him. His glorious face was suddenly tight, the hand on his knee clenching into a fist.

Fighting with drug pushers aside, I didn't know what on earth he thought I could do that would put my person within a whisper of the lowest levels of peril in a sleepy village like Claremont, and it wasn't like he knew anything of my involvement with Adam Fleming.

"I'm still waiting for you to swear you will look after yourself." The steel in his tone bought my attention back to him.

I nodded solemnly. "I swear to you, Arwan, I will do my best to keep myself safe." The tension immediately lifted. "Can I ask one more thing?" I asked after a moment. He nodded. "What lies between us? Who am I to you?"

The next thing I felt was the heat of his hands on my face, his tanzanite eyes just inches from mine. My heart flew into fits, as I drew in his scent to my body like I depended upon it.

"You are my *one,*" he murmured, "and I am yours." I wondered if his words would be the death of me. Then his perfect mouth found mine and, for the first time in my life, I knew what it was to burn.

I kissed him back. I had to. The feel of him, of his mouth moving on mine, was impossible not to respond to. It was the most erotic, pivotal moment of my existence. I couldn't fight him anymore; he'd won, or maybe I'd surrendered. I wanted him, needed him more than I needed anything in my life. I relished in the glorious weight of him pressing me into the sofa, his strong arms around me. My heart flew in my chest as I abandoned all pretence of resistance. Arwan was everywhere, was everything. A moan escaped my lips as the heat of his mouth began to make its way along my jaw, then down my neck to my collarbone in slow, sensual kisses. I couldn't breathe, but didn't care. I just never wanted him to stop.

"Think of me often while I'm gone," he murmured, before raising his face to my mouth for another kiss. His lips were tender and soft on mine, loving.

Then just like that, something changed. My eyes flashed open, my heart still pounding in my chest, as I jolted upright. I groaned loudly and sunk back down into the sofa. Arwan was gone, disappeared. I was completely alone. Only the fragrance of crushed rose petals, that continued to permeate the air, proved he was ever there at all. I inhaled deeply, despite myself.

"Now cometh the pain," I muttered ominously.

chapter

FOURTEEN

I woke in the morning, exhausted. I'd barely managed an hour's sleep. Understandable, I supposed; the night before had been the most arousing and thrilling of my life.

I pulled back the curtains, my limbs heavy and sluggish, and was greeted with the reflection of my own dishevelled appearance. The sun wouldn't be up for another half hour yet. The world outside was black. The days were getting shorter. Winter would be upon Claremont before long, followed by the first coating of snow. As if triggered by my thoughts, the central heating clicked and groaned, before firing into life. I sighed.

I had thought that having answers from Arwan, albeit not the one I desired most, would somehow clear the fog in my mind, allowing me to see the bigger picture with a greater sense of clarity. But the fog had only gotten thicker, denser, shrouding the key to my greater understanding of what exactly was going on here. I was still missing something; Arwan had said as much himself. I wished I'd had the chance to ask him when he was coming home, well, to Avallon

House, anyway. I was already finding the fact that he wasn't there, or for that matter, in this realm, incredibly unsettling. I didn't like it one little bit that he was away. It hurt, literally. My mind kept going back to the feel of his lips on mine, making my mouth throb painfully. I passed off much of the day staring into space for long moments at a time, a hand absently tracing the path of his warm, soft lips on my collarbone.

I worked through Monday at The Shades in a kind of trance. I could hear myself chatting and laughing with the residents at the appropriate moments, while my hands demonstrated how to sculpt the curve of a neck, but my thoughts were never entirely focused on what I was doing.

Arwan had said he wouldn't be gone long, and I believed him, but I had the unshakable feeling that when he did return, he wouldn't be staying long, and that prospect filled me with anxiety. He had forced his way into my life, and against my better judgment, I had somehow allowed it to happen. Now the thought of potentially never seeing him again felt like my very heart were being riven in two. Trust me to fall for the unobtainable. I couldn't help but feel angry at myself. I had known this would happen. I should have fought harder to protect myself, but it was far too late for that now.

I pulled up outside Avallon House bright and early Tuesday morning. I knew before I stepped over the threshold that he wasn't back. I could feel the cloud of emptiness that was his absence, as it seeped through the pores of my skin and hollowed out my chest. Even the dogs were nowhere to be seen.

I tried to keep my mind on the job as I worked away, dusting, vacuuming, and polishing every tangible surface, but even the exuberance of Arwan's collection of art and antiques was unable to captivate my mind. I wanted the man himself. Except that he wasn't a man, was he? Not a human one, anyway. My heart blurred in my ribs every time I acknowledged the fact. Not a man, and yet more of a man than I'd ever known, and this was going to end in disaster. Arwan was going to break me. It was inevitable.

It was late afternoon when I left Avallon House, and the sun was already disappearing over the horizon in a blaze of blood red. I had lingered longer than usual, reluctant to leave in case Arwan might return. But when I couldn't put it off any longer, I pulled the heavy front door of Avallon House shut behind me and slowly descended the white steps to my car.

I drove carefully through the village on my way home; the High Street seemed unusually busy for the time of year. I felt a surge of guilt as I raised a hand from the wheel to wave at Alex humping a large black something along the pavement. I was relieved when, although unable to free a hand to wave, he smiled back at me. Maybe I'd been forgiven for dancing with Arwan Saturday night. I genuinely hoped so. I hated the thought of Alex being angry with me. I smiled for the first time that day.

At first glance, and in the rapidly fading light of the autumn afternoon, it looked like somebody stood on my doorstep waiting for me, and my heart skipped a beat. As I narrowed my eyes and focused, I saw it was a *something* rather than a *someone.*

I took the steps two at a time, curious to see what awaited me, then groaned loudly as I unhooked what appeared to be a witch's garb from the door knocker. I let myself inside and went straight through to the kitchen, flinging my heavily cling-filmed delivery over the nearest chair and rummaging through my handbag for my mobile, to check the date. Thirty-first October. I groaned for the second time and slumped down into a chair. It was Halloween.

At least there was a mask. I was grateful for that. I could hide behind it and hopefully blend in. I had been determined to use my sickness excuse and not go to the party as planned, but when I heard Morag's excited voice shrilling down the phone, saying she'd swing by for me at seven, I didn't have the heart to let her down. Anyway, what else was I going to do all night other than stare at a blank wall, wondering when a certain immortal would walk through my door?

I somehow managed to lace up and tighten the black corset, then tie the two ribbon ends in a secure bow. I slipped the ankle length black skirt over a pair of equally black thick tights, then donned my knee-high boots. The night looked clear, but it would be cold on the High Street. I stood back and examined myself in the mirror. The corset nipped me in at the waist and pushed my breasts to swell above it. The costume, although midnight black, held the faintest sparkle and shimmer in its fabric, and as I moved my hips from side to side, it glittered as it caught the light. My hair was a mess, but for once, that was kind of appropriate, so I just left it to do its own wild thing. Morag had slipped some temporary tattoos in with the costume, and I studied their Celtic knots and intricate swirls after placing them on the inside of both my forearms.

The doorbell sounded, telling me she'd arrived. I grabbed the thick black shawl that completed the costume and snapped the warty hooknosed mask into place. A moment later, I yanked the front door open and was confronted with my mirror image, only in red. After a brief silence, we both erupted into a fit of giggles, two cackling hags. It felt good to laugh after the day I'd had. Morag offered me one of two wicker brooms she held in each hand.

"Your vehicle for the night, madam."

"Omph!" I looked down for the source of my latest bruise.

"Oh yikes, I'm sorry!" I was on my third apology since we'd hit the High Street. This time I'd collided with an overexcited, presumably sugar fuelled, four foot five Freddy Krueger. The gruesome mask suddenly disappeared.

"Sorry, Brook!" beamed a cheeky face before the young man scampered off to catch up with his mates. I stared after the boy, but soon lost sight of him as the cloak of the crowd swallowed him up. "How did that kid know my name?"

Morag grabbed my hand. "I've told you, doll, you've got a glow." I shrugged my shoulders and allowed her to pull me on through the crowd.

Claremont's High Street looked straight out of the set of an old horror movie. Shop fronts had been transformed to resemble haunted houses and creepy castles covered in cobwebs and creepy crawlies. All lighting to speak of was supplied from the innumerable number of flickering grins of the jack-o'-lanterns that seemed to occupy nearly every available crack or crevice. Dry ice smoke pumped from somewhere and swirled about my feet as I followed Morag, weaving through the crowd of ghouls and ghosts. I couldn't believe how into the whole Halloween thing everybody seemed to be, as we walked past the bakery and I snapped round at the feel of twiggy fingers on my shoulder.

"Cake, my pretty?" cackled an associate; witches did not appear to be in short supply tonight. I looked down at the proffered tiny pumpkin cupcake and quickly shook my head. "No thanks," I said, before picking up my pace to catch up Morag.

I didn't want to lose her. The street was teeming with partygoers, all rendered unidentifiable thanks to masks and disguises. Someone had rigged up a sound system, and music belted out into the night.

I breathed deeply as we continued to weave through the crowd. The air was heavy with sweet, spicy scents, like cinnamon and orange, and every now and then I caught the glorious whiff of roasting chestnuts.

"Where are we going?" I shouted so Morag would hear me over the music.

"To the cauldron; I'm supposed to be serving mulled wine. I thought you could help out," she shouted back over her shoulder. Oh, of course, the cauldron. Where else would two witches be going on Halloween?

As it turned out, the cauldron, which was actually much bigger than I had expected, was located about halfway up the High Street and was the source of the spicy, sweet odour. It was steaming and bubbling away, fuelled by an electric plate beneath, keeping the mulled wine it housed nice and hot. There was a small stall set up beside it where people could redeem a ticket and receive a free mug.

"Hi Emma," Morag greeted the bloody zombie we were about to relieve of duty. "We've got the next shift covered," she said, pulling me in behind the stall.

Working the mulled wine stall was more fun than I'd anticipated. Not only did we have the benefit of the heat produced by the cauldron, but we barely stopped laughing from the moment we served our first mug. Everybody was in great spirits, and the banter flowed like the wine. My thoughts were never far from Arwan, but being so busy didn't allow me to dwell on my situation and the complete impossibility of it all. Working the stall was like giving my constantly screwing mind a holiday, and it felt good.

"Hey, wait a second!" I looked over at Morag glaring after three adolescent sized skeletons she'd just served, who were now disappearing into the crowd. She shook her head as her eyes narrowed. The heat from the caldron had made the wearing of masks uncomfortable, and both Mo and I had abandoned them.

"What is it?" I asked.

"I think I just served Daniel and his friends mulled wine!" I pushed a hand to my mouth to suppress a giggle.

"Arghhhh!" she exclaimed. "Bairns! I swear he's going to send me to an early grave!"

After an hour and half, the cauldron was practically dry, and custom had gone the same way.

"Where's everybody going?" I asked Morag. The crowd had begun to thin out, as people seemed to be migrating up to the top of the village, in clusters of varying degrees of drunkenness.

"It's almost ten o'clock; they'll be lighting the bonfire in the field at the top of the village soon." I watched as Morag peered over the edge of the cauldron, then plunged her ladle to retrieve the last of the mulled wine, which she then poured into a mug.

"Is Arwan putting in an appearance tonight?" she asked, feigning mild curiosity. "I know you've been thinking about him on and off all night."

"No, I haven't," I lied turning away so she wouldn't see it written on my face. As I turned, I knocked an empty mug to the ground, and it shattered into pieces at my feet. Morag snorted, amused, making my face burn up. I dropped to the ground to retrieve the broken cup, then looked up to find Morag crouching down on my level, red skirt pooling at her feet in a strangely familiar way as she offered me the final mug of hot wine.

"Here," she said. "Drink; forget Arwan."

The moment she uttered those words, a sharp, hot pain seared through my chest, and all scenery in my peripheral vision buckled and warped. I had somehow managed to accept the mug from Morag, white steam coiled daintily from its contents like waltzing dancers into the night, but I was unaware.

I couldn't escape her words; they echoed through my mind, triggering images, like an old projection in a movie theatre. *"Drink, Brook, forget Arwan."* Every follicle on my body tingled. Then it was another voice that uttered the words in my head, formed by another mouth, belonging to another face, a startlingly beautiful face, framed in familiar wild red hair. Was this the face of the veiled woman of my dreams? *"Drink, Morgen, forget Arwan's betrayal."*

Morag touched my shoulder, snapping me back to myself. While I'd been daydreaming, she'd begun tidying up around the stall, seemingly as oblivious to my mental astral projection as I had been to her actions.

"I've just spotted Daniel, so I'm going to try to catch him up and make sure he's still sober. I'll meet you up at the bonfire, okay?"

"Sure thing," I quickly agreed. Thankfully, Morag was too preoccupied with Daniel to hear the tremble in my voice. I was still crouched on the ground, holding the mug Morag had given me. I rose slowly as she raced off, presumably in the direction of a potentially intoxicated skeleton.

The street was empty now. I was completely alone, with everybody up in the field awaiting the lighting of the bonfire. I jumped at a metallic sound behind me, and turned to see an empty pop can rolling down the cobbled street, pushed by an invisible wind. I watched its noisy progress as it rolled and bounced towards and then past me, as it made its way down the street but abruptly stopped as it collided with a pair of black shoes.

"Why are you out here on your own?"

I gasped. "Arwan!" My heart stuttered in my chest, then raced into a steady gallop. My eyes lost sight of him, and then he was right in front of me, kissing my forehead, then my mouth, sending a thrill of pleasure through me. I put the mug down on the table before it slid from my fingers. It disturbed me how overwhelmingly delirious I felt to see him, to hear his voice, and to feel the heat of his mouth on my skin. I wrapped my arms around his neck, stood up on my tiptoes, and kissed him back.

"You're in one piece, at least," he said after a moment.

"How was your trip?" I asked

"I went home, Brook; I'm on a trip now," he reminded me, smiling. I felt something inside of me fall over. How could I forget? Claremont wasn't Arwan's home or even his world. We belonged to literally different spheres of reality. I pushed to the back of my mind all thoughts of the inevitable pain that would come my way when he went home and permanently left me. I didn't want to waste a moment I had with him.

"You seemed preoccupied when I arrived, deep in thought. Is everything well with you?" he asked, concern suddenly clouding his purple eyes. The words of the red-haired woman once again found a voice in my mind. *'Drink Morgen, forget Arwan's betrayal.'*

"Arwan, who is Morgen?" I hadn't realised I'd even planned on asking him that question. My strange dreams and daydreams were something I felt embarrassed about. I really didn't want to draw attention to them, especially from Arwan, but the words shot out before I really knew what I'd asked. I realised he was looking at me in astonishment.

"Where did you hear that name?" He asked, and his tone told me that he was barely managing to reign in some strong emotion.

"I've been having strange dreams and visions." I told him, reluctantly. He exhaled and a broad smile broke through his features. He looked so utterly jubilant that I couldn't help but smile back at him.

"There's something I want to show you. Will you return to Avallon House with me tonight?"

"Okay," I instantly agreed. Then I glanced down at myself, and felt foolish, suddenly, in my Halloween costume. "But let me go home first and get changed. I'll meet you there in half an hour."

He seemed reluctant to let go of me, but after a moment, his lips found mine in a parting kiss. I would never tire of kissing him, and for an instant, I let myself believe that I, too, was immortal, and that I could kiss him for eternity. Big mistake; how was I going to live the rest of my life when he went his way and I went mine? There would never be another. I could never love another.

chapter

FIFTEEN

It took me less than five minutes to get home. I paced quickly up the hall and went straight to the bathroom, already tugging at the ribbons in the corset. After a bit of a struggle, I finally freed myself of its constraints and shimmied out of the remaining costume. Then I stepped under the hot stream of water from the shower and, for a moment, let it heat my chilled bones, before I quickly shampooed and conditioned my tangled hair.

A few minutes later, wrapped in a towel, I was in the bedroom, digging out a clean pair of jeans and then rummaging in my jumper drawer for something warm. The air outside had felt particularly icy on the way home, and I wanted to wrap up against it. I finally found something suitable and hastily yanked it over my head. I resented the long ten minutes it took to blow-dry my hair before I crossed the hall to the darkened kitchen, looking for the car keys I'd left splayed on the table before leaving for the party. I snapped on the light—and saw instantly that I was not alone.

For one long second, my entire body came to a complete standstill. I could feel my eyes, round and unblinking, in my head, my heart quiet in my chest as an ice sharp chill crept up my spine, bringing with it the realisation that he'd found me. I'd always suspected that one day he would, and yet that didn't detract from the sheer terror I felt at finding him here, in the heart of my home. The place where I had finally begun to feel a chance of hope. It seemed so cruel.

"How..." I stammered, "How are you here?"

My ex-husband, Adam Fleming, sat at my table like he owned it. It had already begun; he was taking over, taking control, and then he would take my life. I realised this as my brain began to register several facts, most importantly the large black gun resting in his lap, with its barrel pointing at me like an accusing finger. But bizarrely, I noticed other things too, like how the lines of his face seemed so much deeper than the last time I'd seen him. His skin tone, once pale, was now grey, like the colour of his eyes, which stared at me with what I could only describe as emptiness. I noticed that his blonde hair, usually styled to within an inch of its life, had been closely cropped in a crew cut; I also noticed that he'd lost weight, making the features of his face appear sharp rather than fine, almost waspish. He obviously still smoked; the faintest hint of tobacco smoke permeated the air as I finally managed to suck in a breath.

"No kiss for your husband?" The gravelly sound of his mocking voice finally kicked my stunned system into action rather than into lockdown. Fight or flight? I heard the chair he was sitting in flip over, and heard something porcelain, my breakfast bowl or maybe my favourite coffee mug, as it smashed to smithereens on the tiles of the kitchen floor. I made it to within three feet of the front door, with my arms outstretched for the handle, before the force of his hand in my hair yanked me painfully to a stop and forced a cry of pain from my lips. My eyes watered as my scalp throbbed in outrage at the assault, but a moment later, the sheer brutality of his actions brought anger rising into my throat like bile.

I tried to twist to face him as my arms frantically lashed out, but his fingers remained tightly wound in my roots, causing excruciating pain with my every swing. Something like "Let go of me you bastard!"

tore from my throat as he let me thrash about. I heard his throaty laugh at my feeble attempts to fight him. Then the cold, hard feel of steel on my temple dispelled my surge of courage. I suddenly felt as if my bones had been eaten out of my body, like a rundown house infested with death watch beetle. *Don't faint. Don't faint. Don't faint*, I chanted in my mind. The last thing I wanted was to lose consciousness, even for an instant. He twisted my hair painfully.

"It seems the backbone you found during my trial is still in residence. Still, I'll have plenty of time over the next few hours to fillet it out of you." I shuddered as he sneered so close to my neck that I could feel his breath on my skin. He inhaled deeply. "Try to run again, and I'll put a bullet in that lovely face of yours." He released his hold on my hair and ran his index finger menacingly down the curve of my cheek, as if the finger were a blade.

"Now," he continued quietly, "we haven't got a lot of time; there's a boat waiting for us at Ross Cove. I want you to pack a bag with enough clothes for forty-eight hours, and I want you to do it fast, like someone's pointing a gun at you." He tapped the gun slowly on my temple, emphasising each word as he said, "Do. You. Understand?" I couldn't speak—my mouth was completely dry—but I managed a nod. Then the gun disappeared from my temple, and an instant later, I felt it prodding my spine.

Heart pounding, I turned slowly and headed for the bedroom, the feel of the gun digging in my back never wavering. I went to my wardrobe and grabbed something resembling a backpack, then began loading it with clothes from my chest of drawers. All the while, he held the gun to my back. My eyes briefly rested on a photo Morag had taken of Ross Cove, that I'd placed on top of the chest several days earlier. Could I distract Adam briefly and place it somewhere strategic? A pitiful clue for when someone came looking for me. It wasn't much of a hope, but it was better than nothing.

"Can you pick up my toothbrush from the bathroom?" My voice trembled and I was glad; Adam would think me far too scared to attempt anything that might lead to someone discovering our whereabouts. He groaned, but instructed me to keep packing as he briefly disappeared for the bathroom. Half a second was all I needed to slip the photo onto the bed, under my backpack.

Adam shoved my toothbrush into the bag, then barked that I had enough, and took the bag from me, swinging it over his shoulder. He took several steps away from the bed, his eyes never seeing my attempt at a clue. I turned to face him.

"Get a move on!" he barked, impatiently using the gun to indicate the bedroom door. I didn't move.

"Are you going to kill me?" I whispered. Tears had welled into my eyes and were now tracing down my cheeks.

The smile that lit his features froze the flow of blood in my veins. "It pleases me you're scared, Brook, it really does, but we don't have time for this conversation at the moment. A certain government-run hotel will be missing my presence fairly soon, and I'm guessing the first place they'll look will be here. So if you don't mind, we'll have our little Q&A in the car."

I choked back a sob. So not immediately, then; I would have to wait for death. To kill me wouldn't be enough. The revenge was in the waiting.

In my preoccupation with getting back to Arwan, I hadn't noticed the strange blue Toyota sedan parked a few yards up the street from my house. I really had become complacent. If he'd come a couple of months earlier, I might have stood a chance, but I'd become too settled, too happy. I'd fallen in love, and it had made me vulnerable, easy to snare, and the big bad wolf had found me.

The village centre was deserted as we raced through; everyone would still be enjoying the bonfire. Was this it? Was tonight the last time I would ever see the people that I cared so much about? I cried some more, wondering how long Arwan would wait before he came looking for me. It didn't matter; we'd be away, and how could he find me if he didn't know where I'd gone? I had absolutely no idea where Adam was taking me after Ross Cove, or how long he intended to keep me alive; he could turn his gun on me at any moment.

It took every ounce of strength I had not to break down and crumple into myself. I wiped my eyes with the sleeve of my duffle coat and forced myself to focus. I needed to believe that Arwan would find me, but if he couldn't, I needed information to help me escape. I couldn't give up. I wasn't the same woman who had spent seven years being the obsequious wife of Adam Fleming.

"How did you find me?" I asked without looking at him. The gun was back in his lap, within easy reach of his hands. I kept my eyes trained on the windscreen and saw what looked like snowflakes beginning to fall through the beams of the headlights as we drove into the night and away from Claremont. Adam reached across me and flicked open the glove compartment. There was nothing inside except a newspaper and a pack of Marlborough Lights. He grabbed the paper and flung it into my lap, then switched on the interior light above my seat.

The paper was folded over in the centre, and I lifted it from my lap with trembling hands and let it fall open. I gasped. It was a photo of Arwan from the night at The Shades, at the party celebrating his wonderful gesture to the people of Claremont. The story hadn't only made local papers like I'd assumed, but had hit the national rags. I studied Arwan's face; he didn't look out of the picture, but instead his profile stared down at what he held in his hands: my sculpture. It would have been obvious to anybody who knew my work that it was one of mine. I felt a new surge of despair sweep over me.

"If I'd have known that one day your little hobby would lead me back to you, I wouldn't have devoted so much time to discouraging it. Funny how life works out, isn't it?"

I could feel him looking at me, a cruel smile in the gravel of his voice, as he waited for me to say something. I took one last look at Arwan's face before slowly folding the paper over again and putting it back in the glove compartment. Then I stared out the windscreen and focused on the snow. It was getting heavier now.

My mind began turning over questions, possibilities. Would Arwan be wondering what was keeping me? Was he pacing the hall of Avallon House, waiting for me to walk through his front door? When he finally went to my house looking for me, would he see the photo I had left, and would it be enough to prompt him to guess my whereabouts? Adam's voice bought my attention back to him.

"I couldn't believe my luck when I saw that photograph in the paper; the rest was easy really," he boasted. "I haven't been idle in the months we've been apart. My business has grown. Jail's great for that, you know; so many likeminded people in one place. I've branched out into new areas. All I had to do was contact a minion in this neck of the woods and give your description, and what do ya know? He knew who I was talking about straight away!" I flinched at the feel of his hand, as it squeezed my knee painfully. "Not surprising, really, someone like you is hard to hide." I could see his leer in my peripheral vision. I fought the urge to shrink as far away from him as possible. I didn't want him to think I was frightened of him. I yanked his hand from my knee but kept my eyes to the front.

"How did you escape?" I asked, and his excitement was almost palpable as he bounced in his seat.

"I was hoping you'd ask me that!" he said, then the tone of his voice dropped an octave. "The same night that I saw your sculpture in the newspaper I dreamt of a red-haired stunner, a total babe." I jerked, struggling to conceal my shock. He had to be talking about the same woman from my own dreams! Who the hell was she, and what was her problem with me?

"Stay with me Brook," Adam said, shaking my shoulder "There's more, but don't worry," He leered "we didn't get naked. No, it was much better than that, she told me she had the power to help me walk right on out of the jail unseen, and I know you'll think I'm nuts, but I believed her, she was so real!" He reached over, and I suppressed a cringe as his fingers skimmed my jaw. "I think she was my guardian angel Brook, and I believe it's thanks to her I'm here with you now." The next time that red-haired psycho girl showed up in my dreams she better look the hell out! "So, I went ahead and came up with a plan," Adam continued, pulling me from a thought bubble that involved my fists, and a lot of red hair. "And now there's a man, with roughly a similar appearance to my own, lying on my bunk, in my cell, awaiting evening register." Adam grinned. "He was my afternoon visitor today, and for £20,000, five minutes before leaving time, he removed his jumper and gave it to me. Underneath, he wore a blue polo shirt the same colour as the standard uniform at HMP Essex. I slipped his jumper over my shirt, and when the whistle blew, telling prisoners to head back to the cells he went in my place. Five minutes later I walked past the screws right out the front door with the other visitors without a soul noticing, just like my hot little guardian angel said!" He ended his account with a flourish. For a long moment he looked back and forth from the road to me, waiting for me to say something. Then when he realised I had nothing to say, he groaned and rolled his eyes. There was nothing left to say.

I stared out of the window, and tried to suppress the trembling of all my bones, watching the snow as it started to run in lines against the black of the night, like we were travelling through space at light speed. It was soothing in a way, hypnotic. For a few seconds at a time, I found I could pretend I was somewhere else, with someone else.

I felt the exact moment that Arwan discovered I'd gone; so did Adam, except that he couldn't possibly comprehend the wrath he'd unwittingly released. The car literally lurched on the road, throwing us both against our belts, as if hit by an unseen wave. For just an instant, the whole world seemed to ripple and shudder with a terrible earthquake, and I knew irrevocably that at its epicentre was Arwan Jones.

"Christ almighty, what was that!" Adam hollered, glaring out the windscreen, his knuckles white on the steering wheel.

We drove on in silence for a while, and I was shocked to realise that my terror was beginning to subside. I no longer had to dig the heel of my boots into the floor of the car to stop my legs from visibly shaking, and my breathing had begun to slow along with my heartbeat. I was drawing strength from knowing that Arwan was looking for me, and it was dispelling my fear and allowing me to think clearly. I was starting to feel more irritated with Adam than frightened. His power was in the fear he was able to generate in people. Not being scared didn't change my circumstances, but it somehow made them easier to deal with; it was emancipating.

I watched him out the corner of my eye as he quickly regained his composure after the earth shuddered, deciding perhaps to dismiss it as an act of nature, which I supposed in some ways it had been.

"You never answered my question back at the house. Are you going to kill me?" I asked without looking at him. Adam laughed without humour, the sound harsh, like cracking whips.

"I'm not going to kill you, Brook—assuming, that is, you do as you're told."

Surprise and relief flooded through me in equal measures. I never in a million years expected him to say those words. In my nightmares, death had always been delivered swiftly and efficiently, with no mercy. I finally looked at him. "I'd thought you would want revenge?"

He met my gaze for a moment, then looked back to the road. "I'm not going to deny that your little stunt on the stand during my trial was...inconvenient, shall we say? I was quite rightly livid, for a period." He rubbed at his jaw thoughtfully, then continued. "They made me see a psychologist in prison, as part of my rehabilitation, apparently. She told me I'm a sociopath, that I am completely incapable of feeling emotion for anyone or anything." His blonde brows rose slightly above his grey eyes as he continued to manoeuvre the road. "The bitch was right, I feel nothing, most of the time...," his eyes met mine again, "bar one exception. The last six months have taken their toll on me, but not for the reasons you might think. Prison's a breeze. It was being away from you that nearly killed me."

Oh dear god, don't tell me he believes he's doing this for love? I looked back to the windscreen, a sick feeling in my stomach. Then it dawned on me that if death wasn't coming anytime soon, it increased my chances of escape and widened the opportunity for Arwan to find me.

The snow was getting heavier by the moment. If it began to drift, maybe he'd have to pull over, and I would have a chance to run for it. It felt like too much to hope for.

"You're it, the only thing I see in a sea of ink and shadows, the flicker of flame that keeps the demons in the dankest corners of my mind." His voice was quiet now, thoughtful, like he spoke only to himself. He was insane. I'd realised that, mere months into our hasty marriage. The shrink was right; he was a sociopath. Those empty eyes didn't lie.

A mobile phone rang out from somewhere on Adam. It seemed to break his contemplation as he rummaged in his jeans pocket to produce a phone. He said nothing, his face emotionless, as he listened to whoever was on the other end, and then after a few minutes, he hung up and shoved the phone back into his pocket.

"Where are you taking me?" I demanded.

"Ireland, initially," he answered. "We're about to meet Duncan Buckie, whose boat's waiting for us, and then we'll be leaving British shores for the foreseeable future."

"Duncan Buckie?" I asked, confused. How on earth was Duncan Buckie connected to Adam?

"That's right; you're acquainted with him, I understand? He's my top man in the West of Scotland. It was Duncan who confirmed your presence in Claremont for me."

Something ice cold began to take hold in the pit of my stomach. "What does Duncan Buckie do for you?" I asked quietly.

Adam glanced at me sideways and hesitated as if debating whether to tell me or not, then shrugged his shoulders with indifference. "He distributes drugs to my dealers on the ground and then helps me launder the money that the sales generate." His tone was jovial; he could have been talking about the weather.

"What kind of drugs?"

"Heroin," he confirmed. Realisation dawned.

"It's you," I whispered. "You've been circulating the contaminated heroin!" Anger flared in my blood as an image of Daniel flashed into my mind. Adam sighed dramatically.

"Ah, yes, contamination is potentially unfortunate for business, but I came up with a solution!" He slapped a hand on my thigh in his delight. "If we could get more kids hooked, then if we lost a few to the contaminated stuff, the numbers would balance out and the income stream would barely be affected. So we dangled a few free hits under the noses of our established junkies and sent them out on a recruitment drive. Very successful, I understand." I stared at him in utter disbelief as he spoke about human lives, with no feeling whatsoever, like the kids he peddled to were nothing but cattle. He clicked his tongue loudly.

"Now don't look at me like that, my love. You didn't expect me to trash a million pounds worth of gear just because of a little anthrax, did you?"

I finally found my voice. "You're an absolute evil..."

"Psycho? So everyone keeps telling me."

"Kids have died! Your lust for money and power has destroyed families." I didn't think there was any way Adam could possibly shock me anymore, until he sniggered.

"Yes, they're dropping like flies, I believe, and not just here—all round the country. You don't expect me to care about that? I have no feelings, remember? It's not my fault; I have mental health issues!" My eyes dropped to the gun in his lap, and I wondered if I could reach it before he could.

"You won't," Adam answered my unspoken question, "and you certainly wouldn't use it, even on a scumbag like me." Our eyes locked together.

"I would make an exception in your case."

He shook his head, smiling confidently. "No, no, you wouldn't." I noticed, however, that his certainty in my predictability didn't stop him adjusting the gun in his lap.

We were getting closer to the coast. The heavily salted air had turned the snow to slush and rain that splattered noisily off the windscreen.

We turned into the car park at Ross Cove and pulled up directly opposite the only other car there, Duncan Buckie's Jaguar, parked under one lonely light post that cast an orange glow over the area directly beneath. A bin chained to its base shuddered and shook violently under the force of the relentless wind rampaging around the exposed car park in moaning, rain-heavy gusts. Although the lighting was poor and the weather didn't help visibility, it didn't prevent me from recognising the ample silhouette in the driver's seat of the Jag.

Adam cut off the engine as Duncan Buckie made his way over to where we were parked. The wind straight off the sea billowed his suit jacket up behind him as he used his arms to try to shield his face from the worst of the rain. Adam rolled his electric window down in time for Buckie's round, moist face to materialise.

"Mr Fleming, it's an absolute honour to meet you," the man spluttered in his almost childlike voice. It was pathetic. Adam ignored him.

"Where's the boat?" he growled. Buckie's head nodded like an enthusiastic puppy.

"Yes, of course, it's docked at a little jetty just below the cliffs. There's a path that runs right down not far from here. It's not an easy passage during the day, and with this weather you will have to watch your step. I see you caught up with your wife." Buckie's eyes flickered past Adam to me.

"Do not look at her." Adam spoke with quiet venom.

Buckie's eyes, suddenly very round, leapt back to Adam. Like everyone that worked for him, Duncan Buckie was terrified of his employer.

"I'm sorry, sir, forgive my impertinence." I groaned loudly, rolling my eyes. Then Buckie produced a set of silver keys and handed them through the window to Adam. "Here are the keys for the cruiser. If you're ready, Mr Fleming, I will show you to the path that leads to the jetty."

Adam lifted his jumper and tucked the gun into the band of his jeans, then turned sideways to face me.

"Get out the car, and don't move until I tell you to. If you run, I will shoot you." His tone was low and deadly, and I knew without a doubt that rather than have me escape, he'd have me dead.

It was hard to hold my feet, outside the car. The wind was strong and bitterly cold, pinching every exposed bit of skin on my body, and the icy rain flew directly into my face. Adam had let me bring my duffel coat, and I pulled its hood up over my head for whatever protection it could offer. As Adam grabbed my backpack from the boot of the car, my eyes darted to the black of the woods that surrounded the cove. I couldn't see for sure because of the distinct lack of moonlight, but I guessed from memory that I was maybe a hundred metres away from the safety of its foliage. I probably wouldn't make it; Adam was fast. I brought my eyes back to him just before he slung my bag at me. He had, no doubt, registered my thoughts.

Mr Buckie's eyes followed Adam continuously. He seemed smaller to me somehow, in defiance of his bulk; Adam did that to people. He reduced big men to nothing with just one glance from his empty eyes.

"Did you bring what I asked?" Adam asked Buckie, roughly grabbing my arm and pulling me to his side.

"Yes, Mr Fleming."

"Well?" he replied with an impatience that threatened to boil over. Buckie scurried back to his car and opened the boot, pulling out a large black sports bag, and carried it over to where we waited. All the time, Adam stood inches from me, thwarting any attempts I might have made to run. Outside of the circle of light provided by the streetlight, we were completely surrounded by black. Snow clouds covered any light from the moon; I couldn't even make out where the land fell away to the ocean. Only the sound of the crashing waves gave an indication. Any path down the cliff face was going to be tricky, that was for sure. C'mon Arwan, there's not much time!

I wondered again if he'd found my photograph and whether it was an obvious enough clue. Not only was I desperate to be in the safety of his presence and away from these despicable men, but I was adamant that they needed to be stopped or more kids would die at their hands.

Buckie put the bag down at Adam's feet like a cowering worshiper with an appeasement offering. Adam kneeled, unzipping the bag, and pulled out a flashlight and a pale blue waterproof jacket, which he put on before rezipping the bag and slinging it over his shoulder. He flicked on the torch and shone it directly at Buckie, making him squint.

"What about the gear?"

Buckie's face flushed red under the torchlight as he stuttered his response. "All the uncontaminated stuff is aboard the boat, and I will continue to distribute the other and, as discussed, place the proceeds in your offshore bank accounts." I couldn't hold my tongue any longer.

"How could you, Duncan? You're responsible for the death of children," I spat. "How can you live with yourself? Everything you buy with the money you make has some poor kids' blood on it, and you walk past their mothers every day in the street, offering your condolences like a pillar of the community."

Duncan's eyes darted everywhere but in my direction. I guessed he couldn't face up to the reality of what he'd see on my face. As pitiful as it was, there were shoots of guilt somewhere within Duncan Buckie, but clearly not enough to make him rethink his choice of career; his greed wouldn't allow it. It was sickening.

Adam pulled the gun from the band of his jeans with his free hand and pointed it directly at me. "No time for sermons. Let's go."

Duncan grabbed another torch from his car and began to lead the way out of the light of the car park, towards the cliffs. Every now and then, I felt the gun in my back, Adam's way of reminding me not to attempt to break for it. Escape was appearing more and more unlikely, and if Arwan didn't find me soon, I'd be on a boat cruising to who knew where with nobody but a sociopath for company.

"This is the path you need to take, Mr Fleming," Duncan said, stopping after only a short walk along the cliffs.

"I'm not walking down there!" I yelled over the sea, pointing down to what appeared to be a path in name only. Under the light of two torches, it looked more like a series of dangerously narrow juts in the granite. One good gust, and I'd be freefalling. I hastily shrugged off the mental image of nose-diving into angry waters, and suddenly realised that the rain had eased considerably and that the wind was dying away to nothing more than a light breeze. Although it was still dark, it wasn't as dark as before, and I pulled my hood down and looked up at the sky, bewildered.

The clouds had dispersed enough to expose the face of the moon. It peeked through the clouds like a silent observer, casting blue light over the earth. Then my skin prickled and hairs lifted at the nape of my neck as I felt it, the brew of something colossal in the atmosphere. The unsettling quiet before the storm-my pulse quickened in expectation. I turned in a full circle, scanning the dark, looking for any sign of him, for any sign of Arwan. I heard Buckie attempting to engineer his escape.

"I erm...um...I'll leave you here, then, Mr Fleming." I guessed Buckie fancied the trek down to the jetty about as much as I did.

"Like hell you will," Adam growled. "You'll take us right down to the goddamn boat."

Buckie's mouth opened and closed in a most unflattering way before he could finally speak. "Yessir, of course, Mr Fleming."

I was surprised that neither of them had noticed the shift in the air, the sudden unseasonal warmth and the static quality it now housed. Adam had gestured impatiently that Buckie should begin leading the descent to the jetty, when something happened that nobody could miss.

The sudden roar of the water was deafening. Adam and Duncan both turned and looked out to sea. I did the same and my bag slipped from my fingers as I gasped in disbelief.

At first there was only one. I could see it clearly in the distance under the light of the moon. An enormous helix of angry white seawater towered hundreds of feet into the sky, fuelled by an unimaginably powerful tornado. After only seconds, the first tornado was joined by a second and then a third, all swirling with unchecked power and fury, eating up water greedily as they spun with seeming mindlessness over the water. Duncan was yelling something, his jowls wobbling furiously, but the high-pitched sound of his voice was lost in the thunder of the gallons of ocean suddenly airborne. I glanced wide-eyed at Adam, who seemed momentarily spellbound. He still held the torch and gun in either hand, but both pointed to the ground, his arms slack in his preoccupation. His eyes stared out to sea, unblinking, as he watched this incredible spectacle.

Unlike Buckie, he wasn't frightened, but awed. I followed his eyes back out to sea and saw that the three tornados appeared to be merging together. I felt a jolt of fear and anticipation as I realised they were undoubtedly now heading in our direction. Duncan was still yelling over the mayhem of the sea, but appeared to give up as he flung his torch at my feet and then legged himself back to the car park. A moment later, I saw the flash of hastily turning headlights. I looked at Adam, still awestruck. My right leg twitched as I readied myself to sprint for freedom. I realised that this might be my one and only chance of escape. But Adam suddenly raised his gun arm without even looking, freezing me to the spot as its barrel pointed at my chest. I let out a defeated breath, realising I'd been holding it since the moment I knew the tempo was on the verge of crashing through the ceiling. Fortunately the tornado appeared to be travelling away from the yellow lights of the fishing village of Ross, but not so fortunately, it was instead heading directly for us on the cliffs.

"You're crazy!" I screamed uselessly against the deafening roar, my arm pointing out to sea. "We're going to die if we stay here!" The three water tornadoes had now merged into one gigantic twisting mass of water. I cupped my hands to my mouth, "We have to run for it!"

"I'll be damned if a storm is going to stop me getting away! Nothing is stopping me getting on that bloody boat!" Where Buckie's high tones were lost to the elements, Adam's indignant growl could not be denied.

I felt the spray of salt water on my face and pulled my eyes from Adam back to the sea. The helix of water was dangerously close to the cliff edge now. I could see something silver, along with giant splinters of jetty wood, caught inside and spinning so fast that it appeared suspended in the water, motionless. I realised that it was the hull of a boat, a big one, undoubtedly Adam's transport out of the country. Then without warning, the water suddenly released its quarry, sending the cruiser sailing over our heads and crashing into the woods, where it exploded into a fireball.

"You son of a bitch!" Adam tossed his torch to the ground, pointed his gun at the towering spry of water, and began firing random shots. The water was so close to the cliffs that I was soaked through from the spray. There was no wind to speak of; it seemed to be confined totally to the energy that turned the water. An urge to run overwhelmed me again, until I saw something else escape free from the water. A large splinter of wood had torn loose and flew directly at Adam, knocking his gun from his hand and staking him through his left shoulder.

I imagined rather than heard the sound of flesh tearing and bone snapping under the assault, and my stomach heaved. I watched, horrified, as his right hand automatically flew to the area of penetration, just as a second stake shot through the air and straight into his right shoulder. At first the look on his face was one of complete incredulousness rather than pain, but then a soundless scream tore from his throat as he lost his footing and fell to the ground. My hands flew to my mouth as he writhed about in agony, desperately trying to pull out the stakes, but the damage they'd caused to his tendons barely allowed him to move his arms at all. Every movement he made only seemed to intensify the agony as he jarred the wood piercing through his body. I could clearly make out the dark patches of moisture spreading out from around the stakes. My instinct was to run the few metres that separated us and try and help him, but the sound of the water was total now. I was sure we were about to get swept up in the mayhem. It was too late to help, and it was certainly too late to run. I shut my eyes and waited.

I reopened my eyes as the deafening roar of the vortex drained away with the last of the water, back to the seabed. And there he stood, on the cliff edge, the image of an all-powerful, vengeful god. He was twice his usual height, towering at least twelve feet, his body free of clothes, exposing the twist and groove of every taut muscle of his warrior's body. In his right hand he swung a giant sword with casual menace, its hilt smothered in jewels, its blade glinting lethally in the moonlight. I dropped to my knees as his eyes, glowing bright green with the power of his fury, briefly rested on me before turning back to what writhed in agony at his feet.

Adam was clearly in pain; he groaned loudly with the intensity of it, but that didn't stop him from desperately trying to inch closer to the gun that had been knocked a few feet away from his hand. Arwan stooped to pick it up, then tossed it effortlessly, miles out to sea. As he did so, I saw clearly every rigid angle of his chiselled face. Arwan was consumed with his fury.

"What the hell are you?" Adam demanded, looking directly into the face of Arwan for the first time. I could finally hear the ring of fear in his voice, something I had never heard before.

"*Retribution*!" Adam cowered at the sound of Arwan's voice, which seemed to rumble from every direction, from the very earth itself. Arwan raised his sword arm high above his shoulder, his glowing green eyes intent on his victim.

"No!" I screamed, scrambling to my feet and forcing my legs to run the short distance to him.

"Arwan." I stood on the tips of my toes, and gently placed my hand on the muscle of his free arm, my head back as I tried to look up into his glorious but livid face. "If you kill him, the blood will be on my hands, because I know you only do it to avenge me." My voice was soft, quiet under the sound of the breaking waves, but I knew he heard every word. "There are families that need to see him brought to justice. Don't rob them of that for my sake."

"I'm sorry, Morgen, I cannot let him live." I didn't notice that he'd used the name that the red-haired woman from my vision had called me; I only saw that he had raised his sword even higher. "Now stand back," he ordered, gently pushing me away with his free hand.

"Arwan, I beg you, do not do this!" I threw myself onto the ground directly in front of Adam, and in the line of the sword. Arwan immediately lowered his arm and the sword with it. I saw pain and anger etched on his face as our eyes locked together for a long moment until he finally spoke.

"You need beg for nothing from me. If you want this...human kept alive, then it shall be so." I let out a long breath and relaxed just a little bit.

"Thank you," I said as he dropped to his knees in front of me, as though the effort of restraining himself from his revenge had momentarily drained all strength from his body. I turned and glanced at Adam, still moaning behind me, then looked back to Arwan. In the brief moment I had looked away, he had returned to his usual height, and the colour of his eyes no longer burned green through the night. I went to him immediately and cradled his head to my chest, as he wrapped his arms tightly around my waist.

"I'm fine," I murmured into the black of his hair. "I'm not hurt at all," I assured him. After a long moment, he rose to his feet and embraced me tightly again. We had both completely forgotten Adam at our feet, now silent despite his pain and watching Arwan's every move with bulging, horrified eyes.

Arwan covered his mouth with mine and kissed me with raw, brutal emotion, and all the shock and fright of the last hour abandoned my body entirely. I fell against the heat of his bareness, and let him drive those emotions out of me.

After a timeless moment, he reluctantly lifted his mouth from mine, a grin tugging at the corners of his lips. I suddenly realised that my left leg had risen and twisted round his thigh, his hand holding it in place, pinning us tightly together. I could feel his desire digging into me, and it was then that I remembered he was stark naked. Not sure what to do with my eyes, I slowly moved to lower and then untwine my leg from his. He turned me away from Adam and led me a short distance along the cliffs, before stopping and turning me back to face him, grinning openly now, his teeth a white flash in the dark. He didn't appear the least bit awkward about his excited nudity, but instead was enjoying the hot flush, no doubt visible to his immortal eyes, that was burning up my face.

"I'm going to get some clothes. I won't be long; wait here till I'm back, and don't worry about him," he said without even looking in Adam's direction. "He's no threat to you or anyone anymore."

"Please don't be long," I begged, my embarrassment forgotten as I realised that I was frightened to be without him.

"I promise you, I will be moments only," he said with such tenderness that it took my breath away. He brushed his lips across my forehead, then walked to where he'd dropped his sword, which he lifted easily from the ground. He turned back to me, and our eyes met briefly before he disappeared.

chapter

SIXTEEN

I sat rocking, chin resting on my knees, upon the granite ground where Arwan had left me, and I stared at Adam's black form through the dark. Other than the feeble lamp in the car park, the only light was a subtle orange glow, provided by the burning boat in the woods some distance away. Thick snow clouds had passed over the moon once more, and I could feel the temperature plummeting. My teeth chattered painfully as the icy rain returned, compounding the moisture in my already soaked clothes.

Adam lay on his side, the only position that wouldn't increase the agony of his staked shoulders. I strained to listen over the roar of the sea as he mumbled incoherently to himself. I guessed he was in shock, as I should probably be. Arwan had done what no mortal had ever been able to do—knock the cockiness right out of Adam Fleming.

I wrapped my arms tightly around my waist as I remembered the image of Arwan, the immortal warrior, in all his might. Arwan was truly otherworldly, terrifying, and yet I only ached for his return.

It was madness. Why did I accept so readily what he was? I had barely finished the thought, when my eyes were drawn by the flash of headlights speedily turning into the car park. I ceased to breathe at the thought of Buckie returning, then exhaled with relief as Arwan appeared directly in front of me, now dressed in black jeans and heavy winter parker.

Before I had a chance to stand, he lifted me into his arms without a word and headed in the direction of his Audi. A moment later, I was in the warmth of its cab and watched as Arwan climbed into the seat next to me. He reached past me into the back and produced a blanket, which he wrapped around my shoulders, his eyes lowered.

"Thanks," I mumbled. He had left the engine idling so the warm air from the heater continued to fill the cab, and it wasn't long before my shivering began to subside.

I waited in an awkward silence for him to say something, but he just gazed out the windscreen, his eyes mirroring the orange flames that continued to lick up above the line of trees from Buckie's exploded boat.

"What are we going to do about Adam?" I asked when I couldn't stand the silence any longer. "He's going to need medical attention pretty quick." That was a gross understatement. I felt a wave of nausea as the image of his body being speared flashed through my mind.

"I called the police on my way back here. They can deal with him." His voice was ice-cold. Right on cue, I heard the sound of a distant siren, and a moment later the inside of the Audi was pulsing with blue light as a single police car tore into the car park. The passenger door that I'd propped myself up against suddenly disappeared from my side, and were it not for Arwan's steadying hand, I'd have tumbled out into the car park.

It was Alex in full cop mode. In one sweeping glance, his eyes took in every detail of my no doubt dishevelled appearance, and I saw the shadow of anxiety that clouded them dissipate slightly when he deduced that I was unhurt.

"Where's Adam Fleming?" he demanded, drawing his baton, his eyes seeming to do a complete one-eighty in their sockets, scanning the area. Arwan flicked on the high beams in a gesture that almost conveyed boredom, and illuminated the grotesque form of Adam who, somehow, had managed to get himself into a sitting position. He was apparently staring out to sea, not thirty feet from where we sat. My stomach turned again at the sight of the giant splinters through his shoulders. I knew that the image would haunt my dreams for years to come. I couldn't imagine the agony he must be feeling, and yet he sat perfectly still, as if simply idling the hours away listening to the sounds of the sea at night. Alex took a couple of steps towards him, eyes narrowed, staring as if his eyes were deceiving him.

"What the f...Is that wood in his shoulders?" Alex was back at my door, but his eyes looked past me to Arwan, wide and white with disbelief.

"Yeah," I said, when Arwan didn't answer. Alex's eyes switched to me.

"And he's alive?"

"Yes."

"Okay, I want you to tell me right now how the hell he came to look like a freaking barbeque kebab!" A muscle jumped in Arwan's cheek, and I felt the slightest shift in the atmosphere; he was struggling to keep his anger in check.

"Tornado!" I yelled, before Arwan could boil over next to me.

"There actually were tornados?" Alex sounded sceptical. I nodded adamantly.

"Yes."

"Earthquakes *and* tornados in the same night?"

I didn't know what to say and started mumbling something about the realities of global warming.

"I felt the quake myself, but I thought the tornados were some kind of prank; there's some steaming drunk people up the High Street tonight."

"I saw them with my own eyes, Alex. Adam got hit by the debris they ripped up," I said quietly, guiltily. Although it wasn't exactly a lie, I knew my face would indicate that I was hiding something. Alex's eyes jumped back to Arwan, who continued to gaze out the window as if these events were of little interest to him. Only I knew otherwise.

"Twice, in mirroring positions?"

"That's what happened," I said, mustering greater confidence. He shook his head, not buying it. He looked over his shoulder to the trees behind.

"Well, thankfully, this one's out of my jurisdiction. You can explain it all to the English cops who are undoubtedly firing up the M8 as we speak. What's burning in the woods?"

"Oh crap, Duncan Buckie!"

"What about him?" Arwan asked, in a dangerously low voice.

I ignored him and told Alex, "You have to arrest Duncan Buckie!"

Alex actually seemed to sway on his feet. "Duncan Buckie! What on earth for?"

"It's him!" I said impatiently. "Duncan's been dealing heroin contaminated with anthrax, Alex. It's him! He works for Adam. He was here before, but he ran off when the tornado came. It was his boat Adam was planning on escaping in, the one that's burning in the woods." I gestured wildly in the direction of the now dying flames. "Search his house, it's there somewhere, all of the contaminated stuff is hidden somewhere in his house, he said so himself." My words finally hit home as Alex yanked his radio from his waist, then looked at Arwan.

"Don't go anywhere!" Then he closed the door and called for more assistance.

I was left once again to the strained silence with Arwan. I shuddered despite the warmth of the cab, as I studied his stony profile and fiery eyes. I should have wanted out of there. Any sane person would be running a mile by now, and yet I felt nothing but the ever constant and unrelenting need to be near him, to somehow try to sooth him. He was angry with me for sure. I could feel it building in the air around us. Why be mad at me? I didn't kidnap myself! I cleared my throat nosily, the sound seeming to rouse him from his thoughts.

"You know, it might have been useful to know you were on the run from your ex-husband."

I licked my lips, dry from the salt spray as I digested his icy tone. "The whole point of being under witness protection is not telling anybody," I pointed out defensively.

"Witness protection?" he scoffed. "You are only safe under my protection." I couldn't really argue with that. Arwan had never failed me, and I wasn't really even his responsibility. I sighed and made my tone gentle.

"I couldn't risk telling anyone, not even you," I tried to explain. "I'm happy here. I've never been happier, even despite all this," I said, releasing a hand from the blanket and waving it in the direction of the cliffs as my eyes moistened with tears. "I'd relive my life with Adam all over again if it meant that one day I'd get away and come to Claremont and find..." My words trailed off. I wanted to touch him, but was frightened, with his mood hanging so heavily in the air. Even angry, he was so beautiful it broke my heart. Silence filled the car again. I wished he'd stop looking out the damn window and look at me. This wasn't my fault, and besides, I was fine anyway, he had found me in time. How had he actually managed to find me? Was it my clue?

"You found the clue? The photo of Ross cove that I left on my bed?" I hoped the slight diversion of the conversation might ease his tension, especially if he had to acknowledge the fact that I'd helped lead him to my whereabouts. Success! He half turned to me, but still his eyes wouldn't find my face. His expression was one of puzzlement, then his mouth formed a half smile, and I was relieved to feel some of the intensity in the car evaporate.

"I must have missed that." I ignored the slight mockery in his tone, just pleased to see him smile, if only slightly. I was determined to keep the ball rolling.

"Then how did you know where to find me?" I waited patiently, watching his pensive expression, until he finally answered.

"I felt apprehensive about letting you walk home on your own. I tried to tell myself I was being overprotective, but the waiting was...*difficult* for me, so I came to get you. I must have missed you by minutes." His tone turned derisive. "There was a message on your answering machine from the police in Essex, warning of his escape from jail." He laughed blackly. "You weren't to panic, though; they didn't think your new identity or whereabouts had been jeopardised."

"Oh, I see," I muttered, imagining for the first time how worried he must have been.

"Obviously your absence and the state of your kitchen told me otherwise," he continued. The emotion that suddenly filled the car was hard to feel, like pain, and I felt my face mirroring his sudden grimace.

"When there was no sign that he'd killed you," he continued, his voice nearly choking on the words, "I realised that a man in his position would most likely want to leave the country as quickly as possible, and a boat out of Ross Cove is the quickest route. I instantly took to the air." His eyes suddenly closed, as he pinched his brow between thumb and forefinger, his voice rough with emotion. "If I hadn't found you when I did, I'd have torn up this whole area. I had no control over myself until I saw you were unharmed."

I reached out to touch his face with the back of my hand, running it down the line of his jaw, making him sigh deeply.

"I don't have a scratch, and once again it's thanks to you." He turned his head and finally our eyes met. I cupped his face, rubbing my thumb in soothing circles on the warm hollow of his cheek.

"This can't happen again," he said, almost to himself. I wanted to assure him it wouldn't, but I knew Adam only too well. If there was a way out of prison, he'd find it, and I knew that inevitably he'd find me too.

"Aren't you worried what Adam will tell the police?" I wondered, letting my hand reluctantly fall back to my lap.

"Other than a lot of nonsensical ramblings, your ex-husband won't have much to say to anybody." His tone was bitter, but there was a current of satisfaction.

"How can you be so sure?" Adam could easily tell the police everything that had happened tonight. Not that there was much chance of anyone believing a word he said, but there were certainly a few elements of the evening's events that might be difficult to explain away. I groaned inwardly at the prospect of having to find answers to some pretty unconventional questioning back at the station, especially when the Essex police arrived. Even if Adam didn't say anything, it was still going to be challenging enough to explain how he happened to come by two wood-staked shoulders in matching places. Alex hadn't swallowed my explanation. One stake I might have gotten away with, but not two.

"No mortal being can look into the green eye of divine fury and keep their sanity."

I had been so consumed with my thoughts that it took a moment for Arwan's reply to sink in. Then I inhaled a sharp breath. Doogie and Stuart had, according to Alex, been exactly the same as Adam now appeared to be: out of their minds. I remembered the bright green glow of Arwan's eyes and felt the hair on my neck stand straight.

"*No mortal.*" Arwan's words echoed in my mind.

"But Arwan," I whispered, "I looked into your eyes."

It appeared that shock had finally found me. I stared numbly into Alex's serious face, inches from mine, as his mouth fired words at me that I couldn't hear. I hadn't realised that Arwan had gotten out the car, and my eyes stared as he walked gracefully past the windscreen to my open door, where he somehow managed to displace Alex. I felt the warmth of his hand at my neck as he tucked a curl behind my ear, then heard the gentle click as he closed the door and shut out the world.

I don't know how much time passed while they stood not far from my window, talking. Moving images flashed through my mind, the same images that had haunted me since the moment I'd arrived in Claremont, playing to the soundtrack of Arwan's words of moments ago. "*No mortal being can look into the green eye of divine fury and keep their sanity.*" What did that mean for me? You can't shatter what's already broken? My parents thought I was unhinged, and they would know, right?

I continued to stare blindly out the windscreen as all the memories, dreams, and daydreams I had experienced slammed unrelentingly over and over in my twisting mind with growing impatience, like they were trying to tell me something. Something like the fact that I was nuts, maybe? I saw the bitter, beautiful woman in red, the white majestic stag and the glorious world he inhabited, and Arwan, always Arwan. I screamed inwardly, sheer frustration pushing me to breaking point. I heard Arwan's voice in my head again, "You are my one", the words he had said to me the night he rescued me from the woods. Words that, in that moment, seemed so painfully familiar to me, just as he did. I'd been aware from the moment my eyes had found his face that he was familiar to me and that I was pulled to him undeniably, and yet how could I possibly have once known and then forgotten a presence like Arwan Jones?

I was suddenly aware of Arwan getting back into the car. I blinked heavily, as if waking from a hundred-year sleep. I could see that there were now more emergency vehicles in the car park, including an ambulance. People in uniforms ran about everywhere, as a fire engine screamed into the other end of the car park, close to the still burning flames of Duncan Buckie's boat.

I watched as two paramedics jumped into the back of the ambulance and shut the doors before the sirens kicked into life and it ripped out the car park followed by several police cars. I realised that I'd been so preoccupied with my thoughts that I'd missed the sight of Adam somehow being manoeuvred from the cliffs and into the ambulance. I was glad.

"I have to go back to Achren."

I turned to meet Arwan's purple gaze, and his eyes were adamant. His words were like a physical blow to my stomach.

"So soon?" I croaked. "You just got back."

"I've spent far too much time away and there are events unfolding that require my attention." It felt like all the air had gotten sucked out the car as I realised that he meant he was leaving on a permanent basis. He must have seen the anguish in my eyes, his tone was so gentle. He had to leave Claremont, which of course I realised meant leaving me too. If I suspected my mind was fractured, I was certain that my heart was.

"Don't cry," he murmured, leaning over to wipe away a tear that I hadn't realised had escaped. I had known this day would come, but I couldn't have prepared myself for the pain and rejection I felt.

"What happened tonight brought home just how fragile you are in your current state." My current state. Did he mean my *crazy* current state?

"I'm sorry! I should have told you about Adam!" I gasped desperately, struggling for breath. He held my face in both his hands, his fingers woven into the thick of my hair.

"You just won't allow yourself to see it, will you?"

"See what?" I asked, exasperated. "What are you talking about? Tell me what I should be seeing!" A moment passed.

"We had plans tonight; do you remember?"

I nodded; of course I remembered. He had wanted to show me something at Avallon House, and then Adam had showed up and ruined everything.

chapter

SEVENTEEN

"After you."

I looked up into Arwan's perfect face as we stood before the oak door of the mysterious room on the second floor of Avallon House. The same one that had called me so unrelentingly once before; the very door that had demanded I see what lay within, which I had almost done until Arwan had frozen me in my tracks and I had reluctantly pulled myself away. The compulsion had lessoned not in the least, and my hand was already on the doorknob, twisting. My pulse quickened as I took several steps into the darkened room, but I could see nothing until Arwan switched on a lamp and I saw an antique four-poster bed hung with royal blue velvet curtains tied back with gold rope.

I knew instantly that the bedroom was Arwan's; his scent permeated the air, making my heart throb painfully in my chest. I breathed the air in, deeply, as though I could store his scent up in my lungs for when he left me permanently. As I stared at the bed, it was impossible not to imagine myself there, naked, folded in his arms. I heard myself sigh, then felt his hands on my shoulders as he gently turned me away from the bed to face the wall behind.

I was presented with two life-size, gold-framed classical paintings, both of which were Arwan's creations. The fact that the paintings were of Arwan's own hand wasn't at all shocking; his work was all over the house. What caused my entire body to tremble with a wave of utter confusion was what the first picture my eyes landed on depicted; me, in a landscape taken right out of the privacy of my own head.

"The day we met." Arwan gestured to the painting my eyes had locked on. I absorbed every detail of the scene before me, so expertly crafted that I could have been looking at a photograph. I knew the place; it was the same orange orchard I had daydreamed about on the first occasion I had lunched with Arwan and he had peeled the orange for me. The sky was just the same, an endless purplish blue, the exact colour of Arwan's own eyes. Even the dress I wore was the same one from all my dreams, white and light like the wisp of a summer's day cloud.

"I had just returned, tired and bloody from battle, and there you were, sleeping under one of my orange trees. The most startlingly beautiful creature I ever saw." I looked at the painted image of Arwan, the armoured warrior atop a shinning black war horse, his impossibly handsome expression one of awe and fascination as he gazed down at my peacefully sleeping form beneath the shade of an orange tree. I sucked in a long breath, utterly disorientated.

"That place, that grove, I know it," I whispered. "But I'm not sure how. Everything's so confusing; I thought it was just a daydream." My pulse thudded loudly in my ears as I looked to the next painting. There we were again, Arwan and I, but this time it appeared we were involved in some sort of ritual or ceremony. We knelt before the great oak tree, the gateway. Our profiles inches apart with our alternate hands clasped, bringing together wide, identical gold wrist cuffs on each of our arms, decorated with the traditional swirls of Celtic design. Between our kneeling forms and the tree stood the majestic white stag that had haunted me since I had arrived in Claremont. Where Arwan and I seemed only to have eyes for each other, the stag looked directly over our heads out of the painting, his eyes brimming with wisdom and intelligence. A shiver ran through my body, turning my skin to gooseflesh.

"What was to be our 'Joining Day." Arwan spoke behind me; his voice held a clear note of regret and perhaps a subtler one of anger. I realised that the painting portrayed some sort of Other-world wedding ceremony, a joining of two people, as Arwan had put it. I turned away from the painting to face him.

"I need you to tell me what's going on, right now." The ring of strength in my voice surprised me. I was tired of being in the dark, when I knew Arwan had the words to bring me to the light. His hands were suddenly firmly at my shoulders, almost taking my weight. His eyes shone purple through a frame of black lashes, holding my own unrelentingly, and I knew that finally the truth of what lay between us was coming and that I was ready to hear it.

"Your name is Morgen. You are an immortal, a potent sorceress of Achren, and I'm taking you home," he said slowly, adamantly. The taut planes of his face showed no hint he wasn't deadly serious.

I now understood the reason that he held his hands so firmly on my shoulders, as the bones disappeared from my legs. My feet remained on the ground, but that was more of a token gesture, for he held me up effortlessly. I squeezed my eyes shut, shaking my head in confusion. What was he saying? It was so hard to absorb, but I knew one thing with absolute completeness. I wanted to believe what he was telling me, more than anything I had heard in my life, but human scepticism told me otherwise. I was a potent sorceress? I could barely shuffle a deck of cards.

"You disappeared three sunsets before our 'joining', our wedding. These paintings were to be my gift to you, but I was robbed of the chance to present them." I fought hard to understand the words that now seemed to flow from his lips unchecked, as though the dam of silence had burst and there was no going back. It was impossible, wasn't it? I could acknowledge that Arwan had always seemed familiar to me, but I was no immortal sorceress, I aged like everybody else. Even Arwan couldn't deny that.

"How can what you're telling me be the truth? You were worried yourself about me looking after myself when you were away. If I were immortal, what could you possibly have to worry about?" I pulled in a deep breath. "And above all else, why do I know nothing of this?" I knew as I said those last words that they weren't entirely true. There had been the dreams, both waking and sleeping. Could they actually be memories of another life?

Anger suddenly shot through his dark features, his grip tightening on my shoulders as he shook me slightly. "You were poisoned," his brow knotted in an expression of anger and incredulousness, "by your own sister!" He tucked me firmly into the crook of his arm and turned me back to face the painting again, as he pointed with his other hand at two women I hadn't noticed initially, in the background of the ceremony.

"It's her!" I gasped. "The one in red, she's been in my dreams, and Adam's, she helped him walk out of prison unseen!" It was definitely the same strikingly beautiful red-haired woman, except that in the painting, her demeanour was tranquil rather than demonstrating the bitterness or anxiety that seemed to surround her in my visions and dreams.

"That is your sister, Annora, the one who tricked you. I'm not at all surprised she aided Adam, and you did see her in your dreams. I tried to reach out to you while you slept, in the hope that some form of memory might return to you, but Annora's poison was much more powerful than anyone could have imagined, and she was already there to hinder me."

"My own sister poisoned me?" I didn't understand why hearing about some figment from a dream apparently poisoning me seemed to hurt so much, but it did. Nor did I understand why I actually believed that what I was hearing was even possible, but again, I did. Maybe I'd seen too much over the last couple of months, that I wouldn't have ever believed possible, to ever doubt anything again.

"She tricked you into believing I'd betrayed you with another, that I didn't love you. The poison you readily drank condemned you to live life after life as a mortal being, remembering nothing of your life in Achren. You chose your fate willingly, rather than staying in your home and living for eternity in my kingdom." My eyes stung with tears as he continued. "You will live and die over and over again until you return to Achren, where a counter potion can be made to restore you to your true immortal self. It's the only way to put an end to this unnatural cycle of your existence."

"Why would she do that to me, my own sister?" I couldn't hide the hurt in my voice.

"It's not clear yet what Annora's motives are, or what plot she's embroiled in, she disappeared soon after you did, but she will be found and the truth uncovered."

A long silence fell between us, but our eyes remained locked together, our faces a breath apart. I wanted to kiss him, to press my lips to his and show him what I felt. He had sounded grave as he spoke to me, and yet all I felt was elation. If what Arwan told me was the truth, and I knew that he would never lie to me, then I could be with him...forever.

"The first time I saw you, the day my car broke down, I could have sworn I'd met you before," I said. "I thought you hated me, and I didn't know why. It bothered me so much that I couldn't stop thinking about you, wondering what I had done to make you hate me so much."

"I was frustrated!" he implored. "I wanted to lift you into my arms and cover you in kisses as I ran for the gateway to take you home. How could I do that? I searched for you for years, and then one day you materialised out of thin air on my doorstep like you were drawn back to me! I couldn't show you how I felt when my eyes, so starved of your face, finally saw you again. I had to control myself, show no emotion. I saw a flicker of something in your eyes, but I could see you didn't know me as you once did. It was like a sword ripping through my chest, but I knew I couldn't rush you into acceptance of what you are, acceptance of me. I knew that if I frightened you, you would run."

His voice suddenly dropped an octave. "But that wouldn't have been the end of it. Oh no. I'd have shadowed your every step for the rest of your life, trying to convince you to be with me, that you belong with me. And if you left this body to enter another, I'd have searched the world over and over again until I found you. You will never be free of me." His words caused my blood to sear in my veins. I realised he didn't understand that what he was saying was like sweet music to my ears, the most incredibly appealing threat I'd ever heard in my entire life. I could feel my mouth trying to form words, but my lips wouldn't give them up. I knew one thing with all certainty. What he said was the truth. I knew I was different; I had always known, and now I knew why. I didn't care whether I was human, immortal, or anything else. I just wanted to be with him.

"All my life, I've felt a little out of step. Different to my parents, separate from everyone around me."

"You *are* different here because this is not your home. Let me take you to Achren where you belong." He didn't wait for my answer, but put his lips to mine and kissed me. I had forgotten until that moment how damp my clothes still were and how cold my skin had become. The heat from his body was like a lick of fire from the sun, and it pulled me to him. I felt the warmth of his hands underneath my jacket, and I shivered against them as he slowly slid it from my shoulders and let it fall to the floor. Then his fingers brushed my stomach, finding the rim of my jumper. I raised my arms, looking deep into his eyes, and he pulled it from me. There was nothing cold about me now—I was as hot as a naked flame.

"I want you," I told him, and by god, I did. The large swell in his jeans told me he wanted me too, badly. He smiled alluringly, and a moment later, the remainder of my clothes had somehow melted into a heap at my feet. I was utterly bare and vulnerable before him. I heard his sharp breath a moment before he kissed me again, and I moaned with pleasure at the deep probe of his tongue as he cupped and massaged my breasts. A moment later, I was helping him out of his t-shirt and removing his jeans and underwear. The time for imagining what lay beneath was over...it was like he'd been carved from bronze.

My trembling hands ran over his smooth chest, taking a long moment to appreciate every taut edge and grove beneath my fingertips. Then my hands moved lower, passing over a muscled abdomen, then... lower still. My tongue moistened my lips as I grasped and stroked the large, hard swell of him with both my hands, watching delighted as his eyes fell shut and he growled like a wild animal. Then before I knew what was happening, he lifted me effortlessly into his arms and carried me over to the bed, moving at a speed that left the room a blur. Depositing me on the bed with a bounce, he straightened and loomed over me at his full height. For the first time in my life, I understood how it felt to feel beautiful and sexy as his eyes, alive in purple flames, travelled slowly and thoroughly over my body, as though drinking in the sight of me. I lifted my hand to his face and he rubbed his cheek into my palm.

"You've no idea how I've ached for you," he said, his voice husky, his beautiful face hard with desire. I smiled a small smile—I was doing my own fair share of aching myself—then I reached for his black hair and pulled him down to me.

"Lay with me, Arwan," I breathed. "You are my One...and I am yours." I felt a shiver ripple through his body as he joined me on the bed.

Epilogue

“It was a beautiful ceremony, Brook, and I just know you two are going to be happy together, you’re perfect for each other.” Morag held both my hands in hers, our last wedding guest, along with Alex, readying to leave.

“Thanks, Mo,” I said, as the look I had seen on Arwan’s face when he turned to watch me walk up the aisle flashed in my mind.

A wedding in the gardens of Avallon House had been Arwan’s idea; he thought I would want Morag and Edith present when we married, along with my other friends from The Shades. As there was no way anyone could attend our joining ceremony in Achren, we decided there was nothing to stop us marrying twice, so we could be official in both worlds. My friends from The Shades, particularly Edith, had been desperate to finally see inside the mysterious Avallon House, and of course it didn’t disappoint. Most of the whisperings however, had surrounded Arwan’s dogs that thanks to Buckie had a bad rep amongst the villagers. But they had mingled with the guests on their best behaviour, endured being stroked and even chased after flying sticks, and it wasn’t long before everyone relaxed around them.

The day had been a success. I had done a great job, even if I said so myself, with the few days I’d had to organise an entire wedding. I had been particularly lucky to find a simple, elegant white gown at short notice from a website, Shotgunbrides.com, whose speciality was maternity wear but who, fortunately for me, stocked several regular designs to choose from as well. Morag had expertly applied my makeup in soft natural tones. She had done my hair too, piling my curls up high on my head, and pulling a few loose around my face. I had been delighted with the end result and I think Arwan was too.

I looked over to where Arwan stood chatting with Alex. It was satisfying to see them at ease with one another. I had wondered how Alex would take the news of our marriage and was relieved when I saw him arrive with Morag. I had high hopes of a blossoming relationship between the two of them, noticing that they had appeared inseparable for most of the day.

"What about you and a certain PC Alex Mcleod?" I teased. "The two of you seemed pretty tight today, and you did practically rugby tackle for my bouquet!" I giggled.

"You noticed that?" she smirked, looking in Alex's direction. "Who knows?" she shrugged. "I've known him a long time, and it feels natural to be with him, you know what I mean?" I looked over to Arwan as he turned and caught my gaze.

"I do, I know exactly what you mean."

"I'm going to miss you, doll, and so is everybody at The Shades. Do you really have to go all the way to New York?"

Leaving Claremont was going to be a wrench, and I hoped I'd be able to visit soon. It was hard to lie to her, but I had no choice, I couldn't tell her where I was really going.

"We have to go where Arwan's work takes us, but I'm going to miss you too, like you wouldn't believe. You're the best friend I ever had." I squeezed her hands. "I'm sure we'll be back soon." Both our eyes had misted up, and we laughed and hugged each other tight. "You and Daniel take care of each other, okay?"

"You ready to make tracks, Morag?" Alex called, as he and Arwan strode over to where we stood wiping away tears.

"You guys were so lucky with the weather today," Alex said, clearly embarrassed to be in the vicinity of two emotional females. "Its winter, and I swear I've got sunburn on my nose!"

Arwan arched a black brow at me, obviously finding the situation amusing. He looked incredible in his wedding kilt and attire. I had to remind myself every time I looked at him that he was mine. I cleared my throat awkwardly and brought my focus back to Alex.

"Aha, very lucky, must be some sort of sun trap here or something...," I said, looking to the crystal clear blue dome above our heads as the words clunked out of my mouth.

"Hmmmm," Alex agreed, dubiously. Subject change required!

"Have you heard from the police in Glasgow yet about Duncan Buckie?" I inquired. To my immense relief, Adam had been sent indefinitely to a high security psychiatric hospital outside of London. His drug peddling days were over, as were those of Duncan Buckie, who was being sentenced for his part in the heroin operation any day now. Thankfully the cops hadn't been anywhere as near as pushy as I had anticipated. In fact, I got the impression that they were just grateful to have recaptured such a notorious and dangerous criminal as Adam, unravelling a multimillion pound drug syndicate that had infiltrated the entire country.

"Not yet, but he's facing at least ten years. I still can't believe he'd be involved in something like drug dealing."

"Huh!" Morag snorted. "For a cop, you don't have much intuition; the guy's an outright flesh creeper!"

Alex rolled his eyes skyward with an indulgent smile. "Okay, Nancy Drew, let's leave these guys to their new life together." Alex's words made my head spin. I was about to embark on a new life, another one.

After more tears and hugs, Arwan and I finally waved Alex and Morag off down the driveway. When they were out of sight, Arwan pulled me into his arms and with warm hands, lifted my chin making me look up at him.

"Did I tell you how glorious you are today, Mrs Jones?"

"Several times," I grinned, "but you can tell me again if you like."

"You're spellbinding. My eyes can't look at you enough..." Arwan's words were interrupted by a chaotic rustling and snapping of twigs from the woods that bordered Avallon House. We both looked to the source, just as a white stag leapt from the foliage and landed gracefully, five feet in front of us.

"Lugh!" I gasped in awe.

Lugh, Arwan had explained, was a divine being, an ageless, endless, powerful entity that represented the voice, eyes and ears of the gods and goddesses of Achren. The stag dropped its head, so low its nose touched the grass, his antlers appearing lethal at such close range.

"My Majesty," he greeted, his words making my insides somersault.

"Lugh," Arwan replied in his own greeting, also bowing low. Still stupefied by the sudden appearance of a being of unspeakable proportions, I remained motionless, gawping. "What brings you here, Lugh?" Arwan asked. "We return at first light."

As Lugh raised his head to answer, I noticed for the first time the anxiety that clouded his eyes. "The gateway faces imminent attack; you must return now, both of you."

My heart was suddenly beating so hard against my chest that I thought it might burst from my ribs and flip around like an earthbound fish at my feet. Go to Achren now, as in right now, this instant? I was in no way emotionally prepared! I thought I had at least another twelve hours to get my head around the next step involved in being with Arwan, and good grief, what was imminent attack supposed to mean, other than exactly that? Was I about to run head first into a battle with who knew what?

In the days since Arwan had shown me the paintings, I had spent many hours probing and asking questions about the place that was once my home. I had the vaguest imaginings of the kinds of creatures Arwan fought, and even just a vague idea was enough to frighten the hell out of me—not forgetting, of course, that Achren also seemed to be home to people who wanted to poison me, primarily my own sister, Annora.

Then there was Rosmerta, the other woman in the painting, who Arwan said was my youngest sister and who had been left devastated when both her sisters disappeared into thin air and left her all alone.

It was just so much to take in, and being asked to face it all at that very moment made me panic stricken. Arwan, seeming to sense my distress, drew me firmly into the circle of his arms, his purple eyes radiating love and reassurance as they gazed down at me.

"It's time to go home." I forced myself to swallow the lump of anxiety that had risen in my throat. Instead, I let the feeling of warmth and devotion that emanated from every atom of the being who held me permeate my immortal soul, and I nodded with an overwhelming feeling of my own destiny. I could face anything as long as he was with me.

"I am ready, Arwan. Take me home."

2342527R00129

Printed in Great Britain
by Amazon.co.uk, Ltd.,
Marston Gate.